No Goi

CW00555979

Robert

(Kent Fisher Murder Mysteries #7)

Copyright © Robert Crouch 2021

ISBN: 9798741647509

One

"Harry Lawson's dead."

I'm not sure why Sarah's telling me as Harry and I fell out over ten years ago.

"The police were waiting for me when I returned home." She folds her arms across her baggy sweater and stares at me, as if it's my fault. "I've been out all night on an emergency call."

That explains the smells of cattle shed and Jeyes fluid, and why she's on my doorstep at seven fifteen on Sunday morning. Her jeans and wellingtons are speckled with muck and straw, suggesting she drove straight here after talking to the police.

"They want me to formally identify the body."

Is that why she's here? Does she want me to go to the morgue with her? I can't think why. She's a veterinary surgeon. She's seen and operated on enough sick and injured animals in her time.

Maybe she wants me to identify Harry.

"Harry had my business card in his wallet," she says, sounding put out. "They asked me about my relationship to him. They asked about relatives, someone close they could contact." She sweeps back her auburn hair, revealing grey roots. "Did he tell you he grew up in a home after his parents overdosed on heroin?"

Harry told me his parents were kidnapped and executed during a conflict in the Middle East in the 1970s. It inspired him to follow in their footsteps and become an investigative journalist.

I'm not sure writing kiss and tell stories about celebrities quite hits the mark.

"Did the police say how he died?"

"They said investigations were ongoing." She glances at her chunky wristwatch, but shows no sign of leaving. "I thought you should know. You and Harry were close once."

I remember the night Harry silenced everyone in the saloon bar of the Red Lion with a drunken outburst. He'd been out of sorts for days, making sarcastic jibes, taunting and provoking me. When Sarah intervened, he pushed her away, accusing her of always taking my side. When I tried to calm him, he thrust me against a wall, pressing his face close to mine.

"Thanks for destroying everything that's good in my life," he said.

Then he crashed out of the pub. The following morning he left for London.

We haven't seen each other or spoken since that night.

"Did you tell the police about the argument in the Red Lion?" I ask.

She gives me a cheeky smile – the one that says she's misbehaved. "There's a lot of things I haven't told them."

I stand aside. "You'd better come in."

She walks around the large puddle, left by the storm that pounded the area for almost two hours last night. Set off by the heat and humidity of a balmy evening in late July, the wind and rain, aggravated by thunder and lightning battered the South Downs. I've already checked to make sure all our animals are safe and well. There's no damage to barns, fences and visitor centre. A couple of the tables and chairs outside the café have overturned, but that's all. The rattle of a stable door in the wind reminds me I need to let the horses and donkeys back into the paddock.

She steps out of her wellingtons, leaving them next to the bristle boot cleaner. Her woollen socks leaving damp smudges on the white laminate floor as she passes. She tilts her head back to look at the roof of the barn, underdrawn by sloping white ceilings, punctuated with Velux windows. Ahead, a central staircase leads to the first floor mezzanine. A stainless steel handrail seems to float over the glass panels that protect the edge and continue down either side of the staircase.

She runs her fingers along the handrail. "Gemma said you'd gone trendy."

Sarah prefers sloping floors, beamed ceilings and brick fireplaces stained with soot.

I leave the front door open for Columbo and follow her up the stairs. At the top she takes a long, sweeping look at my open plan lounge diner, separated from the kitchen by a breakfast bar. She walks straight across to the huge photograph of the Seven Sisters, printed on glass. It dominates the wall behind a white leather corner unit. Smaller photographs of the iconic East Sussex cliffs and surrounding Downland punctuate the glossy white minimalism of the room.

The indifferent sneer never leaves her face as she scans the room. "I can see why Gemma wants to move in with you."

This is news to me. I'm intrigued to discover what Gemma said to her mother. "You don't approve?"

"Are we talking about the décor or my daughter's infatuation with you?"

"Both, as Gemma helped me style the place."

"It's a replica of her old flat. Does it mean you're serious about her this time?"

"It means your daughter has excellent taste."

"I can't say the same for her judgement." Sarah slides onto one of the stools at the breakfast bar and spins herself around. "That's the same make of coffee machine she had."

"She gave it to me as a flat warming present. Would you like a latte, or something bitter, like an espresso?"

"I could murder a full English breakfast." She gazes out through the window at the woodland and gentle hills of the South Downs at the rear of my animal sanctuary. "But you're all smoothies and muesli these days, unless Gemma's tempted you back to the dark side."

"I can poach you an egg or two, laid by our own hens."

"Poaching an egg is like offering me decaffeinated coffee."

I slip the coffee capsule back into the drawer. "I'll make some tea."

A bark downstairs, followed by the eager click of claws on the stairs, heralds the return of my West Highland white terrier, Columbo. He hurtles across to greet Sarah, leaving damp paw prints on the floor. With a big grin, she slides off the stool and kneels to fuss him. While I make tea she calms him enough to examine his eyes, ears, teeth and fur.

4

She glances up at me. "No skin problems?"

I shake my head, well aware of the Westie curse. "I don't feed him wheat, chicken or food with additives, so be careful with the treats."

She holds up the lozenge she's retrieved from her pocket. "It's a vitamin pill, like the ones I use in the practice."

Columbo snatches the treat, wolfs it down, and nudges her with his nose for more. She gives him another before climbing back onto the stool. When she doesn't respond to his barks, he trots across to the corner unit, leaps up onto the blanket and settles to watch us with his big, dark eyes.

"He's a gorgeous dog, so bright and alert." She looks at me and sighs. "Why can't you treat people as well as you treat animals?"

"Are we talking about Gemma?"

"I was thinking about Harry. I know he could be an arse at times, but you didn't have to steal his girlfriend."

"I didn't. She dumped him."

I could tell Sarah how Felicity came to me after Harry struck her in a drunken temper. Sporting a bruised, swollen cheek and finger marks on her throat, she told me how he'd accused her of flirting and sleeping around. Angry and in no mood to return to the flat they shared, she stayed in one of the guest rooms at Downland Manor, unaware he'd followed her.

"Harry liked to hurt people," I say, filling the kettle.

"Well, he can't hurt anyone now, can he?"

We lapse into an awkward silence. While she checks her phone for messages, I pull two mugs out of a cupboard and make tea. "So, what didn't you tell the police?"

"Harry sent me an email in January, told me he was leaving London to work for the *Argus* in Brighton. He met

5

Miranda at an AA meeting last October and they were going to buy a smallholding north of the city and live the good life."

"Why didn't you mention this to the police?"

"A few months after he went to London, he invited me to celebrate his new job with the *Evening Standard*. There was a party at his editor's house. Harry introduced me to his new friends and colleagues like I was his girlfriend. He hardly left my side all evening. When I came out of the bathroom he was waiting for me. He slid his arm around me, telling me how much he wanted me. Next thing I know, he's propelling me into a bedroom, pushing me down onto the bed."

A satisfied smile creeps across her lips. "I left him on the floor with a busted nose and a bruised groin."

I can't help laughing, even though it seems inappropriate.

"When he asked me why I didn't want to meet Miranda, I reminded him of the incident. He said I had an overactive imagination, so I put the phone down. A week later, he sends me a wedding invitation."

I remove the tea bags from the mugs. "I'm guessing you didn't go."

"The wedding was cancelled a week before the big day in June." She places her phone on the breakfast bar to show me a text.

Can't marry Miranda. She was never the one for me.

"He sent three more," she says, scrolling.

You never gave me a chance, Sarah.

You only had eyes for Kent.

If you'd chosen me, none of this would have happened.

"Look at the times, Kent. Harry sent the texts in the early hours of Saturday morning. Twenty-four hours later, he's dead."

Two

While Sarah freshens up in the bathroom, I stare out of the window, wondering how Harry Lawson died. His last text seems to blame her for his troubles. It's typical of a man who never took responsibility for his actions and mistakes.

Did he take his own life to make her feel guilty?

She returns from the bathroom, looking more composed, her hair now tamed into a loose ponytail. "Are you wondering if I carried a torch for you?"

Harry had a flair for the dramatic. She liked to tease. He hid behind wild ideas, she played games.

They both wanted attention.

I turn away from the window. "Why didn't you show the texts to the police?"

"I wanted to talk to you first. What do you think he meant when he said none of this would have happened if I'd chosen him?"

"I'm an environmental health officer not a mind reader."

She picks up her mug, caressing it with both hands. "You've also solved a few murders."

"Was Harry murdered?"

"The police didn't say. Maybe your friend can tell us."

At last, the real reason for Sarah's visit.

"I have lots of friends. Who did you have in mind?"

"Don't be an arse, Kent. Who did you think I meant, your new friend from *Love Island*? She might have amazing tits but she's hardly well-endowed up here." Sarah taps the side of her head and laughs. "Not that you care about things like that."

"Savanna has a first class honours degree in environmental science. She runs a successful beach and swimwear business, as well as her own YouTube channel."

I stop, realising I've let Sarah goad me.

"It sounds like you're smitten, Kent. Where does that leave my daughter?"

"I don't know what Gemma's told you, but she's not moving in here. And so there's no misunderstanding, Savanna's in a steady relationship and not interested in me."

"Then how come I passed her on her way to the donkey enclosure?"

I'm peering through the window at the paddock before Sarah's laughter registers. "Oh dear," she says between giggles, "you have got it bad."

I retrieve my phone from the breakfast bar and ring my friend, Detective Inspector Ashley Goodman. "How are you feeling?" I ask, sensing frustration in her voice.

"Anxious," she says to my surprise.

Like me, she's an expert at hiding her feelings. She's also desperate to return to duty in the Major Crimes Team after three months sick leave. She believes it's dented her chances of going back to her old job.

"I start a phased return tomorrow. It'll be four weeks at least before I'm back full time – *if* the counsellor lets me. He's already delayed my return by two weeks because I refuse to deal with my issues."

"What issues?"

"He won't accept that I don't need to talk about what happened."

"Ashley, someone tried to kill you. You're lucky to be alive."

"So are you, Kent, but no one's psychoanalysing you."

"That's because I handed in my notice."

"Come on, Kent. You've buried it away like you always do, along with the rest of your feelings. Sorry," she says, letting out a groan, "I didn't mean it the way it sounded. I'm saying we're cut from the same cloth. We set our feelings aside, get the job done. Why can't people accept that?"

"Sounds like you need to get back in the saddle. Can I tempt you with a suspicious death?"

"You're not investigating another murder, surely?"

"Harry Lawson, a former acquaintance of mine, was found dead last night. The local officers aren't giving out any details."

"You want me to find out for you?" She sighs, as if I'm always taking liberties. "If I take an interest, the local inspector will want to know why a Major Crimes Team detective is interested. As I'm not officially on duty yet, questions will be asked."

"You could say no, Ashley."

"I will unless you give me a reason not to."

"Harry sent some intriguing texts before he died."

"You haven't shown them to the investigating officer, have you?"

Ashley lives on the other side of the village, so she joins us twenty minutes later, leaving her Audi alongside Sarah's old Volvo in the car park. Columbo barks and goes to greet Ashley, bounding back up the stairs with her, his attention fixed on the treat in her hand.

Dressed in one of her many grey suits and white blouses, she looks fit and healthy thanks to weeks of physiotherapy for her broken leg and injured shoulder. The hours of swimming at Tollingdon Leisure Centre should have helped her cracked ribs and breathing. With her thick blonde hair cropped short and tinted with copper streaks, she looks younger, keener. Even the cynical look that comes from twenty years of investigating murder, rape and violent crimes has deserted her piercing eyes.

She shakes hands with Sarah. "You look exhausted, Miss Wheeler."

"I was called out on an emergency. I knew nothing about Harry until I came home and found a couple of your colleagues on my doorstep. What happened to him?"

Ashley settles beside me on the corner unit. Columbo leaps up and squeezes between us.

"It's all over social media," she says. "Harry Lawson was discovered at the bottom of a private swimming pool. When the storm abated after midnight, people came out of the house onto the patio and someone spotted him."

Sarah's voice is flat and uncaring. "He'd been drinking. He was unsteady on his feet, slurring his speech. He was an alcoholic, inspector. He must have fallen off the wagon."

"Any idea why?"

Sarah shakes her head. She doesn't mention Miranda or the cancelled wedding.

"Why was he outside during the storm?" I ask.

"I wondered that." Ashley gives me a smile and turns back to Sarah. "Detective Constable Bobbie Cook will be at

11

the morgue for the post mortem. After you've identified the deceased, Miss Wheeler, she'll take a formal statement."

"If he was drunk and fell into a swimming pool, why do you need a post mortem?"

"The Coroner will want to consider anything that may have contributed to Harry's death. Like the texts he sent you." Ashley pulls out a business card. "Forward them to me."

Sarah takes the business card and hurries down the stairs. She almost overbalances as she pulls on her wellies and rushes out of the door. Ashley watches through the window. "Did she tell you about the party?"

"No. What party?"

"Councillor Gregory Rathbone invited his well-heeled friends and cronies to a party on Saturday night. The councillor who's now responsible for your department was there."

"Stephanie Richmond?"

Ashley nods. "She dived into the pool and brought Harry Lawson to the surface. She tried to resuscitate him, but it was too late. Not quite how you want to remember your engagement party, is it?"

"Rathbone's getting married?"

"Didn't Sarah tell you?"

I shake my head, wondering what else Sarah hasn't told me.

Three

Ashley declines a cup of tea and ruffles Columbo's fur. "You could come and live with me anytime, but with the hours I keep, it wouldn't be fair. I'd prefer a man, but good ones are a bit thin on the ground."

"I thought you'd finished with men."

"I was hoping to meet one of your hunky colleagues on Friday, but you didn't invite me to your leaving bash."

"I didn't leave."

"Come again?"

"I'm no longer an employee, but I haven't left."

She pauses at the top of the stairs. "It's too early for riddles, Kent."

"Last Monday, the Food Standards Agency rang, unhappy with our inspection shortfall, the merger into Planning, the lack of a plan to deal with another potential shortfall this year. The Agency is carrying out a full audit in five weeks."

"The council asked you to stay on to deal with the audit?"

"No, they assigned Gemma to deal with it."

"She's not an EHO."

"Neither does she have the necessary experience. Every local authority has to appoint a suitably qualified, competent officer to manage its food safety function."

"You." She sets off down the stairs, Columbo racing ahead. "I hope you screwed them for a pay rise."

"I negotiated a six month contract where I work three days a week. Rathbone and his lapdog, Stephanie Richmond, who's Chair of the Planning Committee, only agreed because I factored in inspections of the high risk businesses we didn't visit last year. I also offered to train Gemma so she can continue the work when I've finished."

"Now we're getting to the real reason. You can't bear to be apart from Gemma. I thought you were supposed to be running the visitor centre and café here."

"I still have four days a week with the weekend. A couple of our new volunteers have catering experience."

She opens the door to let Columbo out. "It doesn't leave much time for sleuthing."

"I'll talk to Rathbone tomorrow. He's assigned Kelly to help me one day a week, which is odd."

"Sounds sensible to me. You and Kelly have worked together for years."

I inherited Kelly when the previous Head of Environmental Health resigned. She had no trouble slipping into the role of my PA when I took over running the department for six months.

But I have a feeling all is not well with Kelly.

"Yeah, but Rathbone didn't want me back," I say. "Then last Friday, without telling me, he pulled Kelly out of the call centre. Her line manager sent me a shirty email, telling me I can't poach her staff."

"I'd say he wants Kelly to keep tabs on you, Kent. Maybe you should use her to keep tabs on him."

While Columbo weaves his way through the grass, nose to the ground, we follow the path to the car park. When we draw closer to the Mike Turner Visitor Centre, named in honour of my best friend, who was tragically killed almost four months ago, she stops beneath the sign.

"I still can't believe he's gone," she says, blinking back the tears. "I've hardly thought about anything else these past few months, questioning what we did, what we could have done."

"We couldn't have known what was going to happen."

"I know, but it's made me think about life, my job, what I want. I'm 44 years old, Kent. I'm single, living in a rented cottage, and married to a job they're going to take from me."

"They won't move you, Ashley. You're a great detective."

She looks at me and sighs. "I got careless, Kent. I let my emotions get the better of me. Now I don't know if I've got what it takes."

"You'll soon be running investigations again." I place my hands on her shoulders and give her an encouraging smile. "You're fitter and healthier than you've ever been. You look fabulous too. You're going to knock them dead."

"Thank you. Why don't you come over for a pizza tonight? We can watch *Back to the Future*."

"Make it *Star Wars* and you've got a date."

She sighs. "You and Carrie Fisher. You're so predictable. Okay, I'll indulge your fantasies, but there's something I want you to do first."

"Buy you a gold bikini?"

"In your dreams, Fisher. No, have another word with Sarah Wheeler. Meet her for lunch. Seeing Harry on the slab might loosen her tongue a little."

"Anything specific you want me to find out?"

Ashley holds up her phone to show me a photograph. "This is Sarah's party frock, left on the back seat of her Volvo."

"She was called out on an emergency and changed into work clothes."

"She didn't go home to change though. She brought her work clothes with her. Coincidence, or was she expecting to be called out?"

I shake my head. "Maybe she keeps a spare set of clothes in her car for emergencies."

"And maybe she could have told you about Rathbone's party, but she didn't."

Four

Sarah meets me for lunch in Hampden Park, a short drive from Eastbourne District General Hospital. She's sitting on a bench overlooking the lake, a Pepsi Max in her hand, a packet of sandwiches by her side. Her sleeveless blouse and short skirt show off the deep tan on her arms and legs. When I arrive, she slides a takeaway tea towards me. "I left the bag in."

Careful to avoid the bird poo on the back of the bench, I sit beside her. "How did it go at the mortuary?"

"You were never one for small talk, were you?"

"And you didn't buy me a sandwich."

"I've no idea what you eat these days. I'm not sure I know you anymore."

She never knew me before, despite what Harry's texts suggest.

"When I saw Harry lying in the mortuary, it became real. His death, I mean." She takes a sip of Pepsi, staring out across the lake. "He once told me if he had to die he wanted to go on a battlefield, reporting on the atrocities of war. He wanted to be a hero, not a drunken corpse at the bottom of a swimming pool."

She pulls a chicken salad sandwich out of its packaging and checks the amount of filling. "That's the trouble with dreams – they remind us what failures we are."

She glares at the mothers who walk past with their buggies and pushchairs, forcing her to pull her feet out of the way. Beyond, more mothers help their infants feed the ducks and swans, which stand little chance against the brash gulls. At least most parents purchase seed from the café rather than feeding bread to the birds.

"I didn't know where he lived, worked or socialised," Sarah's saying. "That's how important Harry Lawson was."

"Why didn't you tell me about the party?"

"What difference does it make?" Sarah finishes eating the first sandwich, unaware of the crows and jackdaws massing around us. "I was called out and missed all the action."

"Ashley spotted your party frock on the back seat."

Sarah nods. "I keep some old clothes in the boot for emergencies, like you keep your running kit in yours."

"Why were you at Rathbone's engagement party? You don't like the bloke."

"He didn't invite me. My partner, Stephanie Richmond, did."

"You're in a relationship with the chair of Downland's Planning Committee?"

She laughs. "Gemma looked at me in disgust when I told her my partner was another woman. You're more concerned about Steph being the councillor you have to report to."

I'm more concerned about the alliance I'm facing.

Frank Dean, the Chief Executive, is Sarah's brother and Gemma's uncle. He's working with Gregory Rathbone, a friend of Stephanie Richmond, who also chairs the Planning

Committee. As well as dating Sarah, Stephanie has considerable influence over my new boss in Planning.

It's like an extended family with Rathbone at the head of the table.

"Why was Harry at the party?"

Sarah finishes her sandwich. "He must have talked his way into the house. He was drenched from the storm, dripping water everywhere. When he spotted me, he strolled up with that cocky sneer of his and asked me why I was fraternising with the enemy."

"Did you ask him about the texts?"

"Yes, but Steph came up to rescue me at that point. You should have seen his face when she kissed me. It was like I'd kicked him in the guts."

"Did Harry know you'd be at the party?"

"He said he came to see Gregory's child bride. Katya's in her thirties, for God's sake. She's from Belarus or Latvia, but you'd never know. She speaks good English with hardly any accent. They met at the doctors' surgery when Gregory sprained his wrist earlier this year."

After signing too many redundancy notices, no doubt.

"Now she runs his hotel near Herstmonceux. The Travellers, isn't it?"

"That's right. Why was Harry interested in Katya?"

"You know Harry – always stirring the shit with a stick. He told me to choose my friends with more care and skulked off."

"Do you remember when he arrived?"

She shrugs. "Ten forty-five or thereabouts?"

"I understand he argued with Rathbone."

"It was a few minutes after eleven. I'd had a call about an injured heifer. I saw Gregory rush into the study and slam

19

the door. I heard raised voices, but I couldn't make out what anyone was saying. It was over in a minute, maybe less. Gregory came out, looking his normal charming self."

"How about Harry?"

"No idea. I was on the doorstep, saying goodbye to Steph by then. I saw him come out of the front door a few minutes later while I was driving away."

"Did you see where he went?"

"It was raining stair rods. I could hardly see through the windscreen."

While I've never been inside Rathbone's house, I know the swimming pool is in the rear garden, which is enclosed by a brick wall about two metres high. Harry would have had to walk around the house and find a way into the rear garden to get to the pool.

Why would he do that?

"Is there anything else you remember?" I ask. "Something Harry said? Someone he spoke to?"

She flattens the sandwich carton while she thinks. "He was clutching something to his chest – something under his jacket. He didn't have it when he came out of the front door."

"I thought you couldn't see because of the rain."

"He was turning up his collar with both hands."

Five

On Monday morning, I arrive early at Tollingdon Town Hall, parking my Ford Fusion in the bay I've used for the past nine months. While my old job no longer exists, I've retained my office. There's no space for us within the Planning office, so the rest of the team remain next door. Only Kelly's desk has gone, joining her in the call centre, I imagine.

It feels strange, entering the office I should have left last Friday. Not that I'm a fan of my predecessor's obsession with lavender, which extends to the colour of the walls, the sofa in the meeting area and stationery items like letter trays and staplers. Then I notice Kelly's desk, facing mine. She's on her hands and knees in the footwell.

"I don't think either of us imagined we'd be back so soon."

She shuffles out and brushes the fluff from her sleeves. She's swapped her high heels, short skirt and snug blouse for a more traditional blue suit and sensible shoes, which reduce the saucy swagger in her hips. The bold makeup has gone, draining the fun from her face.

She gives my polo shirt and chinos the once over. "Is this how contractors dress?"

"I'm not ruining a good suit inspecting hot, steamy kitchens with greasy floors."

"You don't have a good suit."

"I thought you'd be pleased to have a break from the call centre."

She presses the button to start her computer. "I don't like being instructed to work for you."

"No one else has your knowledge and grasp of our systems."

"Gemma does." When her computer fails to boot, Kelly glares at me, as if I'm to blame. "But she's far too important to be your assistant. No, send for Kelly. She's only working in the call centre. It's only one day a week."

"Kelly, I can't do the audit without you." I pause as she dives under her desk. "Rathbone's determined to make me take the blame for the inspection shortfall. We can show it was a failure to replace staff and appoint a second contractor that led to the shortfall."

"Shouldn't you be working together to present a united front?"

"That might be difficult as Rathbone doesn't want me here."

"No one wants you here." She emerges, brushing cobwebs from her hair. "Your feud with Gregory Rathbone destroyed this department. It cost Danni her job when she was making a difference. Nigel left because you were spending more time sleuthing than looking after your team. And then you let Gemma back." She clambers to her feet, anger in her eyes. "How could you do that to us?"

"I thought you and Gemma were best friends."

"You're in love with her, Kent. You don't give a shit about our feelings."

"I fought to protect and improve Environmental Health."

She stares at the blank monitor and sighs. "There you go again, always fighting."

"When councillors like Rathbone attack me and the people I care about, the job I love, I'm not going to let them destroy everything."

"What good did all the fighting do? Environmental Health no longer exists." She gives me a sad shake of the head. "Then, when we needed you most, you quit."

"My post was made redundant."

"A post you never wanted. Why did you take it, Kent? You hated senior management. You spent six months antagonising them, knowing you could walk away and go back to your sanctuary and your wealthy father."

It's a damning indictment of my six months as Acting Head of Environmental Health.

"Then why am I here now, trying to protect the reputation of the team and the valuable work we do?"

"You're here to make sure no one blames you for your failures."

On the first floor, the Leader of the Council has an office next to the Chief Executive. They share the same sumptuous carpet, which sinks beneath my feet. I take in the smell of oak panelling, tradition and wealth. The walls, with their Regency style wallpaper and landscape paintings in gilded frames, hark back to a time when the council was a significant player in local affairs.

Gregory Rathbone sits behind a large desk that gleams like a showroom model. He prefers a laptop to a PC, a mobile to a landline and a single letter tray, piled high with folders and papers. This austerity echoes his simple suit, shirt and tie. His thin face is smooth, belying his age, though his black hair, greased and flattened hard against his skull, struggles to mask a bald spot. Naturally, he doesn't have time for small talk. He flaps an indifferent hand at the expensive machine in the corner.

"Grab a real coffee, Kent. Steph's with Neville. She'll be a few minutes."

Neville Priddy, the Head of Planning and Development, is ten years younger than me. His talent for talking the same language as councillors, combined with a ruthless desire to give them exactly what they want, reveals the shortcomings of my approach to management. Now he has his eye on Gemma, hoping to get cosy with the Chief Executive's niece.

I sit at the meeting table. "I heard about the drowning at your house. I hope your fiancée wasn't too distressed."

Rathbone's back stiffens. He places his pen on the desk, regarding me with small, dark eyes. "We're here to discuss the Food Standards Agency audit, not Harry Lawson. But as he was an old friend of yours, you need to know he wasn't invited to my party. I don't know how he got in, or how he found his way to the bottom of my pool."

"Did you tell the police about your encounters with Harry over the years?"

He rises from his grand, almost baronial chair. "I haven't seen or spoken to Harry Lawson for at least ten years."

"Yet he turns up at your house in the middle of a storm."

Rathbone walks across to the window and looks down on Tollingdon High Street. "When I was informed of his presence, I asked him to leave, politely, of course."

"An argument in the study doesn't sound polite."

He turns to face me, his smile as false as the colour of his hair. "Is this is another of your investigations?"

My smile is so sweet it should come with a health warning. "I'm interested in everything you do, Councillor Rathbone."

"Harry Lawson was drunk and sopping wet. He'd already antagonised several of my guests. I escorted him to the front door and made sure he left without a fuss."

"Then how did he end up at the bottom of your swimming pool?"

Six

"What Greg hasn't told you is how aggressive and abusive Mr Lawson was."

Stephanie Richmond closes the door and walks over to the coffee machine. Slim and toned, with short blonde hair, sharp blue eyes and enough jewellery to open a market stall, she has a cultured voice and a disarming smile. In her early thirties, she's one of the new breed of councillors who challenge everything and anything, usually on social media. She's organising Downland's first Gay Pride event, raising eyebrows among many established councillors.

"We shouldn't be discussing Harry Lawson," Rathbone says.

"Nonsense, Greg. Kent's experienced at investigating incidents like these. Maybe he could shed light on what brought Mr Lawson to your house. Sarah's already consulted him."

"Why would she do that?"

Stephanie gives him a conciliatory smile. "We want to know why Mr Lawson turned up at your party. Do you have any ideas, Kent?"

"I didn't know he was in the area. Did you speak to him, Miss Richmond?"

"I went to rescue Sarah." She takes the coffee cup from the machine and heads for the table. "When he realised we were together, he became antagonistic and rather abusive. Then he walked off. I didn't see where he went."

"I was on the landing," Rathbone says. "Lawson spotted Katya coming out of the kitchen and made a beeline for her. When he started making unfounded and unsavoury allegations about her, I went downstairs to deal with him."

"What kind of allegations?" I ask.

"When she was a teenager, Katya fled to this country, fearing for her life. She didn't come across the Channel in an inflatable dinghy, as he suggested. Neither does she organise slave labour at my hotel."

"You argued in the study, I understand."

"No. He was slumped in a chair when I arrived."

"People heard raised voices."

"People heard me. I was angry because he was drunk, because he'd upset Katya, because he'd passed out. I was annoyed because someone let him into the house. I woke him up, dragged him to his feet and escorted him to the front door. I told him to go home. That was the last I saw of him."

"Why didn't you ring for a taxi? It was like a monsoon outside."

"I thought a good drenching would sober him up."

"Instead he walked round the back of your house and ended up in the pool."

Rathbone's phone vibrates and he snatches it off the table, dismissing the call. "The gate to the back garden was locked, as I've already told the police. He must have climbed the wall."

"I thought he was drunk."

"There were footprints in the flowerbeds. He was found in the pool." Rathbone's struggling to contain his frustration. "How else did he get there?"

Maybe someone helped Harry. Maybe it was no accident he was at the party. He brought something with him, hiding it under his jacket.

"The police think he slipped on the tiled surround and fell into the pool," Stephanie says. "His shoes would have been muddy." She fishes her vibrating phone from her jacket pocket and sighs. "Did Adrian Peach ring you, Greg?"

Rathbone nods. "He turned up at the house yesterday with a photographer."

I try not to sound too interested. "Adrian Peach from the *Argus*?"

She nods and takes a sip of coffee. "He's pestered Sarah too. I told her not to talk to him. Now, where were we?"

"Did anyone notice Harry in the back garden?" I ask.

"All the doors and windows were closed, the curtains drawn," Rathbone says. "None of us knew about his tragic accident until the storm passed. You did your best, Stephanie, but it was too late."

I turn to her. "Sarah thought Harry had something inside his jacket."

She shrugs. "I didn't find anything when I tried to resuscitate him. Did you find anything in the pool, Greg?"

He shakes his head. "He had nothing on him when he was in the study."

"Have you found anything that shouldn't be there?"

"Harry Lawson didn't leave an engagement gift, if that's what you mean." His tone tells me he's had enough of my questions. "When I escorted him out of the house he had nothing inside his jacket."

"Could he have gone into the garden before he entered the house?"

She shakes her head. "His shoes weren't muddy when I saw him with Sarah."

Rathbone glances at his chunky watch. "I hope you're going to put as much energy into this audit, Kent."

I nod, my thoughts elsewhere. I've seen the wall that encases his rear garden. I'd struggle to climb the wall, so Harry would have no chance.

Seven

"How did your meeting go?"

Kelly's working at her computer when I return to the office. The pack of plain chocolate digestive biscuits on my desk suggests her mood has improved. I drop into my seat, wondering whether she's right. Did I abandon what was left of my team?

"Where is everyone?" I ask. "I haven't seen anyone from the Food or Pollution teams."

"They started on the district, apart from Gemma. She left you the biscuits, by the way. She said not to eat too many as she wants to meet you for lunch."

At least one person's pleased to have me back.

I glance at the list of emails on my screen. "Has Charlie been in touch?"

"Charlie's on holiday in Wales with Nigel. She's starting next Monday. She asked me to thank you for getting her another contract."

That leaves Gemma, Charlie and me to cover food inspections, complaints and outbreaks. Not much of a thin green line to present to the Food Standards Agency. Their auditors should challenge the level of staffing. I hope they'll insist on more officers, but it won't stop Rathbone employing more food inspectors, who are cheaper than EHOs.

I spot the email from Tommy Logan, editor of the *Tollingdon Tribune*, and ring him on my mobile.

"A little bird tells me you couldn't bear to leave the council, dear boy." His wheezing laugh reminds me of Dick Dastardly and Muttley. "With your hectic business and social life, how do you find the time to protect the beloved residents of Downland?"

"I don't think you rang to congratulate me on my new role, Tommy."

"Only you could abandon a sinking ship and then turn up on the rescue vessel. I'm ringing about Harry Lawson. He drowned over the weekend. You were once fellow rebels, so I wondered if you could give me some background."

"You were fellow reporters, Tommy. Why do you think he went to see Rathbone?"

I notice Kelly, pretending not to listen. I leave the office to continue the conversation.

"Knowing our Teflon councillor as we do, it could be anything," Tommy's saying. "The man has more fingers in more pies than the night shift at a bakery. Did you know Harry joined the *Argus* earlier this year?"

I stop by the stairs. "Did he approach you for a job?"

"He did, but he'd been out of work thanks to his relationship with Tennessee's finest."

"Megan Fox?"

"Jack Daniel's, dear boy. Harry said he'd cleaned up his act and was chomping at the bit for another bite of the proverbial."

"That's more maxims than you can shake a stick at, Tommy." I pause, wondering if Harry was onto one of

Rathbone's scams. "You know Harry liked investigative journalism, right?"

"That's not how I'd describe kiss and tell, though Rathbone's recent engagement could prove interesting."

"In what way?"

"You're supposed to give me information, dear boy. As you're interested in Harry's demise, is there something you want to share with your favourite reporter?"

"What if I talk to Adrian Peach?"

"We both know how fruitless that would be." Tommy laughs at his joke and ends the call. Though tempted to ring Adrian, it would only confirm my interest in Harry's death. That would increase Adrian's interest in me.

The post mortem will reveal anything suspicious.

Back in the office, I find a cup of vending machine tea beside the biscuits on my desk. Kelly's by the window, staring into her cup. When I walk over she gives me an apologetic smile.

"I was out of order, lover. I know you did your best for us."

"It wasn't enough though, was it?"

I wonder how my battles with senior management and people like Rathbone affected morale. Then there's the sleuthing, which sometimes encroached into my work. While I loved every moment, the investigations have left scars. Gemma could have lost her life on at least two occasions. So could Niamh, my friend as well as my stepmother. No wonder she raced back to Northern Ireland after the last investigation.

I never stopped to consider the effect on my team and colleagues. Charlie was a great help with one investigation.

So was Nigel, in his own way. He had the sense to abandon ship. Maybe he knew I couldn't save him or the others.

Here I am again, setting myself for another battle I can't win.

I look down at Tollingdon High Street, at the businesses I inspect, filled with people I enjoy meeting and getting to know. While senior management demanded I keep my distance and remain objective, gaining people's trust and respect leads to higher standards and less trouble down the line.

I thought I could take this into management and make a difference.

"Out there, I worked with people," I say. "In here, I fought with management, even when I became one of them. Now Environmental Health's run by people who have no knowledge or experience of food hygiene, health and safety at work, or any of the other areas we cover."

Kelly joins me by the window. "I know what I said earlier, but no one blames you, Kent. Gregory Rathbone encouraged Danni to get rid of you."

"And you want me to work with him?"

"You don't have to leap into bed with him. You could keep him informed, consult him, compromise." She pauses, expecting a reaction. "Persuade him with facts and figures, not high principles and dreams."

"Is that why you're here – to keep me in line?"

She places a hand on my arm. "I'm here for you, Kent. I had the hump earlier because I lost my job too. A job I loved. If you think we can persuade the Foods Standards Agency to make Rathbone employ more officers and reinstate the department, I want to be part of it."

"And you told me to stop dreaming? If the Agency blames me for what happened, why put yourself in the firing line?"

"Isn't that my choice?" She moves closer, straightening the collar of my polo shirt. "I love working with you, Kent. We think alike, share the same sense of humour. We could make a dream team."

She slides her arms around my neck, her eyes inviting me to kiss her. As her lips approach mine, the door opens.

Gemma freezes when she sees us.

The door slams behind her.

Kelly stares at me, her eyes as hostile as the tone of her voice. "You're not interested in me at all, are you? No, save your lies," she says, stomping away. "I saw the way you looked at her. You're still in love with her."

She's right, but I had to be sure she was working for Rathbone.

But will Gemma believe me?

Can I afford to tell her when her uncle's the Chief Executive?

Eight

I persuade Gemma to meet me for lunch in my café at the sanctuary. It's empty, giving Betty Cooper, a former school meals supervisor, time to clean, polish and rearrange the cake cabinet. She looks a little nervous when I order a jacket potato for Gemma and a cheese and onion baguette, lavished with salad cream rather than butter.

I help myself to serviettes from the dispenser. "How are you finding things?"

"It's quiet, but I like it that way." She hesitates, her cheeks flushing. "I mean, it gives me time to get familiar with everything and take all those temperature checks. I can spend more time with the customers too. Ollie's been a Godsend."

"I thought he was waging war on bindweed."

She smiles, clearly smitten with him. "He always helps me when the deliveries arrive and he's back to clear away when we close. He pops in for tea and a slice of cake mid-afternoon."

I nod, well aware of Ollie's routines.

Betty adjusts her Meadow Farm Animal Sanctuary baseball cap, which looks unsteady on her curly grey hair. My father ordered a hundred of the scarlet caps for the grand opening in May. When few of our visitors and guests took them, he thought it would be good for staff to wear them.

"A white trilby might be more comfortable, Betty."

"Mr Birchill said we had to wear the caps."

"My father isn't running the place. My colleague, Gemma, who will inspect the café from time to time, prefers trilbies. We're not a burger bar."

Betty glances at Gemma and smiles. "She's lovely, isn't she? Slim and so pretty."

I return to the table, pleased my colleague has dumped the sleeveless frocks and sandals with diamante trims for a short black skirt, coffee-coloured blouse and sensible shoes. Until I met Savanna, Gemma was the most attractive woman I'd ever met with her glossy chestnut hair, cheeky smile and sexy eyes, the colour of dark chocolate.

I thought I was in love with her.

But I never missed her the way I miss Savanna.

Not that she's interested in me.

Unlike Gemma, who wants to know what's going on between Kelly and me.

"It's none of my business," Gemma says, scrolling through Twitter on her phone. "I always thought you two should be together. She never stopped talking about you when we were in the Cotswolds."

Ironically, that's what Kelly said about Gemma.

I've never been so popular.

"And she's more your age, Kent."

I can't help laughing. "I thought you were best friends."

Her head jerks up. "I thought we were more than friends. Don't you realise how happy I could make you, Kent?"

"Yeah, but I could never make you happy."

"You could try." She lets out a deep sigh. "I could move here now my mother's serious about Stephanie Richmond. I don't care about her taking up with another woman, but I wish they wouldn't fool around while I'm there. They were making so much noise the other night, I had to go out. And then she starts telling me it's the best sex ever."

Gemma sticks a finger in her mouth like she wants to vomit.

I laugh. "Don't you think you might be protesting too much?"

"Probably, but what are the chances of having a gay father and a gay mother?"

I know her father walked out when she was a young child, but no more.

"You never speak about your father."

"When he left my mother, he didn't keep in touch. He was a musician, always on tour or recording in some foreign studio. When I was thirteen, he rang and asked me if I'd like to live with him for a while. He'd been diagnosed with HIV and wanted to get to know me before he shuffled off. Before he died he said they were the best times of his life."

She falls silent while Betty puts our food on the table. Gemma eyes her jacket potato and baked beans with relish. "That looks so good."

Betty smiles and retreats to the counter. Gemma grabs a knife and fork and plunges in, opening up the potato to release the heat.

"Can I move into the farmhouse now Niamh's not coming back? I'll pay the going rate."

"I'm not sure it's a good idea."

She spears a portion of potato. "Kelly won't mind."

"There's nothing going on with Kelly, whatever you think you saw. Far from disturbing us, Gemma, you saved me from an embarrassing situation."

She doesn't look convinced. "Now who's protesting too much?"

"I've already had one difficult conversation, setting Kelly straight. I don't need another with you. I know you want to get away from your mother, but moving here isn't the answer. Niamh may want to come back."

"She's reopening her father's old bakery in Moy. I've seen the photographs on Facebook."

I bite into my baguette, savouring the tang of the onions Niamh grew in her garden behind the farmhouse. "I'd like to keep all my options open."

"You mean you've promised it to someone else."

Savanna wants to make a film about our work at the sanctuary. She said the farmhouse would make a good base during the shoot. But no one's been round to check the place or confirm details in the last eight weeks. I should ring to find out if she's still planning to make the film, but I don't want to discover she's lost interest.

"We might employ a visitor centre manager," I say. "We might offer accommodation as part of the remuneration package."

"I thought you and Frances were running the visitor centre."

"She's busy running the sanctuary and I don't have the time."

"Then why did you scare Uncle Frank into giving you a contract to deal with the Food Standards Agency. I could have dealt with them."

I can't tell her I want to find out if Rathbone is using Kelly to spy for him.

"How would it have looked, leaving an inexperienced officer to deal with the Agency when I could stay on for a few more months? It happened on my watch, didn't it?"

"It started long before you stepped up, Kent. The auditors aren't stupid. Your opposition to staffing reductions and freezing vacant posts is well documented. They can't blame you, no matter what Rathbone tells them."

"You've no idea what Rathbone is capable of."

"Harry Lawson said that to my mother. He added a few Anglo Saxon adjectives, as you like to call them, but it amounts to the same thing."

"When was this?"

"He called round to see her on Friday evening, the night before the party. Didn't she tell you?"

"No."

"That's when Harry asked my mother to get him into Rathbone's party. When she refused, he said what you just said – you've no idea what Rathbone's capable of. Harry wanted access to Rathbone's study. When my mother told him to leave, he lost his temper."

Gemma pushes her plate to one side and leans closer. "He couldn't believe she was going to Rathbone's party, buying him an engagement gift after everything they knew about him. Harry told her to get out before she was dragged into something she'd regret."

"Was he more specific?"

"My mother never gave him the chance. She marched him down the hall and threw him out, slamming the door in his face. She told me not to say anything. And now he's dead, Holmes."

"Was your uncle at the party?"

"Uncle Frank was on holiday. He'd never get involved in anything dodgy or illegal."

I hope she's right because Harry Lawson's death looks more suspicious by the hour.

Nine

Ashley's tired eyes and dishevelled hair tells me she's only recently woken. She apologies for not treating me to a pizza at her place. Instead she's ordered a spicy curry to wake her up. It's due any time. She slips a treat to Columbo and watches him scoot across the room to his safe corner beside the sofa.

"Have you noticed how dogs can go from sleep to alert in a split second?"

"There's danger around every corner in the wild. You need to have your wits about you and react fast."

"I wish." She yawns again and drops her bag on the breakfast bar. "I arrived home after lunch, dropped onto the sofa and fell asleep. I woke up about fifteen minutes ago, which is why I'm still in my work clothes and looking like I've been out on the razzle. Do people still say that?"

"Depends on how pissed they are." I open a bottle of Becks Blue and slide it across the breakfast bar.

She eyes the bottle with suspicion. "I need something stronger than this. How can they call it beer if it has no alcohol?"

"Try it and see what you think."

She climbs onto the stool, settles herself and takes a sip. "Not bad."

"And low in calories."

"You and your food facts. Mike said the worst thing about meeting you was the number of foods he no longer wanted to eat after your scare stories." She pauses, caught by another memory of the man who was her mentor and inspiration. "I came across his name in a cold case I was reviewing this morning. It was like someone sucked my insides out."

She sips more Becks. "Did you know he joined my gym?"

I can't help smiling at the thought.

"At the start of the year," she says. "He heard me complaining about the women who go there in full makeup and push up bras, posing for the musclebound men who parade past. I wouldn't mind so much, but these women sit around, hogging the equipment while they pose and take selfies."

"You should take up running. It's much cheaper and the company's better."

"I'll only slow you down." She takes another sip of Becks and studies the label. "It's a pity Harry Lawson didn't drink this. He might still be alive if he had."

"He'd definitely been drinking on Saturday?"

"Witnesses at the party said so. He reeked of alcohol, according to Beth. She rang to tell me the post mortem confirmed death by drowning. He had bruising to his elbow and forearms and a bump on the side of his head. There's no evidence it's our faithful friend the blunt instrument, before you ask. It looks like he tripped or slipped, fell forward onto his elbows and arms, and cracked his skull on the pool surround before falling into the water. The storm washed away any evidence from the pool surround."

"Could he have been pushed?"

"Anything's possible as no one saw him fall. The windows and curtains were closed and the rain was ferocious."

"Rathbone has a conservatory at the back, doesn't he?"

"He closed it off because the sound of the rain on the roof was deafening."

"Convenient," I hear myself saying, my mind racing ahead. "But it doesn't explain how Harry got into the garden. The wall's two metres high and topped with trellis. Was there any damage or evidence he climbed over?"

She shakes her head. "It looks like the gate wasn't locked. Rathbone says he locked it that afternoon and no one else has any keys." She smiles. "He leaves it unlocked for the gardener before you ask. That's all I can tell you without getting into trouble."

I pace across the kitchen, thinking. "So, either Rathbone didn't lock the gate as he said, someone else has a key, or borrowed his, or Harry found another way into the garden. Can you access the garden through the study? Or vice versa?"

"Everyone saw Rathbone escort Harry to the front door and throw him out."

"Do you have a timeline?" I ask, certain we're missing something. "Do we know how much time elapsed between Harry leaving the house and drowning in the pool?"

"If you're asking whether he had time to find another way into the garden, I don't know." Ashley pulls her phone from her jacket pocket. "Hi Beth, I'm sorry to disturb you. Yes, I'm with Kent and we'd like to know if Rathbone's study has a door to the garden. Right," she says, nodding. "French doors, locked from the inside, keys in the lock. Yes, I'm sure that's the first thing he'll say. Right, okay, I'll tell him. Thanks."

Ashley lays the phone on the breakfast bar. "Beth wants to know if there's anything you want to contribute to the report she's writing for the Coroner. If there is, she'll come over to take a statement."

I nod, wondering what Harry did after being ejected from the house. From what I've learned, it sounds like Harry was in the study while Rathbone was upstairs with his fiancée.

What if Harry unlocked the French doors, ready to return later, when the party had finished?

My thoughts are interrupted by the arrival of the delivery driver, who pulls up at the entrance. Columbo raises his head and listens, well aware there's food on the way. He can probably smell the curry. His low growl reminds me how he chased the driver last time he called.

That could explain why the driver hasn't entered the car park.

He rings, asking if the dog is safely inside. Though he doesn't sound like he believes me, he pushes open the gate, checking all around. I'm about to go downstairs when Ollie strides across the car park and takes the food from the driver.

"Who's that?" Ashley asks, joining me at the window. She lifts Columbo into her arms so he can look out of the window. The low growl in his throat becomes an excited bark. He starts to wriggle, eager to get outside. When she puts him down, he hurtles across the floor and down the stairs.

"Ollie's one of the new volunteers. He used to work in a bakery, which might be helpful now Niamh's not here to bake cakes."

"Has she sent you the recipes yet?"

I shake my head. "I spoke to her this afternoon. She's offered to supply me from her father's old bakery. She's reopened it with one of her cousins."

Ashley follows me towards the stairs. "Does that mean she's not coming back?"

"She didn't say, but I don't think she will."

I head down the stairs as Ollie raps on the front door. Columbo leaps up, eager to head outside. When I open the door, he's through the gap and barking. Ollie hands me the takeaway bag and then calls Columbo, who stops, looks around and then charges back.

"He often follows me around," Ollie says, his chest swelling with pride inside his overalls. "You're a lovely fella, aren't you?"

He clicks his fingers and Columbo rises onto his back legs. He barks once and Ollie holds out a treat. It's gone in one swift snatch. Ollie clicks his fingers again and Columbo sits.

"I've now cleared most of the borders," he says, "I wanted to make sure I removed every last trace of bindweed before I finished."

He sweeps the grey hair back from his forehead. He may look like a gardener in his overalls, but he speaks like my old English teacher, sounding every syllable. He's trim, fit and healthy, with more stamina than our younger volunteers.

"I appreciate your dedication, Ollie. See you tomorrow."

He glances over my shoulder, interested in who's with me, I guess. "Enjoy your meal, Mr Fisher."

Upstairs, Ashley's removed the plates from the oven. She sniffs in the aroma and dives into the bag for her chicken madras. Once we're settled at the dining table, Columbo waiting below, she mixes the curry and mushroom rice together. We don't speak until we've cleared the plates, mopping up the residue with naan bread. She finishes her second Becks Blue, I help myself to a second glass of skimmed milk.

She takes the plates to the dishwasher, much to Columbo's disgust. She's forgiven when she slips him some naan bread.

"Now we've concluded the most important business of the evening, I'd like to hear about your chat with Rathbone."

"He was more helpful than I expected."

We retreat to the corner unit for comfort. Ashley kicks off her shoes and stretches out, another bottle of Becks in her hand. I make a mug of tea and join her. Columbo leaps up and lies between us, happy to take attention from us both. When I finish relating the main details of my conversation with Rathbone and Stephanie Richmond, Ashley remains silent, her eyes closed. For a moment, I wonder if I've sent her to sleep.

"Something's off." She turns her head to look at me. "Harry's a journalist, investigating Rathbone's activities. From what you've said, Kent, there's something in his study that Harry wants. He finds out his old friend Sarah Wheeler is going to the party and seeks her help."

I've considered something similar. "He thinks Sarah may be affected by what he's investigating."

"We know he holds a torch for her because of the texts he sent." Ashley looks at me. "He sent them the day after he visited Sarah, didn't he?"

I nod, wondering if she's considering something I've missed.

She shuffles to get comfortable. "This is what bothers me. If you were investigating Rathbone, would you tell someone who's been invited to his party?"

"Sarah wasn't directly invited. She was Stephanie Richmond's plus one."

"She's a councillor, so it's likely that Sarah has socialised with Rathbone. Harry's not stupid."

"True, but Harry, Sarah and I had an environmental action group. We had a few skirmishes with Rathbone over the years. Maybe Harry thought Sarah still shared his views."

"Kent, all Sarah had to do was tell Rathbone about Harry's visit and his cover was blown. I'm surprised he trusted her."

"Harry loved taking risks," I say. "He rarely considered the consequences."

"Like blagging his way into the party and insulting Rathbone's fiancée?"

"He could have done that to get her out of the way. Rathbone went upstairs to console her, giving Harry the chance to go into the study."

Ashley doesn't look convinced. "Risky though. Anyone could walk in and spot him. Someone did because they alerted Rathbone."

"What if Harry wanted to unlock the French doors, or get the key so he could return later? He'd only need a few seconds alone."

She shakes her head. "Why draw attention to yourself? Why return to the study while the party's still in full swing? If the rain stops, people could go outside and see him poking around."

"That's why he headed straight for the study after he was thrown out of the house."

"Then he must have had a key for the garden gate." She takes another sip of Becks. "All he had to do was slip the gardener a few quid to borrow the key or get a copy."

"Or ask the gardener to leave it unlocked," I say.

"So, what went wrong, Kent?"

"Someone saw Harry sneaking around the back."

"Or he might have slipped if he'd been drinking. According to the pathologist, Harry's liver was shot. If you were going to break into someone's study for crucial evidence, with a party in full swing outside the door, would you drink?"

"Dutch courage?"

She shakes her head. "An alcoholic knows if he has one drink, it's a slippery slope – or a slippery pool surround in this case."

"What if Harry's drunken state made it easy for someone to make it look like an accident?"

Ten

The aroma of coffee stirs Ashley from her slumbers. She dozed off during *Star Wars*. One moment she was watching, the next she was sleeping, sinking into the corner unit. When I checked on her at eleven, she was lying on her side, snoring away. When I returned from taking Columbo for a short walk, I laid a blanket over her and went to bed.

She was still asleep when I rose at six.

She's not coping too well with her brush with death. I've had some restless nights, punctuated by vivid dreams, but like eating, sleeping has never been a problem for me. Like Ashley, who works unsociable hours, I'm used to being out at night on animal rescues, grabbing a few hours of shut-eye when I can. But the nurse at Eastbourne District General Hospital told me Ashley suffered with nightmares after the incident.

When I place the mug of coffee on the glass table, she opens one eye, staring at me as if I'm a stranger. Then she looks around, a deep frown etched into her forehead. It's only when Columbo stretches forward to lick her face that realisation dawns.

Her cheeks flush. "Have I been here all night?"

I nod.

"Shit. I must look a mess. My throat feels like I've had too much to drink, but my head says not. Why didn't you wake me?"

"You looked so peaceful."

"You said something about checking Harry's flat and his computer, didn't you?" Before I can answer, she throws off the blanket and staggers to her feet. "I need the bathroom."

While she showers, I tip some dried food into Columbo's bowl. This keeps him quiet for about a minute as he devours the lot, pausing only for a drink of water. Once fed, he looks at me, ready to go outside.

I follow him through the door, enjoying the early morning light and residual warmth. The wood pigeons and doves in the woodland are calling to each other. Apart from the birdsong it's peaceful with only the sound of cars in the distance. While I keep an eye on Columbo, who's following all kinds of animal trails through the grass, Frances wanders over on her way back from the paddocks. She only wears khaki tops and combat trousers, which she tucks into Doc Marten boots. She sweeps her long dreadlocks, intertwined with beads, behind her ears and glances up at my flat. "Is that Ashley?"

I look up to see Ashley, wrapped in a bath towel, standing at the kitchen window. She raises the mug of coffee to her lips, glances towards Jevington village and then retreats from view.

"She fell asleep on the sofa."

"Right." Frances saunters off, her grin suggesting she doesn't believe me.

Columbo returns and follows me upstairs, looking for Ashley. She walks in a few minutes later, dressed in yesterday's clothes, her damp hair flat against her scalp. She stops and stares at me. "Why are you smiling like that? Do I look a mess?"

"Frances thinks you spent the night with me."

"I hope you didn't tell her I fell asleep on the sofa. If word gets out you're sending women to sleep..." She chuckles and places her empty mug in the dishwasher. "Still, it's the best night's sleep I've had since ... you know."

I slot a decaffeinated coffee pod in the machine. "Didn't the hospital prescribe anything to help you sleep?"

"I don't like chemicals messing with my brain."

"Apart from Merlot?"

She gives me a helpless shrug. "I thought it would help. I didn't know what else to do."

"You can talk to me, Ashley."

"So you can see what a wreck I've become?" She forces a smile and shakes her head. "I have a counsellor, who says I need to embrace my vulnerability not deny it. But if I end up a blubbing mess, I'll be no good to anyone, will I? I'm a detective inspector because I've accepted the knocks, picked myself up, and come back stronger. You understand that, don't you, Kent?"

I nod. "Now you're sleeping properly you'll soon be back to your old self."

"Does that mean I can spend more nights here?"

"Is that a good idea?" I ask.

"Do you think I'm cold and unapproachable?"

I stop, not sure what prompted the question. "Who told you that – your counsellor?"

"My guvnor."

"I thought you got on well with your boss."

"I did until I almost got myself killed helping you. Now some graduate highflier has taken over my caseload and made a big impression with the suits upstairs. He talks the right bollocks, naturally."

"But he doesn't have your experience."

"He's not cold and unapproachable either." She grabs her bag, ready to leave. "He's charming, good at the job and drop dead gorgeous. I don't stand a chance."

"You'll feel better once you're back full time."

"I need to be back on the job, not wondering how to occupy my afternoons."

"You could always help me."

"Mucking out the stables? I'm not that desperate."

"You could help with Harry. If you get his address, we could take a look one afternoon."

"Even if I was allowed to help you, you're busy preparing for audits."

"Only on Mondays. Tuesdays and Wednesdays are inspection days. And guess who's overdue a food hygiene inspection."

"Our favourite slimeball?"

"I'm going to inspect the Travellers this morning. Rathbone's fiancée Katya manages the place. I can't wait to hear what she has to say about her engagement party."

She gives me a sigh that says I'm beyond redemption. "You're determined to antagonise Rathbone, aren't you?"

"Oh, I intend to do much more than that."

Eleven

The Travellers is more hotel than public house. While tasteful gold letters spell out the name, suggesting class and quality, the fake Tudor beams and leaded windows with PVC frames can't make the building look centuries old. Window boxes and hanging baskets burst with colourful annuals, but their brightness only accentuates the faded and weary banner that advertises Sky Sports. A modern three storey annex houses the hotel, which will soon have a new gym, sauna and swimming pool in the basement. Like the nightclub at the back of the pub, the pool will open out onto its own patio, offering views across the marshes to the coast.

The Travellers has something for everyone – including an outbreak of salmonella at a wedding reception a few years ago.

When I arrive at nine thirty, I settle back in the car and phone Kelly in the call centre. I have to wait a minute or two before her line is free. Despite her friendly greeting, she sounds wary when she hears my voice.

"Can you do me a favour, Kelly? I've arrived at the Travellers for a food hygiene inspection and I forgot to bring the premises file. Could you email me the inspection summary from the last visit?"

"I thought you were going to Tollingdon Community College."

I'm pleased she's checked my diary. "There's going to be a grand opening of the new pool and gym at the Travellers the weekend after next," I say, reading the huge sign in front of me. "Celebrities, several distinguished guests from the world of sport and leisure, and the mayor will be here. As the place is overdue an inspection, I thought I'd better make sure the standards are good. We don't want anyone getting ill at the opening."

"We've got a high volume of calls at the moment. I'm not your personal assistant."

"I don't mind waiting five minutes. Oh, and will you update my online diary to show I'll be at the Travellers all morning? Thanks."

I end the call, saddened to confirm my suspicions. Kelly should have referred me to Gemma. But Kelly needs to update Rathbone. She'll be on the phone to him right now, telling him I'm at his pub. He'll guess I'm here to talk to Katya about the engagement party. Will he tell his fiancée to say nothing or brief her to ensure their accounts tally? With only a few minutes to talk to her, it will be interesting to see which route he takes.

When the email arrives twelve minutes later, I'm confident Kelly's spoken to Rathbone.

I grab my white coat and inspection folder and head inside. Two years ago, Mike and I came here to track down a dodgy mobile caterer. The rooms were wall to wall black with matching floors and ceilings. Now, the booths and partitions have gone, creating a large room that's decorated in neutral tones to highlight the polished woodwork. Seating with plush, plum-coloured upholstery now lines the walls. Uplighters provide a softer glow than the former glare of plasma TV screens and gaming machines.

Like the Goth barmaid, the bar has been replaced.

A woman in a black suit and plum-coloured blouse walks through the swing door from the kitchen at the rear of the room. Her heels beat an aggressive rhythm on the bare boards as she approaches. Slim, with mahogany coloured hair, cut into a crisp bob, she has an air of self- confidence that's intended to intimidate, like the 'don't mess with me' look in her pale wolf eyes. What her welcoming smile lacks in sincerity, it makes up for with dazzling white teeth.

"We've been expecting you, Mr Fisher."

"You have? And here I was, thinking I'd surprise you."

"Thanks to Gregory's keen interest in your work, we can calculate the date of the next inspection from the rating you gave us last time."

If that's the case she would know this inspection's long overdue. Still, she speaks fluent bullshit, so we should get along well.

"Our new chef Terry will be here shortly. Can I get you a coffee while you wait?"

"If you'll join me, Miss Novik."

"It would be a pleasure to sit and explain all the improvements we've made since your last inspection, but I'm needed elsewhere. Terry's best-placed to answer your questions."

"Why, was he at your engagement party on Saturday, Katya?"

That stops her in her tracks. "No. Neither were you, Mr Fisher, but then you weren't invited."

"Neither was Harry Lawson and look what happened to him."

Her forced smile can't take the edge off the flash of anger in her eyes. "I understand he was an old friend of yours."

I nod. "That's why I'd like to find out what happened on Saturday evening."

"Haven't you already spoken to Gregory?"

"I understood he was upstairs when you first encountered Harry."

Another forced smile. "I'll organise coffee."

"Decaff for me."

She pulls out her mobile phone and orders coffee from the kitchen. She sits in the chair opposite me, her posture upright, her hands smoothing her skirt, allowing me a good look at her diamond cluster engagement ring. When there are no creases left in her skirt, she clasps her hands together and looks up.

"Mr Lawson was rude and aggressive. He was soaked to the skin, unsteady on his feet and he reeked of whisky, Mr Fisher. He stood there, staring at my breasts, but I'm used to that."

She's good. No wonder Rathbone fell for her, though I doubt if he had much say in the matter.

"As I explained to the police, Mr Fisher, I tried to calm Mr Lawson and take him into the study. He refused and accused me of recruiting illegal immigrants to work here."

She pauses while a waiter walks over and sets a tray on the table. She makes no move to pour coffee. "Gregory came downstairs to deal with Mr Lawson. I returned to my bedroom."

My bedroom – not 'our' bedroom.

"I was angry and upset, as I'm sure you can understand. That's all I can tell you."

"When did you become aware of Harry?"

"I came out of the kitchen and saw him making a nuisance of himself. As I said, I tried to get him into the study because he was upsetting my guests."

Didn't Rathbone say Harry made a beeline for Katya when she came out of the kitchen? "So," I say, "Harry wasn't aware of you until you confronted him."

"Oh, he knew who I was."

"And then Gregory came down and took Harry into the study."

"Now, let me get this right." She thinks for a few moments. "I persuaded Mr Lawson to go into the study and wait for Gregory. I didn't see Mr Lawson again until he was found in the pool."

I nod, though I doubt if it happened the way she said. Rathbone said he saw Harry make a beeline for Katya when she came out of the kitchen. Rathbone also said he found Harry slumped in a chair in the study.

So did Katya take him into the study or did Rathbone?

Maybe Harry was already in the study.

"You were in the kitchen before you confronted Harry," I say. "Is it close to the study?"

"They're next door to each other. Why do you ask?"

I look straight into her eyes. "I wondered whether you spotted Harry in the study, looking around," I say, my tone casual. "Reporters like to nose around, don't they?"

Her hands smooth her skirt once more.

I smile. "Maybe you spotted him coming out of the study."

"I don't know who you've been talking to, but I've told you what happened. The police have my written statement. And before you pester me with more questions, I didn't see your friend again after I went to my bedroom."

"You weren't there when Harry was discovered in the pool?"

She rises and looks down at me with a sneer. "Are you asking me for an alibi, Mr Fisher? Maybe you'd like to check my passport to see if I'm an illegal immigrant, as Mr Lawson suggested."

"I meant no offence, Miss Novik. I'm simply trying to find out what happened to my friend."

"Your friend was drunk. When Gregory threw him out he got into the back garden and fell into the swimming pool."

"Thank you for your time. I know you have a lot to do, what with the opening of your new gym and swimming pool. I'd love to take a look after I've finished in the kitchen."

"That won't be possible."

"We need to add it to our pool water sampling programme, that's all."

"There won't be any water to sample unless the contractors resolve the fault with the filtration system."

"You don't seem to be having much luck with swimming pools, do you?"

"Please report to Chef when you finish your inspection." She strides away, calling over her shoulder. "I have nothing further to say to you."

I reach for the pot of coffee, sensing she's already said more than she intended.

Twelve

The beefy chef walks into the dining area. Small and built like a bull, he has a shaven head, tattoos on his forearms, but the cleanest whites I've seen since I pressed mine this morning. He looks me over like a steak he wants to tenderise. His handshake almost crushes my hand.

"Terry Phelan," he says in a scouse accent. "I'm glad you're here, Mr Fisher, because I've found a body in the freezer."

While I've lost count of the number of chefs who've found bodies in freezers, his laughter's infectious and not what I expected. I could say the same for the large, open plan kitchen. Gone are the old units, the rusty cookers and dented stainless steel worktops I found on my last inspection. The grey tiles with dirty grouting have transformed into white plastic cladding that runs from floor to ceiling, covering every wall. From fridges and freezers to dry goods store, to preparation areas and wash up, everything is top quality and more than compliant with the law.

It takes less than an hour to complete the inspection and examine records. When we squeeze into Terry's tiny office, the only question marks involve the food handlers and their training and knowledge.

"Most of them speak some English," he says, shuffling into his chair. "Mind you, I'm one to talk with my accent."

I sit opposite on a chair that creaks ominously. His desk looks like it fell off the back of a lorry, travelling at speed. Among the manuals, folders and boxes of antibacterial hand wash, there's only enough room for an old laptop. More boxes, stacked on the floor, contain disposable gloves, hairnets and paper caps. He stretches across to a bookcase filled with manuals, ledgers and trade magazines. He extracts a ring binder, which he passes to me.

"Kat trains them, but they don't stay long, which is why there are so many records."

"What do you do if there's a problem with communication?"

"To be honest, you only need to show the people once and they get on with it. They don't talk much either, which is great. I don't know where they come from, but they're grafters."

I hand the binder back and pull out the pad with my report forms. "I'm impressed, Terry. You must enjoy working here."

"Kat's a great boss. She's demanding, but fair. She works longer hours than the rest of us and I can't remember the last time she had a day off. She expects everything to be right and she doesn't tolerate slackers or mistakes."

"Yes, I can imagine she's difficult to please."

"Kat's not had it easy," he says, his tone suggesting he's rather taken with Katya. "She was raped by the people who brought her and her sister to England. Instead of the promised job in a swanky Brighton hotel, she was forced into the sex trade. She lost her child, got separated from her sister, and was beaten if she stepped out of line or tried to escape. But Gregory Rathbone rescued her and here she is, transforming his business."

"That's some story."

"She's some woman. She deserves a top hygiene rating, wouldn't you say?"

"You've earned it, Terry. I'll complete the details upstairs if that's okay. Were you here when the new kitchen was fitted?"

"No, I've only worked here for six months, but Kat leaves me to it. She lets me adapt the menu and create new dishes, especially for weddings and parties."

"Did you do the catering for her engagement party?"

"Only the finger buffet. I prepared it here and took it over to the house. Now that's a grand place. Have you seen it?"

"Only from the outside."

He laughs. "Aye, Kat's housekeeper is harder to get past than a doctor's receptionist. Vera she's called – Vera Slater. When I arrived at the gates, she refused to let me in because I didn't look like any chef she'd ever met. I had to call Kat to get through. Then Vera refused to let us take the food through the house. We had to go through a gate and through the back garden. Nice swimming pool and Jacuzzi," he says, reaching for his phone. "I took a photo on the way out."

"I hear someone fell into in the pool," I say, studying the photo.

"That's why Kat didn't want me to go over and collect anything," he says, as if everything makes sense now. "I thought it was Vera, being awkward. She got the right hump when I had a nosy at the pool, telling me I was holding up Green-Fingered Glen, who needed to mow the lawn."

"He's the gardener, right?"

"He's not keen on Mrs Slater either. She checks his work like Hercule Poirot before she'll open the gate so he can leave."

"Does she control all the gates?"

"She controls the days you can visit. She's in charge of housekeeping here at the hotel three days a week. That leaves two days at the house when Glen can do the garden. He tried to change his days to avoid her, but no luck."

When the sous chef beckons him, I head upstairs. Without prompting, a cup of tea arrives, brought by the same waiter as before. He hurries away before I can strike up a conversation. Hearing a ride-on lawnmower outside, I walk over to the window and spot Green-Fingered Glen's van close by. Though tempted to talk to him, I make a note of his mobile number. Back in my seat I consider what Terry told me.

If Vera Slater locked the gate after Glen finished his work last Saturday, how did Harry Lawson get into the garden?

Who unlocked the gate for him?

If only Vera Slater, Rathbone and Katya have keys to the gate, one of them must have allowed Harry to access the garden last Saturday. While this leads to some interesting conjecture, I wonder if someone made a copy of the key.

Hearing the lawn mower once more, I realise there may be another way into the garden.

I hurry around the back of the Travellers and stop beside Glen's van. He waves when he notices me and pulls up on his ride-on mower a few moments later. I hold up my badge and raise my voice to be heard above the sound of the engine. "I understand you look after Gregory Rathbone's garden."

He removes his baseball cap to reveal a sweating bald head. "What of it?"

"Terry Phelan suggested I had a word with you."

Glen, whose fingers are more nicotine yellow than green, pulls a pack of cigarettes from his shirt pocket. "I only cut the grass and tidy the borders."

"How do you get your ride on mower into the garden? It's too big to fit through the gate at the side of the house."

"Well spotted. Why do you want to know?"

"A friend of mine had an accident on Saturday evening."

"You mean the reporter who drowned in the pool?"

"How do you know he was a reporter?"

"He asked me the same question you just did."

I glance at my watch. "Do you want to break for lunch so we can talk?"

He puts the cap back on his head. "I've got grass to mow."

"Can you tell me how you get your lawn mower into the back garden?"

"I don't. I use Mr Rathbone's mower. It's similar to this one."

"How did he get his mower into the garden?" I ask, sensing I know the answer already.

"Why don't you ask him?"

Unwilling to admit defeat, I try a different angle. "Is there another way into the back garden?"

"Reporter asked me that too."

"What did you tell him?"

"I suggested he rang the doorbell."

He takes a final draw on his cigarette and flicks it away.

63

Back at my car, I glance across at the hotel annexe, weighing up my chances of speaking to Vera Slater. If she helped Harry get into the back garden, she might feel anxious now he's dead. He had a way with women when he turned on the charm. They seemed to gravitate towards him, keen to listen to his exaggerated stories and escapades as a hunt saboteur. Being a reporter for the *Tollingdon Tribune* helped. He specialised in lifestyle features, which meant free tickets for shows and galleries, offers of meals from restaurants and an easy way to entertain women.

He also ensured our activities to disrupt hunts received good coverage.

Did Harry charm Vera Slater?

When Katya strides out of the hotel, looking like she's ready to kick someone, I climb into my car. I'm already going to get enough grief from Rathbone when she tells him about the conversation we had. I won't compound it by demanding to inspect the hotel.

Vera Slater will keep. I don't want to talk to her here – or at Rathbone's home for that matter. That's assuming she'll talk to me. If she trained at the Green-Fingered Glen school of public relations, I may as well quit now.

I need a backup plan.

I'm halfway to Wartling when I realise Adrian Peach at the *Argus* could help me. As a colleague and a reporter, he may know what Harry was working on.

Stopping in the layby near the entrance to Herstmonceux Castle, I ring Adrian. He'll be delighted to learn I'm investigating Harry's death, but for all the wrong reasons.

Adrian picks up on the first ring. "I was wondering if you'd ring me, Mr Fisher."

"You were?"

"Yeah, Harry said you'd contact me if someone killed him."

Thirteen

Adrian drowns his burger with ketchup. "Harry liked to be dramatic, but I never expected him to wind up dead the next day."

We're sitting at a table on the terrace of the Beachy Head pub, looking across the South Downs towards Belle Tout lighthouse and Birling Gap. With the sun high in its trajectory, the heat is intense, despite the pleasant breeze. Hundreds of visitors, from dog walkers to foreign students, stroll along the undulating hills, looking out at the sparkling sea. Far too many people venture close to the edge, oblivious or unconcerned about the fragile state of the chalk cliffs as they take selfies or peer at the sea below.

"Idiots," I say, shaking my head.

"Harry said you formed an action group to deal with people who damaged the environment up here." Adrian shovels some chips into this mouth, more interested in me than the tourists putting their lives at risk. "What did you do?"

"We took action."

He laughs. "What sort of action?"

"Reciprocal. We targeted people, like the ones who have barbecues on the Downs. They used to scorch the grass with their portable barbecue trays. Occasionally, one would cause a fire, especially during a hot, dry summer. Then there's the danger to wildlife when you leave behind a hot, barbecue tray, dripping with animal fat."

"How did you deal with it?" Adrian asks.

"We returned what they left behind."

I don't tell him how we tracked down the offenders and pushed their waste food and litter through their letterboxes after dark. If the letterbox was large enough, we'd force the remains of the portable barbecue through.

We adopted a similar approach with dog owners who didn't clear up after their dogs.

As Harry worked for the *Tollingdon Tribune*, he would go round the next day to find out how people reacted to our actions.

"Make the punishment fit the crime," Adrian says, nodding in approval.

Though he eats like a horse, Ashley describes him as wiry as a whippet. Young, alert and keen, he has a nose for a story and the tenacity to chase it down. While it goes with the territory, he's interested in the people behind the stories and news. He gave Mike Turner a glowing obituary, focusing on his achievements and the people whose lives he'd changed.

It doesn't stop me wanting to keep Adrian at arm's length, even though he may have information that will help me.

Then again, I have something he wants – access to Savanna.

When he met her at the official launch of my animal sanctuary, he followed her round like a puppy, desperate for attention. When she finally gave in and suggested a selfie, he couldn't resist. She posted it on Instagram later, saying some reporters have no respect for privacy. Behind them was the sign for the ladies toilets.

"Let's concentrate on Harry," I say, keen to move things along. "Do you know why Harry went to Rathbone's party?"

"I didn't know Harry was going there. Weeks ago, he claimed he was onto something big. He'd raided the archives for stories and features about Rathbone. That's why I wondered if it had anything to do with your action group. You and Rathbone have clashed a few times over the years."

"I thought Harry was in London."

"He's written regularly in the *Argus*. I'm surprised you haven't noticed."

"I don't read newspapers or watch the news."

"I don't suppose you have much time with your sanctuary and all this sleuthing. So what's with this environmental health contract? You hardly covered yourself in glory when you were running the department. Or are you going to blame Gregory Rathbone?"

"Let's stick to Harry. We both want to know what he was investigating and why he died. So, why don't you tell me what you know?"

He puts his knife and fork down. "Harry's mobile phone and notebooks are missing. I only found out yesterday, when I called at the mortuary. They're not in his desk at work. Ditto his flat."

"Did you ever meet Miranda, his fiancée?"

"I had an invite to the wedding. Then Harry came in one morning and said it was all off. He didn't seem upset or angry and wouldn't talk about it. Miranda was devastated.

When he left for work that morning, he kissed her on the cheek, said he couldn't marry her and not to wait up for him. He'd already cancelled the wedding the day before."

"Have you any idea what went wrong?"

"Harry was always up and down, bipolar even. Some days he could take on the world. Other days, he could drive you crazy with his moody silences and cynical remarks." Adrian dips another chip in ketchup. "I think there was another woman."

"Why do you think that?"

"Little things. The way he talked on the phone sometimes. A silly smile he thought no one noticed. Some mornings, he'd saunter into work like he'd lost his virginity. I've no idea who she was before you ask."

"Did he ever talk about Sarah Wheeler?"

"Gemma's mother? No never." He pauses and thinks for a moment. "Miranda refused to believe there was anyone else. She blamed the newspaper for Harry's behaviour. She claimed we didn't support him or believe in him, so I've no idea what he told her about work."

"Harry always blamed others for his mistakes," I say. "If he was onto something, but couldn't convince your editor, he might have complained to Miranda about it."

Adrian shakes his head. "Harry wanted all the glory. That's why he was dismissed."

"Slow down, Adrian. When was Harry dismissed?"

"Last Thursday afternoon. I don't know the details as I wasn't there, but Harry claimed someone had sabotaged his investigation." Adrian picks up the last chip and leans forward. "The day before he asked me if I'd found a memory stick in my car. When Miranda threw his stuff out a few weeks before, she scattered his belongings on the front drive. I helped him collect them."

"Did you find the memory stick?"

"We spent an hour searching my car, but no memory stick. When I asked him why it was important, he said the bitch has probably taken it. I said Miranda wouldn't do that. He said she was many things, but never a bitch."

"So who was he referring to?"

"Good question. Back in the office, before he left, Harry made a phone call and then rushed out. I don't know why he used the landline, but I checked the last number he dialled." Adrian pauses, like a TV presenter about to announce a game show winner. "I don't know who he spoke to, but he rang Downland District Council."

Fourteen

While Adrian goes inside to order himself another lager shandy, I pull out my notebook. I need to cross reference the details he's given me with what Sarah's told me. If I can create a timeline, I might make some sense of what happened to Harry.

January of this year – Harry emails Sarah, says he's returning to East Sussex to buy smallholding, going to marry Miranda. Sarah not interested in meeting her. Harry rings to find out why, she reminds him of time he sexually assaulted her. He denies all knowledge of incident.

Following week – Harry sends Sarah invitation to wedding in June.

Week before the wedding – Harry walks out on Miranda, sends Sarah text about always picking wrong person. He's also working on big story, but won't tell anyone what. (Rumours of another woman? Did he tell her?)

Thursday last week – Harry can't find memory stick. He wonders if it's in Adrian's car after they collected Harry's belongings when Miranda dumped them in the driveway back in June. When memory stick not found, Harry says 'the bitch probably took it', but he's not referring to Miranda? (Is there another woman?)

Thursday afternoon – Harry makes phone call to Downland DC. (Is this where the 'bitch/other woman' works?) Harry's sacked and accuses editor of sabotaging investigation.

Friday evening – Harry calls on Sarah. (Why didn't Sarah tell me this?)

After midnight on Saturday morning – Harry sends three texts to Sarah, implying he was in love with her.

Saturday evening – Harry gate crashes Rathbone's party. (Is Harry caught in the study?) He's thrown out but later found drowned in swimming pool. (How did Harry get into back garden?) His phone and laptop are missing.

"Have you worked it out?" Adrian gestures to my notebook as he drops into his seat, an expectant look on his face. "What do we do next?"

I close the notebook. "Are you suggesting we work together?"

"We're both after the truth."

He's after a story, but I say nothing, curious to see what he has in mind.

"You've spoken to Sarah Wheeler," he says. "You can find out who Harry rang at Downland. Your friend, Ashley, knows what the police and Coroner's Officer are doing."

"What are you going to contribute, Adrian?"

"I'll find out what happened at the party. Gregory Rathbone loves getting his name and picture in the papers. I'll offer him a splash on the devastating effects of the drowning on him and his fiancée."

"What about the missing memory stick, mobile phone and laptop? Could someone have taken the memory stick from Harry's desk?"

"Harry would have noticed."

"Not if he was drinking."

He looks thoughtful for a moment. "I'm not sure I've ever seen him drinking. Harry never came to the pub with us."

"His liver was on its last legs, Adrian. Him too, I guess."

"You mean he got drunk and fell into the swimming pool?"

"That's how it looks."

Adrian gives me a suspicious look. "Are you fobbing me off?"

I pocket my notebook. "You're a reporter. You want a good story, like your editor."

"He suggested we work together." Adrian drains his shandy and leans forward, his face animated. "We get an exclusive about how you investigate. You get access to our resources and contacts. I could be Dr Watson to your Sherlock."

"Holmes and Watson were friends."

He laughs, not taking offence. "You might get to like me."

"Would I have a say in what you printed?"

"We wouldn't print anything until the investigation was concluded. If we don't work together, we might print something that could affect your investigation."

"If Harry was murdered, his killer won't want you nosing around. Are you prepared for that, Adrian?"

"I've been threatened by experts. It goes with the territory," he says, as if it's a daily event. "You were almost killed twice on your last investigation. What's it like, coming so close to death? How do you deal with it?"

"I don't think about it."

He studies me, not convinced. "Someone slammed a door earlier. You flinched and looked over your shoulder, an anxious look in your eyes."

"It took me by surprise," I say, having no recollection of the moment.

"No one else jumped." He rests his chin on his knuckles, studying me. "I've interviewed soldiers, who served in Iraq and Afghanistan. I interviewed one soldier from the Falklands war in the 1980s. He still has nightmares and panic attacks. He also sat with his back to the wall like you, keeping an eye on everything and everyone."

Ashley taught me that, but I say nothing.

He checks his watch. "Gemma said you'd deny it."

"You spoke to Gemma?"

"Easy," he says, raising a hand. "I'm only saying I don't know many people who can do what you do and shrug it off."

I learned the hard way.

When my mother walked out of her marriage and took me to Manchester as a seven year old, I wanted to die sometimes. For years she lied, blaming me for her problems, especially after she'd drunk too much. It wasn't fair, but there was nothing I could about it. All I could do was lock the anger and frustration away, until one day I couldn't take any more. I lashed out at a boy who taunted me and he beat the shit out of me.

That's when I wondered if I was as useless and pathetic as my mother kept telling me.

A teacher found me and took me to the first aid room. She listened to my woes and said there was always something better over the horizon, including the life I wanted to live.

74

The following week, she introduced me to the library.

"When I was eleven, I read Sherlock Holmes," I say. "I wanted to be as smart as him, to solve the puzzles no one else could solve. When I discovered Agatha Christie I wanted to solve a murder."

"And now you have. How did it feel when you solved your first murder?"

I slide my notebook into my pocket and get to my feet. "Talk to your editor and give me your proposals for how we might work together."

Adrian grabs his phone. "You won't regret it, Kent. We'll make a great team."

Ashley wouldn't agree, but then I'm not going to tell her.

Fifteen

Ashley has her own demons to vanquish. Like me, she has her own way of dealing with them. The last thing she needs is me dragging her into another investigation.

After Adrian leaves, I sit in the car, thinking about my childhood and how I took refuge in books. Sherlock Holmes, Hercule Poirot, and ultimately James Bond, took me into alternative realities where the good guys were invincible and always won.

When life with my mother became difficult, I escaped into this reality. I felt safe and important there, someone who could make a difference. Even when Atticus Finch lost the court case in *To Kill a Mockingbird*, my belief never wavered. It made me more determined than ever to fight for fairness and justice, especially in my alternate reality.

Sometimes, when I think about the six investigations I've completed, I wonder if they belong to an alternative me. While I don't need a phone box like Superman, do I transform into Super Sleuth, as Tommy Logan likes to call me?

Is that how I cope?

That's why I say little to Ashley. As a police officer, she faces the prospect of injury and death every day. It's her reality, not some romanticised notion gleaned from books.

Then there's Gemma. We rarely talk about the investigations and the scrapes. It means I don't always check to make sure she's okay.

Would she tell me if she wasn't?

I head over to Sarah Wheeler's house, arriving a little after six. While she attends to the sick and injured animals of Tollingdon in the surgery next door, Gemma walks through from the kitchen, carrying two mugs of tea. She places them on a small table and removes her jacket, laying it over the back of an armchair. When she sits beside me, her subtle perfume and dark sexy eyes remind me how crazy I was about her.

"My mother won't finish surgery for another hour."

"I came to see you," I say, not sure where to begin. "I wanted to talk about our investigations."

"Are you going to start a blog like I suggested?"

"No, I'm talking about you being attacked, injured and shot. People have died as we searched for the truth. How do you cope with it all?"

"What's brought this on? Are you having trouble?"

"No, I wanted to know if you were okay. I keep meaning to ask, but..."

"You don't like the touchy feely stuff." She chuckles and settles back. "I usually talk to Kelly. She's like a big sister. She listens and doesn't mind if I talk gibberish. She always knows what to say to make me feel better, especially where you're concerned. I know she looks confident and in control, but she's had a tough life. She understands how I feel."

77

"I want to understand how you feel."

From the look on her face, I don't think she believes me. "If you want me to open up, you have to give too, Kent. You can't clam up because you don't want anyone to know you're struggling. Not everyone will see your struggles as a weakness and take advantage." She takes my hand. "People who care about you, who love you, will want to help you. But you have to let them. You have to trust them."

"Trust isn't one of my strong points. You know that."

"You trust me on investigations, Kent. I don't understand why you can't talk to me about what matters."

I've always been hopeless at expressing how I feel. As a child, I spent so long keeping my feelings to myself to avoid ridicule, embarrassment and disappointment, it became a way of life.

Gemma leans closer. "Has Mike's death left you feeling vulnerable?"

"Grief I can handle."

"Then why are you here? What do you want?"

"I want to make sure you're okay after our last case."

"It's only taken you four months to ask, but thanks for your concern. Sorry," she says, backing away. "I appreciate your concern, but I'm not sure what you want."

Neither am I. Once, I thought it was Gemma, but I made a mess of everything. I kept wondering if there was something better over the horizon.

When Savanna walked into Meadow Farm my brain turned to mush.

It's not like she's even interested in me. I doubt if I enter into her thoughts.

Yet I can't stop thinking about her.

I keep hoping she'll turn up one day to tell me she's dumped her partner.

I haven't felt like this since Barbara Booth smiled at me in the sixth form.

I turn to Gemma, aware of the silence. "I want you to help me investigate Harry Lawson's death," I say. "I want to make sure you're ..."

"Up to it?"

"No, your mother's involved."

"Involved in what?" Sarah strides into the room, accompanied by a cocktail of animal smells and disinfectant. Her crocs thud on the vinyl floor as she heads into the kitchen. "My six fifteen failed to show so I thought I'd have the cuppa no one else thought to make me." A cupboard door slams and she marches back into the lounge. "You've used all the tea bags, Gemma."

I hold out my mug. "Have mine."

"What are you doing here, Kent?"

"Is that what you said to Harry when he called round last Friday?"

Sarah glares at her daughter. "You told him."

I stand up and step between them. "Why didn't you tell me, Sarah?"

She grabs the mug from my hand and takes several mouthfuls of tea. "As he walked away, Harry said it would be my fault if he wound up dead."

Sixteen

Sarah shrugs and drinks more tea. "You know Harry, prone to emotional blackmail when he couldn't get what he wanted."

"What did he want?" I ask.

"He wanted me to unlock the French doors in the study."

"So he could enter from the garden?"

She nods. "I told him to piss off."

"Did you say anything to Rathbone?"

She shakes her head. "I never thought Harry would come to the party, let alone walk in as bold as brass. I tried to avoid him, but I was too slow."

"Why didn't you tell me on Sunday?" I ask.

Her receptionist looks around the door. "Miss Wheeler, your next appointment's here."

Sarah drinks the rest of the tea, thrusts the mug into my hand and follows her receptionist.

Gemma lets out a deep sigh. "If you want my help with Harry Lawson, I can't stay here. It's bad enough when she's fooling around with Steph Richmond in the bedroom without her wondering if I'm spying on her." She gives me her best pleading look. "Can I stay at the farmhouse?"

"I'll think about it. First we need to consider what Sarah said. If Harry wanted her to let him into the study through the French doors, he must have arranged for the garden gate to be left unlocked. Only three people have a key – Rathbone, his fiancée, Katya, and Vera Slater, the part time housekeeper."

"Someone could have made a copy of the key."

"Agreed, which moves the housekeeper to the top of the list. We need to know when she's working at the house. If you ring the Travellers tomorrow morning, we'll know whether she's working there or at the house."

"Rathbone will go apeshit if you visit the house to interview her."

"I'm not going to visit her at his place. No, we need to find out where she goes when she finishes working there."

"Follow her home and speak to her there?"

"Exactly, we need to know more about her first. Does she have an axe murderer husband? Does her brother cut keys for a living? Did she clean for Harry? As soon as you know where she's working, let me know."

"What are you going to do?"

"Find out where Harry lived and take a look. Then there's Miranda. They were due to marry in June and Harry called it off the week before. Why? What caused the breakdown?"

"Or who."

I go through the details of my timeline, including what Sarah and Rathbone told me about the party and events beforehand. "Harry's phone and laptop are missing."

Gemma breaks into a wry smile. "Rathbone has to be involved. There's something in his study that Harry wanted. Any ideas, Holmes?"

"Harry told colleagues at the *Argus* he had a big story, but wouldn't say what it was."

"Have you been talking to Adrian Peach?"

I nod. "He wanted my help."

"Mine too. He's asked me out for a drink later. While he's kind of cute, I think he's more interested in my mother."

"He wants to talk to her about the party, I guess."

"I turned him down, but I could change my mind. Do you want me to find out what he's up to?"

I wonder if Adrian will tell her about the partnership he hopes to broker with me. Maybe I should warn her.

Or maybe I should hang fire. If Adrian says nothing about working with me, he might offer Gemma a similar partnership.

Things could get interesting.

Seventeen

Rathbone enters my office at nine o'clock on Wednesday morning. He pauses in the doorway and clears his throat so I'm forced to acknowledge his presence. Dressed in a blue pinstripe suit and complementary tie, he looks more accountant than councillor. Then I spot the suede shoes that owe more to Elvis than coordinated fashion. With his shiny, slicked back hair, he only needs to grow some sideburns to enter a lookalike contest.

He makes a show of closing the door and strolls across to the meeting table, taking a seat at its head. "What happened to Danni's bowl of sweets?"

I remain in my chair. "She must have taken it with her. Gemma's got some Bombay Mix if you're peckish."

He frowns and pulls his jacket sleeves over the cuffs of his shirt. "I stopped by to thank you for the top hygiene rating you awarded the Travellers yesterday. Katya was delighted, as you can imagine. She's put a lot of time, effort and money into charting a new course for our hotel and conference centre."

"I'll ask Kelly to upgrade the property description on our database. Public house with motel annex doesn't have the same ring, does it?"

His laugh is as genuine as his election promises. "You never could take a compliment, could you?"

"Depends on who's complimenting me."

"Perhaps it's the way you treat people, Kent. Where does interrogating Katya fit into a hygiene inspection?"

"The questions about Harry Lawson preceded the inspection. I won't be billing the council for the time it took, if that's what concerns you. Katya seemed happy enough to answer my questions."

"She was talking to an environmental health officer who was about to inspect her business. She didn't want to do or say anything that might affect the outcome."

It's my turn for a humourless laugh. "Katya wasn't in the least bit intimidated by me or my questions. Why would she be if Harry's death was an unfortunate accident?"

He rises, but not to the bait. He walks over and plants two hands firmly on my desk. "You are contracted to prepare for an audit and inspect overdue food businesses. Is that clear?"

"If I've unintentionally antagonised your fiancée, please accept my apologies. I thought she would prefer to talk to me rather than a journalist, looking for a scandal."

Rathbone's frown brings his eyebrows together. His voice drops to low and menacing. "I'd terminate your contract, but you'd have an extra three days a week to make mischief."

He walks out, leaving the door open. Relieved to be free of his bad breath and aftershave, I settle back.

Gemma strolls in, casting a puzzled glance after Rathbone. She closes the door and grins. "Don't tell me he's sacked you already."

"No, he realised it would give me five days a week to investigate Harry's death. Have you located Vera Slater?"

"She's having trouble with her Schnauzer. Don't," she says, trying not to laugh. "I had enough trouble keeping a straight face when her colleague told me. Vera works at the Travellers on Wednesday, Thursday and Friday each week, leaving Monday and Tuesday for Rathbone."

"Has Vera visited a local vet by any chance?"

She slides onto the chair on the other side of my desk. "I'm not checking my mother's records, if that's what you're thinking."

"It'll be quicker than going through the electoral register. Unless you'd rather stake out the hotel and follow her home one afternoon? I thought not. So, how was your date with Adrian Peach?"

She tilts her head from side to side. "Okay, once he stopped asking about you."

"I didn't realise he was a fan."

"He wanted to know what it was like working with you, catching killers, that kind of thing. Either he's planning to write your biography or he's genuinely mesmerised by you."

"Then why did he ask you out for a drink?"

"He's fishing. He spent a weekend with Anna Westcott for a feature he's writing. He's clearly besotted but she kept talking about you. I think he's jealous, so he wants to find out if there's anything between you and Anna."

"I don't know an Anna Westcott. Who is she?"

"You're winding me up, right? It's Savanna's real name."

"Adrian spent a weekend with Savanna?"

She rolls her eyes. "I don't think he slept with her, if that's what you mean. He approached her during the grand opening for your sanctuary. Then, out of the blue, she rang and invited him to her house near Ditchling. She's a got an indoor swimming pool, which you'd expect as she designs swimwear." She pauses and looks straight into my eyes. "You never mentioned she's shooting a film at your sanctuary."

"I didn't know she was going ahead. These so-called celebrities say things and then forget about them."

"Adrian said she's rather taken with you, especially your concerns for the environment and wildlife."

"Stop, Gemma. You're making me blush."

"Not as much as when I mentioned Savanna. Adrian said the two of you spent a lot of time together at the launch. She was well-impressed with your flat apparently. She's a fan of minimalism, which probably explains the skimpy swimwear."

"Savanna was escaping from my father. She had some ideas on how we could raise our profile on social media. That's where Columbo comes in."

"Do you still keep your PC in the bedroom?"

I can't help laughing. "Subtlety was never your strong point, Gemma."

"You're the one who likes everything she posts on her Instagram and Facebook pages."

"I share them to promote her business and the sanctuary."

"I don't know why you're protesting so much, Kent. Anyone can see she's drop dead gorgeous."

"Savanna has a long term partner."

"I know." Gemma clasps her hands together, as she always does when she has something interesting to reveal.

"Adrian told me about Johnny Spender. He owns lots of residential and commercial properties in the area, including the cottage Ashley rents. He wasn't happy when he found out his letting agents rented it to a police officer."

"Interesting."

"Oh, it's gets more interesting. One of Spender's flats in Alfriston was ransacked on Monday." She dips into her bag and pulls out a keyring. "Guess who lived there."

Eighteen

"How did you get the keys to Harry Lawson's flat?" I ask.

Gemma taps the side of her nose. "You're not the only sleuth in town."

"I'm surprised Adrian gave them to you."

"He didn't. Beth from the Coroner's Office dropped them over. Harry was an orphan. He died without relatives."

The penny drops. "So the council will have to bury him."

She nods. "Beth arranged to meet the letting agent there so she could go through Harry's personal possessions. When she arrived, the door was unlocked and the place trashed. It could be a burglary, of course."

"Or someone was looking for something," I say. "Are you off to the flat now?"

"That was the plan until Johnny Spender bent my ear. He wants his workmen in there today to clear the flat and get it ready for new tenants at the weekend."

"So you told him you couldn't visit until tomorrow."

She nods. "Then I realised Sylvie's on leave this afternoon and not back till Monday. I'm not allowed to visit on my own in case someone claims I took something valuable."

I nod, having written the policy last year after a distant relative made a similar claim against us. "You could ask Neville Priddy to go with you, show him what we do."

"He didn't know we buried people who died without relatives."

"Don't be too harsh, Gemma. He's only a head of service."

"True, but he's authorised you to accompany me this afternoon, purely as an observer. It saves you from begging me to take you, more's the pity."

"I'm surprised Neville authorised me, considering Harry drowned at Rathbone's house. Our council leader won't be happy when he finds out."

"Then you'd best get out on the district where he can't find you."

Gemma hands me a printout of the email authorising me to go with her. I grab my folder containing all the paperwork I need for food inspections and prepare to go. Hopefully I won't encounter any problems during my inspections or this afternoon's visit will have to wait.

"I'll see you in Alfriston at two o'clock," she says. "Don't forget to bring the protective clothing and kit we'll need. You remember where it's kept, don't you?"

"As a contractor, I don't have keys to the storeroom. See you later."

As I exit the town hall onto Tollingdon High Street my mobile rings. I step to one side to take the call, aware of the tension in Ashley's voice. It's only the third day of her phased return, but she's clearly not enjoying it.

"I need to move out of the cottage," she says. "Can you pop by this lunchtime?"

I glance at my watch, wondering if I'll have time. "I thought you had another month before the tenancy expired."

"The landlord sent an electrician to the cottage this morning without telling me. He's only condemned the wiring and said I need to move out. When I took the tenancy, the letting agent told me the kitchen was only rewired a few years ago."

It sounds like Johnny Spender's getting impatient.

"I've got a couple of inspections to do and then I'll see you at the cottage. We'll sort this out."

She sounds relieved. "I was hoping you'd say that."

I walk down Victoria Road for my first inspection at a delicatessen, wondering why Spender's so keen to get Ashley out of the cottage.

Does Savanna know how he conducts his business?

I dismiss the thought, knowing it's nothing to do with me.

My father worked in property development. He must have come across Spender.

With a mental note to ring him later, I focus on the food hygiene inspections, which pass without incident. It feels good to be back on the front line, helping businesses to improve their standards and ratings. I'd much rather discuss temperature control than performance indicators.

What possessed me to become acting Head of Environmental Health?

My concerns about Kelly and the way Rathbone was treating her.

At the moment everything seems to involve Councillor Gregory Rathbone.

At ten past one, I join Ashley in her kitchen. While I make a cursory examination of the plug sockets, she retrieves two chicken salad baguettes from the fridge and places them on the small table in the corner.

When I take a seat opposite her, she says, "They're modern sockets. How can they be dangerous?"

"I'm not an electrician, but I reckon a new tenant will move in the day after you leave."

"That's what I think." She tears off a chunk of baguette with her teeth and devours it in seconds. "Yesterday I put in an offer to buy the place. I said I'd match any sensible offer already on the table. The agent said she'd mention it to the freeholder. Then an electrician turns up this morning while I'm at work." She pauses, her expression grim and angry. "I had a quick look round before you arrived. He's been rifling through my drawers and cupboards. He was careless in my knicker drawer."

"The freeholder has an aversion to police officers," I say. "You might want to check out Johnny Spender, in case he has a record."

"He doesn't." She tears off another mouthful of baguette. "A few years ago he owned a hostel for the homeless in Brighton. Alongside the usual winos, dropouts and people with mental health issues, we had information that a significant number of young women passed through the place."

"People trafficking?"

She shrugs. "Two weeks of surveillance revealed nothing, so the guvnor decided to pay a visit and put the pressure on. Spender was so clean, he sparkled, inviting my guvnor to take a look around inside and see the wonderful work he was doing to support people forgotten by society."

"You don't like Spender, do you?"

"I wouldn't have taken this place if I'd known. I dealt with the letting agents. It was perfect, I was in a hurry, so I didn't check." She pauses for another mouthful of baguette. "I can understand him not wanting me here, but the tenancy expires in a few weeks. Why the rush?"

"Are you going to make him wait?"

She drops the baguette and hurries away, tears streaming down her cheeks. I catch up with her in the garden, staring at the South Downs. I stop beside her, hand her a tissue and wait until she's ready to speak.

"I love it here." She sniffs and balls the tissue. "But since the hit and run, my self-confidence is all over the place. One minute I'm ready to take on the world, the next I want to hide in the toilets. The slightest noise wakes me up at night. Sometimes, I can see the Range Rover bearing down on me. I only have to hear a car engine revving and my heart pounds." She turns to me, mascara streaking her cheeks. "What the hell am I going to do, Kent?"

I slide my arms around her and pull her close, running my hand over her hair. "Why don't you take my spare room until you're back to your normal self?"

"That would set tongues wagging. What about the farmhouse?"

When I hesitate, she steps back. "No worries, Kent. I've got colleagues who can spare a sofa for a couple of weeks."

"No, you're a mate, Ashley. The farmhouse is yours." I smile, not sure what I'm going to tell Gemma. "You need to feel safe while you put your troubles behind you."

"What would I do without you?"

She kisses my cheek and hurries inside. When she emerges from the bathroom, looking her normal efficient self, I've finished my baguette and made her a coffee. As she cradles the mug in her hands, she manages a hesitant smile.

"You promised the farmhouse to someone else, didn't you? I thought so," she says, reading my eyes. "I'll be fine, Kent. Mike wouldn't want me to quit, would he?"

"No, the farmhouse is yours, Ashley, for as long as you need it."

"It could be months."

"Then we'd better agree a suitable rent. Start packing and we'll move you in tomorrow," I say, heading for the door. "I'm off to Alfriston now to look at Harry Lawson's flat with Gemma. It's another of Johnny Spender's properties."

"Small world."

I stop and turn, jolted by an unexpected thought. "Look, this may be nothing more than a coincidence, but someone with a key went into Harry's flat and ransacked the place. It's not the letting agent, so –"

"It must be Spender. I reckon he came here too. But why? I have no connection to Harry Lawson."

"You don't need to be Einstein to work out you might be helping me investigate Harry's death."

Her face pales. "Maybe I will take your spare room tonight."

Nineteen

It's a short drive from Jevington to Alfriston, but long enough to help me realise I'm making spurious connections. Johnny Spender has a large property portfolio. Harry and Ashley are two of many tenants. The only link is me and my conspiracy theories.

Mike Turner dubbed me Konspiracy Kent.

His sudden incursion into my thoughts reminds me how much I miss his common sense and bullshit detector. He would have told me reporters make enemies. He would have reminded me how anyone could ransack Harry's flat.

"Anyone with a key," I say, thinking aloud.

It reminds me to take a look inside the farmhouse before Ashley moves in. Niamh left most of her belongings there when she returned to Northern Ireland. I don't think she planned on staying for more than a few weeks, but maybe her old home and haunts brought back happy memories. She was only seventeen when she came to London.

She'll be happier with Ashley in the farmhouse.

At least I didn't promise the place to Gemma, though I'm not sure how she'll react when she discovers I've let Ashley stay there.

And to think I didn't really care what others thought.

You're going soft, Fisher. Since you met Savanna, you're acting like a lovesick schoolboy with a crush on your English teacher, Miss Austen.

Nonsense and insensibility.

But it felt real at the time – until Barbara Booth walked past in her sports kit.

Gemma's parked in front of an old Victorian semi-detached house on West Street, north of the free car park in Alfriston. Brick built with an orange tiled roof, sash windows and an inset porch, the house is now two flats. Harry occupied the ground floor, bagging the bay window. The net curtains look as faded and lifeless as the geraniums in the window box.

She unlocks the front door. "Any problems with the food inspections? Neville's asked me to monitor your work."

"Will you be prioritising my work now you're becoming a manager?"

Her dark eyes gleam. "You never complained when I used to tell you what I desired."

"You were naked at the time."

"Your appraisal could be exciting."

We walk into a hall with an original tiled floor that leads to two doors. Despite the high ceilings and fanlight above the door, it's a dark hall that needs a bigger bulb and a tickle with a cobweb brush. A small table, coated with dust, holds a variety of leaflets and letters, none addressed to Harry. Gemma unlocks the left hand door, which opens into a smaller hallway. The kitchen is straight ahead. The door to the left takes me into a living room that has a window to the back garden. Beyond is a bedroom.

Gemma stares at the chaos around us and hands me some disposable gloves. "My student digs looked like this after a party."

Whoever broke in here emptied every cupboard and shelf, not that there was much to tip out. A sofa and matching armchair have been flipped over and the backs and bases slashed open to reveal the padding and foam.

"You should see the bedroom," she says, summoning me. "Harry's clothes are all over the floor."

The room's almost identical to the living room, apart from the bay, which once contained a dressing table. It's now on its back, mirror smashed, drawers on the floor. A few socks, items of underwear and handkerchiefs lie scattered on the floor. A couple of shirts, some jeans and a tatty pair of trainers that look like they were retrieved from the tip, lie in front of open wardrobes, heaved away from the wall.

"It doesn't look like Harry kept his savings under the mattress." I examine the slashes cut into the stiff and stained fabric. The pillows suffered a similar fate. I walk over to the small computer desk. "Do we know if they took his laptop?"

"I can ask Beth."

I peer behind the desk. "Where are the notebooks and pens, Gemma? Where's the diary, the stationery, the memory sticks? Where are the photographs, the nick knacks we all keep?" I kneel to peer under the bed. "Where's the duvet?"

She looks around. "He didn't spend much time here, did he?"

In the living room, I walk over to the fireplace and switch on the electric bar fire. When nothing happens, I flip a light switch. An energy saving bulb comes to life.

No heating, no duvet, no personal possessions.

Gemma's right – Harry didn't spend much time here.

"Did anyone speak to the tenant upstairs?" I ask.

"The flat's been empty for months."

Yet Spender wants Ashley out of her cottage pronto to make way for new tenants.

On the shelf in the alcove beside the chimney breast, I check the small pile of paperbacks, selecting the cryptic crossword book over the autobiographies of sporting legends. I flick through the pages, resisting the temptation to read the clues. It looks like Harry's completed the first twelve crosswords and then given up. His neat writing fills the margins as he tried to make sense of the clues.

"Put it back, Kent. We're looking for anything that might help us with Harry's death."

As Harry hated cryptic crossword puzzles, I slip the book into my jacket pocket. I follow Gemma into the kitchen, where every cupboard door is open.

My feet crunch on pasta, rice and lentils as I walk around, avoiding the pots, pans, trays and cutlery strewn across the vinyl tiled floor. A small drop leaf table lies upside down in the corner. Two chairs lie on their sides, the padded seats and backs cut open. Smears on the dusty worktops suggest someone climbed up to check the tops of the wall cupboards.

I look under the sink, finding an old bottle of bleach, some washing up liquid and a wash-up sponge that's supporting new strains of penicillin.

"Do you want me to check the bathroom?" I ask, peering through the window. "I'm surprised the neighbours haven't complained about the overgrown garden. The SAS could remain undetected out there for months."

She closes the door of the fridge and frowns. "Are we missing something, Holmes?"

"Refreshments," I reply, stepping into the bathroom. "Take a look at this."

She hurries over. "What have you found?"

"Either there's nothing in here worth taking," I say, glancing round the tidy bathroom, "or our burglars found what they wanted and didn't bother coming in here."

Gemma lifts the toilet seat and quickly puts it down again. She stretches over the basin to open the wall cabinet above, revealing a packet of sticking plasters, a blister strip of paracetamol and a tube of Athlete's Foot gel. Some nail clippers and tweezers complete the personal grooming selection.

I step onto the rim of the bath and check the top of the cabinet. "Nothing," I say, leaping down. "No smell of cigarettes and no ashtrays. No alcohol, no bin bag with empty bottles and no tumblers or glasses. Nothing that cries out Harry Lawson."

She opens the packet of sticking plasters and tips them out. When she shakes the packet, something small and black tumbles out, pinging off the side of the washbasin to land in the plughole.

She takes the tweezers and extracts a micro SD card, holding it up like a trophy. "I wouldn't call this nothing."

Twenty

When I phone Coroner's Officer Beth Rimmer, she confirms she found no personal items of Harry's at his flat or at Rathbone's house. "I've no idea what's happened to his mobile phone," she says, "or his wallet and credit cards. According to my colleagues, there's been no signal from his phone or any activity on his bank account or credit cards since his death."

"Either someone took them or he put them somewhere safe."

I pause as the waitress at Totally Tea places our cakes on the small round table. She ignores my smile and weaves her way back through the tables in the garden to the main café. I lean forward and cut into my slice of chocolate orange sponge.

"When we worked as hunt saboteurs, we were often running about in the woods or tussling with the hunt people," I tell Beth. "We didn't want to lose anything valuable, so I left my stuff at home. Harry locked his in the glove box of his car."

"There's no record of him owning a car since he was banned for drunk driving in May this year. He collided with a deer in Ashdown Forest and swerved into a ditch at the side of the road. When officers arrived, they smelt alcohol and breathalysed him. His car was a write off."

Didn't Harry and Miranda cancel their wedding in June?

"Was it late May?" I ask.

After the sound of a mouse clicking, Beth confirms my suspicion. "Is the date significant?"

"Curiosity. Is everything okay with you?"

"I'm busy, as always, but ticking along. Ashley seems to be struggling though. I popped in for a chat yesterday and she looked wiped out."

"Are you sure she wasn't bored senseless?"

Beth laughs. "Like the rest of us, she's not one for paperwork, but the spark's gone from her eyes. A few weeks ago, she couldn't wait to get back. The new guy they drafted in from Surrey to cover her sick leave has made quite an impression. She's worried she'll be transferred out of the Major Crimes Team."

"She's had a lot to deal with, Beth."

"And like you, she's brushing it under the carpet."

It sounds like Beth's holding me responsible. "She's seeing a counsellor," I say.

"Because she has no choice. You're the one she listens to, Kent. You need to talk to her. She could have died in that hit and run. She's realised she's not invincible and doesn't know how to deal with it."

"I'll do my best," I say, certain Mike's death has more to do with Ashley's state of mind. He was the father she never had. "If you find out any more about Harry –"

I stop, realising she's disconnected.

Gemma licks the cream from her finger doughnut. "How's Ashley? Beth said she was back at work."

It's time to break the news. "Ashley has to move out of her cottage due to electrical problems. I've said she can stay in the farmhouse."

"She's lucky to have a friend like you," Gemma says, without missing a beat.

I should quit while I'm ahead, but I want to tie up everything in one hit. "I know you wanted to move in there, but it's an emergency."

"Don't worry," she says, her voice soothing. "Once the works are completed and she's back home, I'll move into the farmhouse. It gives us more time to plan a housewarming party. What do you think?"

I think there's no way to stop Gemma moving into the farmhouse.

Back in the office, I write up the reports for this morning's inspections and update the database as I used to before moving into management. My visits this morning confirm how much I've missed being out on the district, dealing with real people, not those who live in a rarefied atmosphere. The moment I walked into the delicatessen and showed my ID card, it was like old times.

Adrian Peach threatens to destroy the mood by calling me on my mobile. "My editor wants us to pool resources."

"You're editor's obviously a comedian."

"No, he's serious. He thinks it's a brilliant opportunity."

I should have known Adrian was too young for puns. "You realise there are things I can't share with you if they could affect a court case in the future."

"Like what?"

I don't tell him it will be most things. "Evidence."

"I can't share my sources, so no worries. Do you want to meet?"

"Before we do, are you aware of Harry's conviction for driving while over the limit?"

"Sure. I used to give him a lift sometimes. What about it?"

I'm wondering who gave him a lift to Rathbone's party.

"The case went to court a couple of weeks before his wedding to Miranda was called off," I say.

"Miranda got it into her head that Harry was seeing someone else. She reckoned he'd gone to see her the night he got breathalysed."

I want to point out that Harry was breathalysed months before the court case, before he cancelled the wedding. "Do you think this other relationship was serious?"

"I don't think there was a relationship. Harry could be a charmer with the women. That's how he picked up Rathbone's scent."

I pick up my pen. "Go on."

"Harry met someone close to Rathbone. He never mentioned her name, before you ask."

"Not even a clue?" I walk over to the coat rack and retrieve the puzzle book from my jacket pocket. "Did Harry like crosswords?"

"No idea. He knew more words than anyone I've ever met. That's why he was so good at obituaries. He did plenty after he lost his wheels."

I open the puzzle book, flicking through to the thirteenth crossword. On a previous case, a murder victim left some clues to his past using crossword clues. Has Harry done the same?

"Do you know anything about this woman?"

"No. What's this about crosswords? I never saw Harry doing one."

"I found a puzzle book at his flat in Alfriston. It was the only thing that suggested he lived there. Could he have been living or staying somewhere else. Miranda's place? Do you have an address for her, Adrian?"

"I called round this afternoon, but Miranda wasn't there. The neighbours said the police were there yesterday as someone had broken in and trashed the place. The police secured the place. I couldn't get in."

"She wasn't there at the time, right?"

"The neighbour saw her leave early on Sunday morning with two holdalls. She must have heard about Harry's death."

She left too early to have heard about it on the news.

So who told her?

Twenty-One

I call Gemma into the office to talk about the SD card we recovered from Harry's flat. She knows we can't check it at work without IT scanning the card for nasties and asking us some awkward questions.

"I could bring it round with a pizza, like old times." A sly smile accompanies the suggestive look in her eyes. "Then we could retire to your bedroom, like we used to."

"I don't keep the computer in my bedroom anymore. I have a study now."

"Pity," she says with feeling. "Do I need to bring a pizza for Ashley?"

I pause, realising how complicated my investigation has become. I don't want to work with Adrian Peach, though I need his help. I need Ashley's help, though she's not allowed to work with me. And Gemma wants us to investigate together like we used to.

"Let's stick to you, me and Columbo for tonight," I say. "Harry knew something that cost him his life. If he slipped and fell into the pool, why did someone trash his place, Miranda's too? They're looking for something."

Gemma holds up the SD card. "But we found it."

I can't believe the intruders missed it. Maybe they planted it for us to find.

Once she leaves, I ring Kelly. "Can you spare me five minutes?"

"I can't leave the call centre."

"I'll come to you."

"If it's about the audit it'll have to wait until Monday. I'm not your PA, Kent."

"A friend of mine, Harry Lawson, rang the call centre late last Thursday afternoon. I'd like to find out who he spoke to."

"You should talk to my boss, Brenda Keegan."

That's the next part of my plan. At the moment, I want to confirm that Kelly's doing Rathbone's bidding.

"What if I said it was linked to Councillor Rathbone? Harry Lawson drowned in his swimming pool over the weekend. You can understand why I don't want to make this public."

Kelly takes a while to answer. "Okay, I'll check. Meet me at the smoking shelter in ten minutes."

"I didn't know you smoked."

"There's a lot you don't know about me, Kent."

I end the call and go straight down the rear stairs to the first floor. I hurry along the corridor to the main staircase that leads down to reception on the ground floor. Once through the door to the Chief Executive's suite, Council Chamber and committee rooms, I slip into the kitchenette used to provide refreshments during meetings. Glad that Alf's not there, I close the door a little and wait. If I'm right, Kelly will be along at any moment to visit Rathbone in his office opposite.

A minute later, I hear the door to the suite open. I peer through the narrow gap and see Kelly approaching. She stops outside the door to Rathbone's office. She's about to knock when Alf calls to her.

"He's out, Miss Morgan. Would you like to come into my kitchen and wait? I've got some chocolate hobnobs, if you're interested."

Shit! This wasn't supposed to happen.

"I'm on my way out, Alf. Another time maybe."

"Just say the word, Miss Morgan."

To my relief, she walks towards the Council Chamber. Alf watches her, a huge smile on his face. Then he pushes open the door, showing no surprise when he sees me. People are always popping in for a chat and a decent cup of coffee.

"If you're after a cup of Columbian best, I've only got enough for the Planning Committee meeting this evening," he says. "Thankfully, the Chief Executive's at a conference this week or I'd be in and out of his office, the number of meetings he chairs. And if you're after Councillor Rathbone, he left fifteen minutes ago." Alf walks to the window and peers out. "His car's not there, so he must have gone for the day."

"Did I hear Kelly a moment ago?"

He nods. "There she is, walking across the car park. Lovely mover, isn't she?"

I join him at the window and watch her strut from the councillors' stairwell across the car park to the smoking shelter. "Was she looking for Councillor Rathbone?"

He nods. "I don't know how she puts up with him. Anyone would think she's his personal secretary, the way he treats her. Some days she's in and out of here like a yoyo. Not that I'm complaining, mind. She often has a cup of coffee with me afterwards. She likes to hear all the gossip."

And relay it back to Rathbone, no doubt.

Though pleased to have evidence that Rathbone's using Kelly, it's all circumstantial. I don't want to believe Kelly's been deceiving us all this time.

"Good to see you, Alf."

Though the councillors' staircase is the quickest route to the car park, I don't want Kelly to see me coming out that way. I return to the staff staircase and join her a minute later. She stands a few metres from the smoking shelter, arms folded and eyebrows dipped, watching me with troubled eyes.

I stop a few feet away, pushing my hand into my pockets. After a few more frowns, she speaks, her voice as empty as the look she gives me.

"I took the call from Harry Lawson."

"Why didn't you tell me when I rang?"

"I'd forgotten about it until I checked the log. The call was short. He wanted to speak to you, but you weren't answering your phone. He said he'd ring you at home."

She doesn't blink or break eye contact as she speaks – like me when I'm telling a whopper.

She starts walking. "Someone's collecting me."

I watch her walk to the entrance and then out of sight.

Back inside the town hall, I go straight to Brenda Keegan. Her office is a glass-walled tribute to transparency in the corner of the call centre. What you see is what you get, which is an organised and efficient manager who speaks as she finds. A tall and elegant woman, she has long fingernails that don't chip or break when she types.

When I enter her office, she gives me a warning look. "I hope you're not planning to steal Kelly for another day a week."

"Actually, Brenda, I may not need her help for the full six months."

"Five months and three weeks?" She laughs and encourages me to sit. "That's good news. Every day she spends with you, Kent, the less likely she is to return here."

"I was hoping to have a quick word, but she's not at her work station."

"She had a migraine so I sent her home. Anything I can help you with?"

I slide into the chair. "We're arranging a funeral for a man called Harry Lawson. He died without relatives, so we have to bury him. He rang here late last Thursday afternoon."

"You want to know who he spoke to."

"He's a complete mystery, Brenda. There may be someone in Housing or Benefits who's dealing with him."

"Who might pay for the funeral, you mean?" She laughs and turns to her computer. After a few mouse clicks, she says, "Tom took the call at 16.53 and forwarded it to Kelly. He didn't speak to anyone else and the call lasted a little over two minutes. There's no recording, if that's what you're hoping for."

"Could I speak to Tom?"

She points to the blonde-haired man at the work station nearest to us. He's using a headphone and mic. As he talks, his animated hands suggest frustration. The person on the other end could be saying, "You're the fourth person I've had to explain this to."

When he finishes the call he gives me an expectant look. After a brief introduction, I ask him if he remembers Harry Lawson's call.

Tom turns to face me, his voice low. "Yes, he was an arrogant so and so. He refused to give me his name at first, saying he would only speak to Kelly. She was taking a call, so I couldn't put him through."

"He asked for her by her first name?"

Tom thinks for a moment and nods. "I offered to take a message, but he said she never returned his calls so he would wait. Kelly didn't want to talk to him, so I suggested she record the call, but she didn't. She didn't say much either. When she finished, I went over to make sure she was okay, but she was on the phone to someone else. She said something like 'You have to do something about him'. Then she hung up. She jumped out of her chair and walked past me as if I wasn't there."

Is Kelly the bitch Harry referred to?

"Do you know who she was talking to?" I ask.

"Am I going to get in trouble?"

I shake my head. "All calls are logged, Tom. I can ask Brenda, if you prefer."

"It was Councillor Rathbone's extension."

Twenty-Two

Gemma makes light work of her pizza. She devours it before I finish updating her about Harry's death, taking care not to say anything about Kelly. Gemma pinches a potato wedge from my plate and nods. "Good work, Holmes."

I set my tray on the coffee table and slip a slice of pepperoni to Columbo. He wolfs it down and turns to Gemma, pawing her leg, aware she's kept some pepperoni back for him. She ruffles his fur and makes him sit before she lets him have his treat. She turns to me, a mischievous glint in her eyes.

"Shall we get down to it, Kent?"

She pads across the floor in her bare feet and loads her plate into the dishwasher. "Why was Harry so determined to go to the party?"

I join her by the dishwasher. "I think he wanted something that was kept in the study."

"Do you know what it was?"

I shrug. "Evidence of some kind?"

She slots my plate into the dishwasher. "Maybe the answer's on the SD Card."

While I have my doubts, we need to check.

I grab a couple of bottles of Becks Blue and follow her into the study. Most of my old furniture and equipment is here. I replaced my old PC with a laptop, which sits on a desk I bought from a charity shop. My collection of Scooby Doo toys has a new home on top of a cabinet I bought to go with the desk. There's room to spread out, lots more storage and a whiteboard on one wall for brainstorming.

Gemma looks impressed. "Almost everything a private eye needs."

"What's missing?" I ask, sitting in my chair.

"A femme fatale, of course."

Gemma pulls up a chair and sits beside me. Columbo settles under the desk, resting his head on his paws. She inserts the card and a short list of files comes up on the screen. Mainly pdfs and photographs, they're news reports about slave labour and people trafficking, culled from news channels and newspapers.

After a few minutes of checking the files, I sit back. "None of the reports are local or recent. Can you imagine Rathbone being involved in something like this?"

"He's more likely to cut down ancient woodland to build houses." She takes a sip from her bottle. "There's nothing from Harry here."

"There's nothing that warrants hiding the card in a bathroom cabinet."

"If they'd already found what they wanted, Holmes, why trash Miranda's place?"

"Exactly," I say, wishing I could make sense of events. "We need to find Miranda before they do."

Hoping she might have Miranda's mobile number, I ring Sarah. Councillor Richmond answers, sounding out of breath. "Hello, Kent, it's Steph. Sarah's indisposed. Can I take a message?"

"I'll ring tomorrow, Miss Richmond. Sorry to disturb you."

"Call me, Steph. We're not in the council chamber now."

"You chair the committee that oversees the department that employs me, Miss Richmond."

She purrs with laughter. "That doesn't mean we can't be friends. You may even grow to like me."

From what I hear, she's a councillor who cares about the area and the people she represents. She's young, dynamic, and an environmentalist with an interest in protecting Downland's green and pleasant land. Rathbone hails her as a rising star, a breath of fresh air. She's the youngest committee chair in the council's history, halving the average age of the current crop.

"You may be right, but you're still a councillor. Enjoy the rest of your evening."

Gemma rests her head on my shoulder and looks up at me like a puppy that needs a home. "Can I stay? They'll be at it all night."

When Ashley pulls up at the front gate in a hire van at eight thirty on Thursday morning, Frances and I are briefing the volunteers for a busy day ahead. I ignore the toot of the horn and turn back to the volunteers, who are enjoying tea and Danish pastries in the café.

"Now it's the school holidays, we'll have more children running around, so take care and gently remind parents about handwashing. Ollie, are you okay to help Betty in here when it gets busy?"

"Anything for a slice of your lemon drizzle cake," he says, giving Betty a friendly smile.

She blushes a little, but likes the compliment. "I'll make it a big one, Ollie."

"Okay, any questions?"

The volunteers finish their tea and follow Frances outside. Betty clears away the tea cups and plates, pausing to look me over. "I hope you're not having trouble sleeping, Mr Fisher. My father had a terrible time after the Falklands War. He used to wake in the night in a cold sweat, a terrified look in his eyes. Sometimes he would shout and scream."

"I'm sorry to hear that," I say, not sure where she's going with this.

"People tried to kill you, Mr Fisher. You're lucky to be alive."

Another toot of the horn distracts me.

"Your friend Gemma said they tried to blow you up. I do some cleaning at her mother's house on Saturdays, in case you're wondering how I know. She looks after Sonya – my cat. It all helps when you're on your own, doesn't it? My father was the same."

"He was?" I ask, wondering if she took him to the vet.

"If he heard a bang or an unexpected noise, he jumped like you did when your police woman friend slammed the van door." She gestures outside. "She doesn't look too pleased, does she?"

Betty takes the plates into the kitchen, nodding to Ashley as she enters the café, dressed in a white coverall. She spots the plate on the table and takes the remaining Danish pastry, tearing into it. A smile fills her face. "Better than sex."

"I thought that was chocolate."

113

"At the moment it's any food." She laughs and takes another large bite. "My guvnor gave me a couple of days off so I thought we could start early. I never unpacked most of my stuff when I moved in, so it won't take long."

"I was going to ring you about Miranda, Harry's former fiancée."

"I heard someone broke into her house."

"That's why I need to get hold of her. She could be in danger."

"Rewind, Kent. Are you linking the break in to the one at Harry Lawson's flat?"

I reach into my pocket and pull out the SD card, sealed inside a labelled plastic bag. "We found this in the bathroom cabinet at Harry's flat."

"We?"

"Harry has no family so we're burying him. I helped Gemma look for personal effects, details of friends, bank accounts."

"I don't know many people who keep bank statements in the bathroom." She hands the SD card back. "DC Bobbie Cook's dealing with Harry's death. Did you find anything useful on the card?"

"News reports on people trafficking and slave labour – nothing specific to Rathbone. It could be research, cobbled together off the internet, but there's nothing to show that it's Harry's work."

"He thinks the intruders put it there." Gemma strolls into the café with a towel wrapped around her head. "Do you have a hairdryer, Kent?"

Ashley, who's about to devour the last mouthful of her Danish pastry, seems to lose her appetite. "Gemma, you're looking well. I'm moving into the farmhouse so we'll be

114

neighbours. Join me when you're ready, Kent. I'd like to hear more about Harry."

She strides down the path, hurling the last of the Danish pastry into the bushes. Betty sighs and shakes her head. "Didn't she like the Danish?"

"You had Danish pastries?" Gemma stares at me in disbelief. "You could have told me."

"You were sound asleep, despite Columbo's best efforts to rouse you."

"No one rouses me the way you do, Kent." She gives me a provocative smile and strolls out of the café.

Betty collects the remaining cups. "Were you talking about the poor soul who drowned at the weekend?"

I nod, watching Gemma scoop up Columbo. She laughs as he tugs the towel from her head.

"He came to Miss Wheeler's house," Betty says, "while I was cleaning last Saturday morning. Almost took the door off its hinges with his banging."

"Harry Lawson?"

"He wasn't pleased when I told him Miss Wheeler was shopping with Miss Richmond. Now, she's a nice woman, ever so polite and helpful."

"Did he say why he was calling?"

Betty shakes her head. "He said she mustn't go to the party. Then he held up a brown envelope and said he had some photographs for her. I offered to take them for Miss Wheeler, but he said she'd know where to find them if anything happened to him."

She gasps and looks at me with horrified eyes. "Do you think he knew he was going to die?"

Twenty-Three

I sit Betty at the table and make her a cup of strong tea. She's upset because she didn't leave a note for Sarah. "I was running behind and I had to go shopping. I didn't remember till I got home. If I'd written a note, Miss Wheeler could have done something."

"Sarah spoke to him at the party," I say, sitting opposite. "Are you sure Harry said she would know where to look if anything happened to him?"

"I think so. Will I have to talk to the police?" Her hand trembles as she reaches for her cup of tea. "Could you talk to your friend, Ashley? I don't want to go to the inquest and have all those people watching me, thinking it's my fault because I forgot to leave a note."

"No one's going to think that. Now are you sure you'll be all right? I can ask Ollie to come over."

She shakes her head. "I don't want him to think badly of me."

"I'm sure he won't. Was Gemma at home when Harry called?"

"She goes to the gym on Saturdays. Most evenings too – unless she's here with you. She's such a bonny girl. But you already know that, don't you?"

When I return to the flat, Gemma's dressed and seated at the breakfast bar, tucking into toast. She confirms she was out on Saturday morning.

"I'll ask my mother if she knows where Harry put his photographs. Do you have any ideas?"

"We had some secret locations where we left things for each other, like photographs, details of hunts we planned to hit."

"You were pretty close back then, weren't you?"

"At first, but Harry only confided in me when he had to. He liked to confide in Sarah. I guess it made him feel important, knowing things I didn't."

"Do you think the intruder was looking for the photographs?"

"Your mother never said anything about Harry's photographs when I spoke to her on Sunday morning. Maybe he didn't say anything about them at Rathbone's party."

"I'll ask her." Gemma jumps down from the stool and ruffles Columbo's fur before slipping him some toast. She checks her appearance in the mirror and nods. "I could update you over one of Betty's lunches, if you fancy."

"I'll be stuck with Ashley today. She doesn't have much furniture, but it still has to be loaded into the van and unloaded at this end."

"You'll have to clear Niamh's stuff too. She didn't take anything with her, did she?"

Niamh's agreed to let Ashley move into the house, providing she leaves everything as it is. Ashley's plan to store her furniture in the garage goes astray when we discover it's filled with Niamh's old belongings from Downland Manor.

"There's space in one of the smaller barns," I say.

While we clear an area, I update Ashley on my progress with Harry Lawson's death.

She stops sweeping and leans on the broom. "Do you think he took the photographs to the party to show Sarah?"

"I've been thinking about that. What if Harry wanted her to see the photographs, but they weren't intended for her? He was hiding something under his jacket when he arrived, but not when he left."

"You think he wanted to show them to Rathbone." She considers for a moment. "Are we talking blackmail?"

"Or a story he intended to publish."

Her lips curl into a grin. "They had to act fast. Then they realised Harry had stashed the originals. That's why they turned over his flat. Bravo, Kent."

"Don't forget Miranda's house. She left before they got there. I think Harry warned her."

"Do you think she knows where the original photographs are?"

"She might. Before they split, Harry might have told her what he'd uncovered about Rathbone. Can you track her down?"

Ashley's sigh suggests it's not going to be that simple. "If her parents report her as missing, maybe, but it won't be me who follows it up. She could have trashed her own house to send us in the wrong direction. Have you considered that?"

At the moment, there's too much to consider. "Maybe I'll ask Adrian Peach about Miranda. He worked with Harry at the *Argus*."

"You mention Miranda and Adrian will know you're investigating Harry's death. He's already hassled Sarah. If he finds out Gemma's helping you, he'll be like a dog in a butcher's shop."

I consider her words as we return to the truck. "There's another possibility. What if the killers were searching for something that had nothing to do with Harry's photographs?"

She groans. "I knew you were going to make this even more complicated."

"I'm struggling to envisage Rathbone getting mixed up in people trafficking. But I can imagine his fiancée Katya employing illegal immigrants as cheap labour."

"There are plenty of migrants coming across the channel." Ashley jumps up into the truck and manoeuvres the sofa onto the lifting plate. "And the future Mrs Rathbone has expensive tastes. Beth told me the engagement party was a pretty lavish affair."

"Katya's running the Travellers for him. They've spent a fortune on the place, but he has no other businesses to help fund the works. Well, no legal ones."

Ashley grins as she lowers the sofa to the ground. "So, either they've had a windfall or they're making money on the side."

"Does that mean you'll check it out?"

"It's not my ball to kick," she says, her voice strained. "Not that I'll be kicking anything other than my heels. There's talk of restructuring." She turns away to move the sofa. "If they find out I'm helping you, Kent, they'll transfer me to Hastings."

"Moving here's not going to help, is it? Unless ... you told them where to stick the job, didn't you?"

119

She doesn't answer.

"Maybe you returned to work too early. You need more time to ..."

"More time for what?" She spins around, tears brimming in her eyes. "More time to make silly mistakes? My guvnor tells me to keep my distance and I move in next door to you. Is that the behaviour of a rational woman? No," she says, with a weary shake of the head, "it's the behaviour of a frightened woman. I'm getting too old to work all the hours God sends, running on adrenaline and cups of coffee, fighting a system that makes it harder for me to do my job."

"But you love your job."

"I love this place." She glances around and draws a breath. "I could run the visitor centre."

As much as I want to make her feel better, it's not the answer. "You'd be bored senseless within a week. We're restless – driven. We want to make a difference, even if we know it's impossible sometimes."

My voice dies in my throat as Savanna saunters into view. She pushes her hands through her gleaming hair and lets it settle over her tanned shoulders. She looks amazing in a powder blue shirt, knotted above her waist, and matching shorts, both sporting her logo. Even though there's an angry glint to her blue eyes, they still turn my brain to mush and my legs to jelly.

She walks up to me, ignoring Ashley. "Thanks for screwing my plans, Kent."

Twenty-Four

"I have a feeling this is my fault." Ashley gives me an apologetic shrug and turns to Savanna. "Is this about the farmhouse? You wanted to use it while you were filming."

"You must be the detective Johnny spoke to." Savanna peers into the truck, wrinkling her nose in distaste. Then she glares at me. "You agreed to let me use the farmhouse while we were filming. I've spent months setting this up. Then first thing this morning, Johnny says you don't want me to film here."

I'm about to protest my innocence when the penny drops. Before I can confirm my suspicions, Columbo joins us, leaping up at Savanna, his tail wagging. She drops to her knee to fuss him, unable to stop him clambering up to lick her face. She slides a hand underneath him and gets to her feet, smiling as he pushes his nose under her hair to nuzzle her ear.

I can't believe I feel jealous. What's wrong with me?

"Why don't you take Columbo back to my flat," I say. "I'll join you in a minute."

Her look tells me I'd better not keep her waiting.

I turn to Ashley, wondering what she said to Johnny Spender, knowing he was Savanna's partner.

"You said the filming wasn't going to happen," Ashley says, a defiant look in her eyes. "When Spender shows up to tell me the cottage is a death trap, he asks me if you're about to discuss the filming next week."

"You told him there wasn't going to be any filming."

"I needed somewhere to live."

"You could have stayed in my spare room until the filming was over."

"Yeah, like Gemma's going to agree to that."

"What's Gemma got to do with anything?" Then I recall Gemma coming into the café earlier. "You assumed she'd moved in with me, didn't you? She stayed the night to get away from her mother and Steph Richmond."

Ashley pushes the button to raise the ramp. "Tell Savanna she can go ahead with her precious filming."

"Where will you go?"

"What do you care?" The ramp jolts to a stop, almost discharging her to the ground. She sways back and grabs onto the sofa. "I didn't want you getting mixed up with Spender, okay?"

"You didn't want me spending time with Savanna."

"They're both bad news, Kent. She can't be blind to his business dealings, or the people he mixes with."

"What sort of people?"

"People we're interested in."

"People like Rathbone?"

"He's small fry." She sits on the arm of the sofa, considering her words. "Spender's now a member of your father's casino in Brighton. It's filled with the kind of people Spender wants to meet – people with money, influence and no scruples."

"With that level of cynicism you should have no trouble getting your old job back. Then again, you have something in common with Savanna. She's hates casinos and all forms of gambling. My father wasn't impressed when she turned down his offer to be his VIP guest."

Ashley doesn't look impressed either.

"If you're suggesting she knows nothing about Spender's gambling, it's time you looked beyond the big blue eyes, Kent. Trust me, she knows about Spender's interests. Ask her if you don't believe me. You've got the perfect opportunity to get to know her better with this film you're making."

I want to dismiss Ashley's sneering words, but beauty doesn't equal honesty and integrity, does it? Everything I know about Savanna is filtered through the haze of fantasies.

Ashley gets to her feet and hauls the sofa back into the truck. "Think about this, Kent. If Spender's involved in Harry Lawson's death, how will Savanna feel when she finds out you said nothing?"

Twenty-Five

Getting to know Savanna should have been a dream assignment. She would be consulting me about animals, seeking advice on how best to film them without causing anxiety or stress, marvelling at my skills and compassion. We'd have to spend days together. And if there was any late shooting, she'd stay over in the farmhouse.

Now I'm not sure what to expect.

The media branded her the Ice Queen after her brief appearance in *Love Island*. But watching her play with Columbo on the floor in my flat, I see only warmth and love. She knows exactly what he wants because she loves animals.

In my books that makes her compassionate and caring.

"You're amazing," I hear myself saying.

She looks up and smiles. "You're the amazing one, caring for all the animals, making sure they live out the rest of their lives in peace. I've read about the cruelty and suffering some people inflict on animals. I'd like to do the same to them."

"Me too."

"How do you set aside the anger when you see what people have done to these poor creatures? What if you can't save them? What if they die?" She's padding across the floor in bare feet. "How do you deal with it, Kent?"

"You make sure the ones that live have as good a life as possible."

"What must you think of me, Kent?" My stomach tightens as she stops before me, looking into my eyes. "I roll up and accuse you of messing up my plans when Johnny never spoke to you. That's one of the reasons I sent him to Jevington."

I wonder if Spender sees himself as a messenger.

"Johnny's not good with people in authority," she says, strolling across to the window to look out at the Downs. "His mother died from an overdose when he was four or five. He went into care, but he never talks about it. When you read about some of the things that happened in those places..."

She shudders and falls silent. Columbo nudges her leg with his nose and whines. She scoops him up and lets him lick her face. "Frances told me how you rescued him, how you sit and talk to him, discussing your cases and troubles." She ruffles his fur and looks into his eyes. "I wish I had someone like you."

"Columbo's a great listener," I say, reaching for the kettle.

"Sure, but I'm hopeless at expressing my feelings. That's why they branded me the Ice Queen. Johnny's the strong, silent type, so imagine what it's like after dinner at my place."

My place, not our place.

"Maybe you need a dog."

She sets Columbo on the floor. "We're busy people with businesses to run. Sometimes, we don't see each other for days."

Hearing a diesel engine below, I look out to see Ashley driving away. "What does he do?"

"He likes to surprise me with holidays in the Cayman Islands."

Is that why she's here – to tell me she's off on holiday?

She grabs her phone from the worktop. "I need to talk to Wayne, my production manager. I usually bring him along to assess the project, make all the necessary checks."

Maybe she didn't bring Wayne because she isn't going to film next week.

"Did you send Johnny to tell me you were off on holiday?" I ask.

"I knew nothing about a holiday until he showed me the tickets this morning. We had a monster argument. That's when he told me you didn't want your sanctuary associated with sleazy swimwear."

Is she angry with me or her partner?

"When we discussed this at the grand opening of the sanctuary, Savanna, you sounded so excited about making a film here. But you never followed up, so I thought you'd lost interest. What's a small animal sanctuary on the edge of a village compared to the glamorous world of swimwear?"

She looks at me with those sultry blue eyes and cancels the call to Wayne. "Kent, it's you I'm interested in. Can't you see that?"

If she'd said that yesterday, my emotions would be turning summersaults of joy. Today, I know I can't compete with the Cayman Islands.

"You solve murders," she's saying, animated now. "You rescue animals. You protect people in your work. You're strong, fearless, a local hero."

My disappointment hasn't dulled my ability to recognise bullshit. "What do you want, Savanna? Why aren't you packing for your holiday?"

She looks down at Columbo, as if she'd prefer to talk to him. "I'm not sure about Johnny. I was hoping you could help me."

She picks up her phone, taps and swipes, and then places it back on the counter. "This is a photograph of an email on Johnny's laptop."

Local Property Developer Harbours More than Tenants in Shoreham.

Johnny Spender, who owns many properties along the South Coast, was unavailable for comment following accusations that he is harbouring illegal immigrants in his properties.

It's the kind of speculative piece Tommy Logan would print in the *Tollingdon Tribune*.

Do you really want me to print this?

Harry Lawson.

I look at the date. Harry sent the email last Friday evening, the day before he drowned. "You need to show this to Ashley," I say.

Savanna snatches back the phone. "No way. She's a police officer. Can't you find out if it's true? I've checked online every day and the *Argus* hasn't printed the story."

"Harry's death might have prevented him from submitting the story. Why were you checking your partner's emails?"

127

"Last Friday evening, Johnny was shouting down the phone, threatening all sorts of grief and retribution. When I asked him what was going on, he said it was nothing he couldn't handle."

"So you took a peek at his emails."

She nods. "He's been on edge for weeks. The slightest thing sets him off. Then this morning, he tells me he's booked us two weeks in the Cayman Islands."

"You think he's making a run for it?"

"I don't know what to think. We could investigate Harry Lawson's claims, couldn't we? You do this sort of thing all the time."

"You mean I could investigate. You're going on holiday."

"I've got too much to do," she says, shaking her head. "I can't drop everything at a moment's notice."

She hurried straight over here though.

"Won't he be suspicious if you don't go on holiday with him?" I ask.

She gives me a wry smile. "I wouldn't be surprised if he takes someone else instead."

There's no emotion in her eyes as she speaks. Is it bravado, or is she trying to tell me Johnny Spender's history? If that's the case, and she rushed over here, what does she want?

Not that long ago, I'd be thinking my fantasies were about to come true.

"Would you forward the photo to me?" I ask, playing wait and see. "I can contact Harry's email provider to find out more."

She nods and scoops up her phone. For a moment she looks at me, all manner of emotions flickering across her eyes. Then she's on her way. Before she shuts the front door behind her, she calls up the stairs. "I can't wait to start filming on Monday."

I can't wait to phone Ashley.

Twenty-Six

Tollingdon Furniture Supplies occupies several interconnected units on a small retail park on the northern edge of the town. Built in the 1950s, the buildings are a mixture of brick and corrugated sheet cladding. According to the sign over the main door, the business has traded since 1971.

It's a shame they haven't cleaned or repainted the sign since then.

Ashley parks her Audi in the corner of the car park, next to some weary shrubs that stop litter blowing into the road. She sits there, fingers drumming on the armrest.

After our disagreement earlier, I wasn't expecting her to ring me with the address of Miranda's workplace. When I forwarded the details of the email Harry sent to Spender, Ashley phoned straight back.

Maybe she's having second thoughts.

"Let me do this," I say.

She shakes her head. "My guvnor will put me behind a desk unless I show what a good detective I am. If he disciplines me for using my initiative and coming here, I may as well quit the force now."

While I understand how vulnerable she feels, interfering in a local investigation will not win her any friends. "If I can find out what happened to Miranda, you won't need to risk your career, Ashley."

"No offence, Kent, but why would Mark Steele tell you anything when he didn't tell the uniforms? He's Miranda's deputy, before you ask."

I point to a couple of old sofas, dumped in the alley that runs alongside the building. "That's a public footpath, so they're guilty of fly tipping. The sofas also provide harbourage for rats, which is a serious public health risk. And who knows what health and safety contraventions I'll find inside. Letting me try doesn't make you any less of a detective."

"Okay, you can take the lead, Kent. It's the least I can do after the information you gave me about Johnny Spender. Harry's editor at the *Argus* knew nothing about the story. There's no reference to Spender on Harry's work computer."

"It would be great to find a link between Spender and Rathbone."

Ashley raises a finger. "Let's walk before we sprint."

"Talking of running, you need to stay out here in case Steele legs it."

"Why would he do that?"

"If we're looking for Miranda, there's a chance the guys who turned over her place have already visited here. What if they threatened him?"

"I'll pretend I'm a customer, looking for a chaise longue. I can intercept him before he reaches the exit."

"Give me a moment," I say, heading for the alleyway.

The two sofas look old. While companies often take away old sofas when they deliver new, these were dumped here from the nearby housing estate. I take a couple of photographs and return to the entrance. Ashley's gone inside already, captured on the CCTV camera above the door. It closes behind me, cutting off the fresh air needed to dilute the unmistakable fumes of new furniture.

The store's divided into room areas, each hosting the appropriate units. An elderly couple are testing reclining armchairs, supervised by a patient sales assistant. Ashley's in the bedroom area, which is nearest to a staff door. A young man in a suit sits behind a desk, watching her, ready to pounce if she shows any interest.

He looks up when I approach, straightening the huge knot on his colourful tie. He looks disappointed when I ask for the manager, Miranda Tate. He gives my ID card a brief glance and picks up the phone.

"Mark Steele, the deputy manager, is supervising a delivery in the warehouse. I'll see if he can spare you a few minutes."

"I know the way." I push through the door, which opens into a dimly lit corridor with an office, kitchenette and staff toilet to one side. The door at the end leads to a small warehouse at the back of the store. It's filled with a mixture of new furniture, wrapped in polythene or cardboard. Old items are piled against the wall beside the roller shutter doors that lead to the service yard. Like the workers ahead of me, I ignore the instruction to wear a hard hat and hi-vis jacket.

"You're not allowed in here," the older one calls, turning away from a truck that's waiting to be loaded. Short and stocky with a head of spiky brown hair, he weaves past some sofas. "This is a high risk area. You need to leave."

I hold up my ID card. "Environmental Health."

He doesn't look at my ID. "If you're here about the sofas in the passageway, I'll tell you what I told the last bloke from your council. They're nothing to do with us. Take a look round the adjoining estate. You'll find more furniture in the front gardens than on our shop floor."

"I'm looking for Mark Steele."

"That's me. What do you want?"

"I need to talk to Miranda Tate."

"If it's to do with the store, you talk to me. If it's not, you shouldn't be in here."

Having fended off the police, he's confident he can dispatch me. Somehow, I can't see a complaint about rats troubling him.

I turn and make my way back. In the corridor, I check the toilet and kitchenette before heading into the manager's office. It's small, hot and stale, with a cluttered desk, an old PC and a dirty printer overheating in the corner. Every shelf buckles under the weight of manuals, box files, and spare handles, hinges and fittings. Printouts of every email from head office obscure most of the noticeboard, which shares the wall space with a leave planner, peppered with various coloured dots and tiny writing. After foraging among the printouts, I locate the sheet that contains staff details, including contact numbers and emails.

Someone has drawn a line through Miranda's details.

"What are you doing in here?"

Steele fills the doorway – width wise at least. Though he's trying to look menacing, there's a nervous flicker in his eyes.

"If you won't help me find Miranda, you leave me no choice."

He folds his arms across his barrel chest. "The police won't see it that way."

I pull out my phone and call Ashley. "Can you join us, Detective Inspector Goodman? Mr Steele's being obstructive."

When Ashley comes through from the shop floor, Steele backs away, looking nervous. "I thought you were from Environmental Health."

"I hope you haven't been harassing this gentleman, Kent?"

Steele looks at me. "You're Kent Fisher? Can you come back on Saturday?"

"Why, will Miranda be here?"

"I've no idea, honest. I'm not even sure if she's alive." He looks from me to Ashley. "She's dead, isn't she? That's why you're here."

"What makes you think that?" she asks.

He gestures to the shelf behind the desk. "It's inside the health and safety folder."

"What is?"

"An envelope, addressed to you, Mr Fisher. Miranda told me to give it to you if she didn't contact me before Saturday. She's not going to, is she?"

Steele watches me remove the lever arch file from the shelf. A padded envelope drops out, landing on the cupboard beneath. The unmarked envelope feels like it contains a book.

"Is this it?"

He nods.

"Mr Steele," she says, her voice stern, "why do you think Miranda's dead?"

"I told him where to find her. He was worried sick."

"Who, Mr Steele? Who did you tell?"

"Her husband, Harry Lawson."

Twenty-Seven

Steele sticks to his assertion that Harry Lawson visited him on Monday. He describes Harry as someone who looked a lot older than his hair. He had a beard, wore dark glasses and leather gloves and spoke with a posh accent. The rest of the description was filled with words like normal and average.

To make it worse, the grainy CCTV footage for Monday confirms Steele's description.

"It could be anyone," Ashley says when we emerge from the store. "Do we think the person posing as Harry threatened Steele? He looked nervous to me."

"You'd be nervous if you'd seen Harry's ghost."

"Don't, Kent. I'm in no mood for your jokes. And what's this all about?" She opens the cryptic crossword puzzle book and reads out the inscription inside the cover. "My phone's not the only mobile with a view of the Cuckmere."

She riffles the pages and tosses the book to me. "You fancy yourself as Inspector Morse. Why don't you tell me why she left you a puzzle book? Better still, tell me how she knew you'd visit her place of work."

"How did she know she had to get out of her house before it was trashed?"

"Someone tipped her off."

"Why not Harry Lawson? He had a cryptic crossword book in his flat. It wasn't brand new like this one, but they're part of the same series."

Ashley rams home her seat belt, turns the key in the ignition and drives away. "Only you could notice something like that."

It sounds like an insult. "I noticed because Harry hated cryptic crosswords. He thought in straight lines, not laterally. Not that I'm much better at solving the puzzles. Gemma's streets ahead of me. When we were investigating Anthony Trimble's death, he left clues in a cryptic crossword book."

Ashley looks thoughtful. "Was Harry aware of this?"

"It came out during the trial, so he could have read about it. The press started to call me Endeavour Fisher."

She laughs. "I'm not sure that's an improvement on Jessica Fisher. But we know where Harry got the idea. He's been thorough in his preparations, I'll give him that."

I nod. "He thought someone might want to kill him."

"He made plans so you would investigate if he died. He sent those texts to Sarah, knowing she'd come to you for help."

Something flashes through my mind, but it's gone before I can catch it.

Ashley slows as we approach the traffic lights. "So Endeavour, where do we go from here?"

"Let's go to where a mobile overlooks the Cuckmere. Sunshine View Caravan Park," I say, responding to her puzzled frown.

"Mobile homes," she says, accelerating away. "Is that where Miranda's holed up?"

I settle back in the seat, not sure what to think. We soon speed past my old sanctuary and the overblown entrance to Downland Manor Hotel, formerly the Fisher family's ancestral estate. My life has transformed since my first investigation when a fatal workplace accident turned out to be murder, and so much more. It prompted Colonel Witherington to ask me to find his missing wife. Then Anthony Trimble died mysteriously in a luxury care home, leaving a trail of crossword clues. Then Ashley consulted me as an environmental health officer when she investigated a cold case that linked to a café I once closed down. The body was found on land that became Sunshine View Caravan Park.

I wonder if Harry deliberately selected the site because of my previous investigation.

As we drive over the Cuckmere River, Ashley breaks the silence. "Why do you think Miranda agreed to help Harry? She must have been pretty cut up when he cancelled the wedding."

"Maybe she still loved him. Maybe she realised she might be in danger too."

"I'm glad one of us knows what we're doing. Since Mike died, I've been struggling to join the dots."

I reach across and squeeze her hand, aware of how vulnerable she feels.

The last investigation has made me more aware of my own mortality. While it never occurred to me I could die, when death reared up at me it was Gemma who occupied my thoughts. She's been with me from the start, helping me on most of my investigations, making me laugh, spotting the clues I missed. She's never let what she's experienced dampen her spirit or how she feels about me, despite the way I've treated her at times.

I need to put that right.

Niamh's suffered too. Like other people close to me, she's not escaped the fallout from my investigations.

By shutting off my emotions to cope with what I do and see, I've also shut out the people who care about me.

"I'm here for you," I say, noticing how thin and tired Ashley looks.

With views across the Cuckmere valley to Litlington, Sunshine View Caravan Park, south of Alfriston, is the perfect place for a restful holiday and rambling. There's not much else to do until the new owners finish building a leisure complex, containing a bar and restaurant, gym, indoor swimming pool and computer games area. Erin Perkins at reception looks disappointed when we decline the offer to look at the architect drawings and illustrations.

She directs us to Miranda Tate's mobile home, situated less than fifty metres from where the body in Ashley's cold case was buried.

The home looks like any other on the site, except the curtains are drawn. A look underneath reveals some old plant pots, several picket fencing panels and a rusty watering can. We walk around the rest of the home before returning to the steps that lead to the door. Ashley raps on the door's glass panel. When no one answers, she raps again, calling out. She tries the handle and seems surprised when the door opens. A wave of heat bursts out, flushing us with a stale odour.

"Miss Tate, are you home? Police, Miss Tate."

139

She turns to me. "There's no smell of a body and no flies, but someone's made a mess in there. We'd best get some gloves from the car before we go inside."

Once we have gloves, Ashley heads straight down the corridor to the bedrooms, leaving me to check the lounge/kitchen area. Someone's emptied every cupboard and shelf, ripped out the bench seat cushions and tipped the contents of a waste bin onto the worn carpet. Checking the date on the only sandwich box, it looks like Miranda was here at some point over the weekend, maybe after she fled from her house.

Ashley looks relieved when she returns. "Pillows and mattresses ripped apart, but no bodies. No clothes in the wardrobe, no toiletries in the bathroom. Have you found anything to suggest she was here at all?"

I point to the sandwich box. "I doubt if the person who did this stopped for a bite to eat."

"Good point. It looks like Miranda's still one step ahead of the bad guys, whoever they are. That's the good news. Unfortunately, they're one step ahead of us, which is the bad news."

"What if she's already dead?" I ask.

Twenty-Eight

While Ashley files a missing person alert for Miranda Tate, I visit the neighbouring homes. Despite the breeze, the afternoon sun sends the temperature into the low eighties. Most people are out and about. At the fourth home, an older woman in a yellow kaftan and orange shorts opens the door. Her curly purple hair tumbles around a face that's lined and deeply tanned, contrasting her hazy green eyes. She sways as she studies me, almost spilling the contents of her cocktail glass.

"I'm Blossom." She ignores my ID card and beckons me inside. "I don't often have a handsome young man coming to see me."

From the reek of alcohol on her breath, I'm not surprised. I remain on the deck and point across the grass. "Do you know the occupant of that home?"

"Only saw her once, like I told the man who was looking for her."

"When was this?"

"Yesterday evening? Or was it the evening before? The days all blend into one out here. He woke me up, banging on the door like those couriers who leave parcels. But these foreign types don't have manners and breeding, do they?"

"He wasn't local then?"

"No, Brighton." She laughs and takes another sip of the clear liquid in her glass. "Poland or Rumania, I'd say. I'm not at my best when my karma's disturbed."

"Could you describe this man?" Ashley asks, heading up the steps. "I'm a police officer."

"Yes, you have that aura about you. And no, I can't describe him. It was getting dark and I needed a drink. I told him no one lived there." She giggles and leans closer. "I didn't say she left a couple of days ago. I closed and locked the door, but I could hear them arguing."

"They? I thought you said there was one person."

Blossom looks at me as if I'm insolent. "There was someone else in the car."

"What sort of car?" Ashley asks.

"A red one, parked on the road."

"Male or female?"

"Cars don't have sexes. But she was definitely a woman – though it could have been a man. I wasn't wearing my contact lenses at the time."

Ashley's expression says we're wasting our time. "Thank you, Mrs ...?"

"Blossom de Ville. Miss Blossom de Ville."

"My colleagues may want to take a statement from you."

"Do you want me to tell them about Gregor?"

Ashley turns back. "Who's Gregor?"

"I heard the name while they argued. Gregor," Blossom says with a flourish. "Sounds like a villain."

"Could it have been Gregory?" I ask.

"Gregor sounds more romantic, don't you think?" She giggles and closes the door.

Back in the car, Ashley smirks. "Gregory Rathbone's a councillor. He fiddles his expenses and tax returns. He gets builders to supply inflated quotes while he has work done on the cheap."

"He also runs a hotel that employs foreign workers. Maybe that's what Harry was investigating."

"Do you really think Rathbone would risk his political career and the perks he enjoys by using illegal immigrants and slave labour?"

As much as I want to bring down Rathbone, she's right. "What was Harry investigating?"

"No idea, but I know where you can find lots of clues." She grins and points at the puzzle book.

"Joke all you like, Ashley, but when I work out the key to unlock the clues, we'll find out what Harry was up to."

"I'd offer to help, Kent, but I don't understand the clues, let alone the answers."

Thankfully, I know someone who can help.

While I make tea, Ashley heads for the whiteboard in my study and starts updating. With all the excitement, she seems to have forgotten I'm off limits. I give Columbo a shrug, wishing we were alone so I could take stock of what I've learned and identify what I've missed. Maybe I could answer the question that gives me the most grief of all.

Why did Harry go to Rathbone's party?

It's like having the name of a song on the tip of your tongue.

Harry knew he might not come out alive.

He prepared for the worst.

He even persuaded Miranda to help him, knowing he'd put her life in danger.

Typical Harry – always thinking of himself.

I remove the tea bags from the mugs, add a little extra milk to tone down the colour, and join Ashley in the study. She's still scribbling away.

"What do you think?" she asks, stepping back. "Do you think we're getting somewhere?

I look at the details, the connecting lines, the questions.

"Not really. We still don't know why Harry went to the party. Why did he pester Sarah and send her those texts? Why does she keep withholding information?"

"Maybe you're putting too much emphasis on Rathbone and his party, Kent."

"Harry died there. If he wasn't investigating Rathbone –"

"Then Harry went to see someone else." She points to the whiteboard. "Any ideas?"

Twenty-Nine

Ashley gulps down her tea, waiting for Coroner's Officer Beth Rimmer to email a list of the people who attended Rathbone's party. When her mobile rings, Ashley glances at the screen and grimaces. The conversation is short, prompting only monosyllabic responses from her.

She flops back into the chair. "My guvnor."

"I guessed that from the way you kept saying sir."

"He wants to see me at eight tomorrow morning. I don't think he'll be sending me back to the Major Incident Team. Maybe it's for the best."

Not sure what to say, I remain silent.

"You're supposed to tell me the rules and red tape make it impossible to do the job, so I'm better off out of it. You should remind me I spend half my time filling in forms and reading procedures so villains don't walk free on a minor technicality."

"I know how much you love your job."

"My job's gone. I can resign with dignity and become a private detective."

She drinks the last of her tea and thuds the mug onto my desk. "I didn't do anything wrong, did I? When we realised Miranda Tate was missing, possibly dead, I rang it through." She's on her feet, propelled by anger and frustration. "So what if I was on leave. We're never on leave. We spend our lives being suspicious of everyone and everything. Mike told me to remain sceptical and challenge everything."

"Ashley, why do you want to throw in the towel?"

She stops pacing, confusion pushing the anger from her face. She manages a helpless shrug.

"I'm not sure I can go on like this, unsure of everything and anything. Some mornings I don't want to get out of bed because there's nothing to look forward to. I miss Mike. I miss the way he looked after me. He was always there for me. Why did they kill him, Kent, and spare me? Why wasn't I killed when the Range Rover struck me?"

I wrap my arms around her and hold her close, letting her weep. When she's cried herself out, I let go, wishing I could fix her.

"You didn't die because it wasn't your time. You've still got work to do, a job you love. It's in your DNA." I pass her a tissue from a box on the desk. "Why would your boss want to lose the most dedicated, tenacious and gifted officer he has?"

She dabs her cheeks. "What if I have to do more counselling?"

"You need to talk to someone who can help you through this."

She shakes her head. "You help me through this. Being with you means more than you'll ever know."

Her phone buzzes, distracting her. "The list we wanted. Now we can work out who Harry might have gone to see at Rathbone's party."

She turns to the whiteboard, back in work mode, as if nothing happened. It's not long before she's on her laptop. She's still hunched over it when I go to bed at midnight, the mug of tea I made her untouched.

When I wake at six thirty on Friday morning, Columbo's not lying on the bed as usual. Ashley hasn't slept in the spare bedroom. She's not in the study, though Columbo's lying behind the desk. He raises a sleepy head and yawns. I sit in the chair and ruffle his fur, wondering if he spent the night here.

On the desk I find a list of names from Rathbone's party. A separate sheet of paper contains three names – Gregory Rathbone, Sarah Wheeler and Harry Lawson. Sarah and Harry were once cautioned for possession of cannabis. Rathbone was charged with supplying cannabis and other Class B drugs, but never prosecuted.

Ashley rings while I eat breakfast. She sounds bright and confident, like her old self. "This is about drugs, Kent."

"I saw your notes. Did you work through the night?"

"I had to contact a former DI to get the lowdown. The main prosecution witness was one of Rathbone's accomplices. She disappeared a week before the trial. As her evidence was crucial, the CPS couldn't proceed. Rathbone walked, along with his partner in crime." She pauses for a breath. "Harry found the witness, though not in a conventional way."

"What do you mean?"

"Her name was Mary Collins, but she'd changed her name to –"

"Miranda Tate," I say, joining the dots. "So, that's why he called off the wedding. He found out she was part of Rathbone's drug dealing network."

"Now Rathbone needs her out of the way so she can't give evidence against him."

"Your guvnor should be impressed."

"I hope so. Have I missed anything?"

"I don't think so. Why didn't Harry take his evidence to someone like you?"

"He was a reporter." She says it as if it explains everything that's wrong in the world. "He wanted the story and the glory."

"It's hardly a major scoop. Rathbone's a local councillor, not some government bigwig or celebrity."

"Harry was an alcoholic, Kent. His liver was shot. His days were numbered. He wanted to go out in a blaze of glory, righting a wrong."

"Showing the woman he loved what he could do," I say.

"I didn't peg you as a romantic, Kent. Anyway, I think Harry had more than Rathbone in his sights."

"The partner in crime you mentioned? Who is it?"

"You're not going to like this. Rathbone's partner in crime and co-defendant eighteen years ago was Kira Novik."

"As in Katya Novik – Rathbone's fiancée?"

"No, as in Katya's sister. But you know Kira as Kelly Morgan, your former PA."

Thirty

I'm still struggling to believe the news half an hour after finishing the call with Ashley. Kelly Morgan is Kira Novik, accused of helping Rathbone deal drugs. At least it explains Kelly's recent behaviour. It doesn't make me feel any better though. For ten years, I've trusted her. We've laughed and joked our way through three heads of service, including me, constantly belittling and taking the piss out of councillors like Rathbone. We've shared secrets, covered up mistakes, and heaven knows what over the years.

Now I know why Rathbone was always one step ahead of me. Danni too. He knew what we were doing, what we were thinking, what we were planning. And he never did anything to make us suspicious. That took some skill, especially for someone who likes to show how clever he is.

I can't afford to underestimate him.

Was that Harry's mistake?

"Kelly, you were a drug dealer." Saying it doesn't make it any easier to accept. "You were Gemma's Maid of Honour. She confided in you."

Columbo barks and paws my leg, hoping for the leftovers from my breakfast bowl – not that I've eaten much.

While I want to confront Kelly, she mustn't know Ashley's investigating her.

I can't tip off Brenda Keegan at the call centre either.

On Monday morning, I'll have to go into the office and pretend nothing's changed. If Kelly suspects I know about her past...

But what do I know?

"I don't know where she lives or what she does in her spare time," I tell Columbo. "I've never detected a hint of an East European accent. I can imagine her lap dancing though."

Kelly once told me she'd mentioned her time as a lap dancer during her interview. It sounded like the kind of joke she'd make. Now I'm wondering if she was an illegal immigrant, lured into the sex trade. It doesn't explain how she hooked up with Rathbone or became involved in drug dealing.

Where's the evidence Harry gathered about her?

Did he hide it somewhere for safe keeping?

My gaze settles on the puzzle book from his flat. It's the one item that doesn't sit with his direct, impatient character. "How am I going to find out, little mate?"

Columbo tilts his head from side to side, as baffled as me.

A knock on the front door sends him racing down the stairs, barking out a warning. Betty calls out. "Are you decent, Mr Fisher?"

"Come on up," I say, sounding like a game show host who's lost his way.

Columbo follows her up the stairs. She places her handbag on the worktop and studies the room for a moment.

"Would you mind if I made myself a cup of tea before I start?"

"Start what?"

"You said I could clean for you, earn some extra cash. I can come back later if you're busy."

"No, carry on. And don't bother with the study."

She nods and picks up the crossword book, scanning the pages. "Inspector Morse was good at these. I used to love watching him." She places the book back on the worktop and looks around once more. "Where do you keep the Dyson?"

I point to the utility room door. "It's in a cupboard. Why don't you have my tea, Betty, and I'll get out of your way."

I grab the puzzle book, collect the one from Miranda, and head downstairs, pursued by Columbo. Outside, he veers off to greet Frances, who's on her way back from the kennels. Like almost everyone who knows him, she has a treat ready. If he didn't have the free run of the sanctuary, he'd be overweight.

"I'll be in the farmhouse while Betty cleans the flat," I say as we walk. "Do we have any groups booked in?"

"No, you have plenty of time for your crosswords. Come on, Columbo."

She heads off towards the paddocks. Columbo weaves through the grass beside her, sniffing the ground. I nod to Ollie, who's emptying the rubbish bins in the car park, and continue to the farmhouse. Though Niamh left three months ago, her presence is still here in the furniture and in the kitchen where she baked before setting up a confectionery business.

I pick up one of her cake racks, realising how much I miss her and her exquisite tiffin.

As I settle at the kitchen table, hoping to make sense of the puzzles, my phone rings, displaying a number I don't recognise. The woman's voice sounds faint.

"Do you have the second puzzle book?"

"Yes. Is that you, Miranda? Where are you? We need to talk."

She's already ended the call.

A few moments later a text arrives.

Your fourth and final clue. Timing matters.

Thirty-One

I stare at Miranda's text, wondering what happened to the previous three clues. My call goes straight to voicemail. My reply to her text isn't delivered.

Either my number's blocked or Miranda used a burner phone.

Unable to contain my frustration, I slap the puzzle books down on the dining table, creating a cloud of dust. Looking around, I realise no one's been in here for weeks, maybe months. It needs a good clean. I leave a message for Ashley and go in search of cloths, dusters and Niamh's old hoover.

A couple of hours later, during a break for a cup of tea, Ashley returns my call.

"That was a long meeting," I say, sounding more sarcastic than jokey.

"We had a lot to discuss. My guvnor thanked me for uncovering Rathbone's drug dealing and the connection to Harry's death." She pauses for a slurp of something. "I've seen the post mortem report. Harry's clothes reeked of alcohol, but he hadn't had a drink that evening."

"But everyone said he was drunk."

"We need to wait for the toxicology reports to see what else was in his system. At least my guvnor now accepts

Harry was murdered. He wants me to liaise with CID to find Miranda Tate. I'll have to continue counselling, but I'm back on the team."

"That's brilliant news."

"I'm more relieved than excited. From the look he gave me when I entered his office, I thought I was finished. When he went through the things I shouldn't have done, I was ready to resign. Then he told me good officers always showed initiative."

"Let's celebrate at the Bells tonight."

"I'd love to," she says, sounding uncomfortable, "but you're strictly off limits. It's a condition of my return to duty. I shouldn't really be talking to you now. So, what's this about Miranda's text?"

I tell her about Miranda's phone call. "Do you want me to forward the text she sent?"

"Sure. Why didn't you mention the previous three clues?"

"I didn't know there were any clues."

"There are hundreds in those puzzle books. When you find the three that matter let me know."

Ashley ends the call, sounding like a detective rather than a friend. I shrug, knowing she needs her job. I can't blame her for that.

Turning to the puzzle books, I wonder if she's right. Maybe the three clues are in there. If only I knew what I was looking for. Tired of cleaning and staring at clues that make little sense, I drive to Sunshine View Caravan Park, hoping to catch the people I missed yesterday. When I climb out of the car, Blossom waves me over. She points to the home next to Miranda's.

"Jeremy West spoke to her last week. He owns the van and rents it out. He pays me to do the cleaning between guests, but he'll have to pay me double to clean up the mess in there. It looks like someone went berserk."

I thank her and head for West's home, skirting around the Nexus SUV, parked outside. The timber steps lead to a lavish decked area that runs along the side of the home and wraps around the front. Potted plants, burdened with flowers, burst out of ceramic pots and troughs, drawing the bees, butterflies and ladybirds from the nearby hedgerows. Several tomato plants, attached to canes, rise up through the flowers.

"The tomato's Moneymaker," West says, stepping out onto the deck. "Highly appropriate for a wealth advisor, wouldn't you say?"

Unlike a mobile home, I'm tempted to say.

He's tall, slim and looks more like an athlete than a financial adviser with his toned muscles and short cropped hair. Dressed in shorts and vest top, his flip flops slap the decking boards when he approaches, hand outstretched, smile revealing Hollywood teeth. He raises his Ray-Ban sunglasses to reveal intense hazel eyes. His accent lies somewhere between Jack the Lad and senior civil servant.

"Did you call yesterday, looking for Miranda?"

I nod. "Kent Fisher."

"You're the guy who solves murders. So what happened over there? Looks like a bomb hit it. Was Miranda hurt?"

"I don't think she was there when it happened."

"Have you any idea who trashed the place, or why?"

I shake my head. "When did you last speak to Miranda?"

"She rang me on Friday morning to let me know she was leaving early. Ironic, considering she only stopped by twice

155

– the day she arrived and last Friday when she left the key in the key safe."

His ushers me into a home larger than Blossom's. It has a separate kitchen and lounge area, all tastefully furnished and decorated in pastel tones. The tan leather sofa faces a huge TV, currently tuned to Bloomberg. A couple of fans move hot air around, helping it back towards the open windows. On a table in the corner, a laptop nestles among broadsheet newspapers. With no photos on display, no pictures on the walls, and not a hint of anything decorative, I suspect West spends his time making money.

"Did Miranda say anything about where she was going?" I ask.

"No. I imagine she was returning home wherever that is."

"Don't you take people's addresses when they book?"

"She didn't make the booking." He gestures towards the sofa and takes a seat in a matching armchair by the window. "Why are you interested, Mr Fisher?"

"She was engaged to a friend of mine, who's no longer with us. Can you tell me who made the booking?"

He leans over to the table and grabs a copy of the *Argus*. Harry Lawson's on the front page. "It says police are treating his death as suspicious. Is he the friend you referred to?"

I nod.

"He paid in advance for two weeks. That's all I can tell you." West places the newspaper back on the table. "At least I know why he never showed. Do you think that's why Miranda never showed?"

Was Harry planning to spend time here with Miranda? Had they patched up their differences? Was he trying to protect her?

I shrug and ease myself off the sofa, my head filled with more questions than answers. "Thanks for your time, Mr West."

"Miranda had a visitor on Thursday morning," West says as I open the door.

"Blossom never mentioned anyone calling."

"Blossom goes shopping on Thursdays. She also dozes off most afternoons. I didn't see the visitor, before you ask, as I was busy on the phone, but I saw a Land Rover pull away around midday."

"Did you notice the registration number?"

"No, but the name on the back door was Sarah J Wheeler, Veterinary Surgeon."

Why was Sarah visiting Miranda last Thursday?

What else hasn't Sarah told me?

Thirty-Two

Sarah makes no effort to hide her displeasure before she lets me into her house. It's a little after two thirty and she's on a late lunch, if the half-eaten sandwich in her hand is anything to go by. Dressed in her white coat and smelling of disinfectant, she steps back into her hall, retrieving a cup of coffee from the phone table.

"I hope this isn't a social call. I have dental surgery to perform at three."

"You came to me about Harry," I say. "You wanted my help. Yet every time I take a step forward, I find something else you haven't told me. You called at Sunshine View Caravan Park last Thursday morning."

"There was no one home. There's nothing to tell."

"Why did you go there?"

"I was fed up with Harry badgering me." She takes a slurp of coffee to wash down the last of the sandwich. "He had a bee in his bonnet about Gregory and wouldn't let it rest. Then Harry started telling me he'd always loved me and how he regretted not telling me all those years ago."

"How did you feel about that?"

"I told him I'd never had any feelings for him, but he refused to believe me."

"Did you tell him about Steph?"

"No, but he found out at Gregory's party, didn't he?" She laughs and heads into the living room. "When Steph spotted him badgering me, she came over and kissed me on the lips. You should have seen him squirm. He said I'd made the worst decision of my life."

"Harry never struck me as homophobic."

"I'd bruised his ego, that's all. Would you believe me if I said I'd never looked at a woman until I met Steph? He didn't. Neither does Gemma."

Sarah passes me a photograph from the sideboard. She's with Stephanie Richmond. Neither of them is aware of the camera as they gaze into each other's eyes, clearly in love.

"I met Steph three months ago at some dreary local business function at the town hall. I'm not even sure why I went. One minute I'm eating canapes, bored rigid by some planning officer, the next I'm looking into the most wonderful eyes I've ever seen." She shivers with pleasure. "I'd never felt so excited and so scared at the same time. I couldn't take my eyes off her."

I return the photo. She looks at it, a rare smile passing across her lips.

"Gemma was horrified when I rolled in with Steph and took her straight upstairs. Gemma thinks I've always been gay. She believes it drove her father away when she was a child, even though she knows he was gay. She forgets there's been no one in my life since he walked out."

"Why did you go to see Miranda?"

"I rang her and asked if she was in touch with Harry. She asked me to stop by Sunshine View Caravan Park, but she wasn't there. I would have waited, but I had visits to make."

"Did you tell her Harry was pestering you?"

159

"I had to tell her why I wanted to see her. She said Harry had always been obsessed with me. She knew about our EnvirAvengers group, our past together."

"Why did she invite you over? Why couldn't you talk on the phone?"

Sarah hesitates. "I don't know. I never thought about it at the time. Do you have any idea?"

"Did you know Harry was dying?"

"You mean he took his own life?" She says it as if it's what she'd expect from someone like Harry. "He was needy and emotionally dependent, a fantasist. When reality shattered his illusions, he couldn't cope."

"He didn't have long to live, Sarah."

"What difference does it make? Harry spent his life digging up dirt, raking through people's private lives to fill column inches. He believed councillors like Steph and Gregory were corrupt because it went with the territory. Why should I feel sorry for the guy? In case you've forgotten, he assaulted me."

She strides past me towards her practice, leaving me to make my own way out.

Back in my car, I can't help wondering why she came to me about Harry's death.

He was obsessed with her and she hated him. Miranda didn't stand a chance.

I'm about to set off when Gemma drives into the car park. The sparkle in her eyes reminds me of the moment I first saw her.

I wanted her so much it hurt.

Is that how Harry felt about Sarah? Did the hurt become so intense it drove him to assault her?

Was it enough to drive him to suicide when she rejected him again at Rathbone's party?

I ring Adrian. He must know more about Harry's state of mind than anyone.

"Kent, I was about to ring you." Adrian sounds pleased with himself. "I'm meeting Miranda Tate this evening."

"You tracked her down?"

"She rang me. She's been laying low for a couple of weeks."

"Yes, at a caravan site near Alfriston."

"No, she's in Brighton. I'll let you know if I find out anything useful."

He ends the call so quickly, I know he's lying.

Why is Miranda talking to Adrian when she sent me the fourth clue?

Thirty-Three

Gemma leans into the car and chuckles. "You look like you've got constipation."

"If you're referring to my deductive skills, you're probably right."

"Who were you talking to?"

"Adrian Peach has found Miranda Tate. Or she found him."

"Sounds like you need to update me, Holmes. Do you fancy a late lunch?"

Though tempted, I need to be careful what I say as my investigations involve her mother. Then there's Kelly's past with Rathbone. If I tell Gemma, two of us will be pretending everything's normal. Kelly will soon get suspicious.

With Ashley under orders to stay clear of me, Adrian chasing his own story, and Gemma too closely involved, it looks like I'm working on my own.

"Can we take a rain check?" Then, seeing the disappointment on Gemma's face, I suggest we have a pizza with Frances like the old days. "Shall we say seven o'clock?"

"As long as I can stay over," Gemma says. "It's not much fun when your mother's bonking away all night in the next room."

My phone saves me. I pick up, wondering what Ashley wants.

"I hope you don't have any plans for this evening, Kent. I'm going to cook you something special to say thank you for being the best friend a mixed up detective inspector could wish for."

"I thought I was strictly off limits."

"You are from tomorrow morning. That's when I officially return to my old job."

"In that case," I say, "I can offer you something more interesting this evening."

Back at Meadow Farm, there's a stranger chatting to Frances. Though his laughter lines and paunch tell me he's in his fifties, his surfers' hair, Hawaiian shorts and vest top suggest he's not so good at maths. His animated hands have a life of their own, waving a clipboard around like a lethal weapon. As long as he doesn't refer to me as dude, we'll be fine.

"This is Wayne," she says. "He's here about next week's filming."

"I thought Savanna had cancelled," I say, shaking his hand.

"If she'd cancelled I'd hardly be here, would I?" He looks me over, his frown and pursed lips suggesting he's not impressed. It doesn't look like Hollywood will be calling soon. "You're the guy who solves murders?"

He looks so surprised I'm not sure if I should laugh or feel offended. "Were you expecting Bruce Willis?"

"No, someone younger."

Frances puts a hand over her mouth, desperately trying not to laugh.

"From the way Savanna described you, I was expecting *Casualty* with animals. She wants me to make your sanctuary shine." His expression suggests it could be his greatest challenge to date. He consults his clipboard and points to the paddocks. "We'll need to smarten up the horses and donkeys for the camera."

"They've had lives of terrible abuse and neglect. What do you expect, thoroughbreds?"

"No worries, Mr Fisher. I'll source some horses from the riding school next door." He scribbles on his pad as he speaks. "Now, where's your dog, Columbo?"

"He's in makeup, having his fur blow-dried."

Wayne continues to make notes. "Great name, by the way. He's the perfect rescue dog for the kennels – fun and feisty. The other three dogs aren't so ..."

"Visually appealing?"

"Friendly. They started growling when I went up to them."

Frances turns away, stifling more giggles.

"They've been mistreated in ways you don't want to know, Wayne. You're a stranger. You invaded their space. They're bound to feel defensive. You can show how anxious and nervous they are in your film. People need to see the effects of the terrible treatment some owners inflict on their animals."

"Won't that put people off taking rescue dogs?"

Frances steps in. "The people who visit us love dogs and want to make their lives special. We can take you to visit dogs we've rehomed so you can see how happy they are now."

"I'm not sure the budget will stretch that far. I'll check with Savanna and be in touch."

When he's out of earshot, Frances says, "He's concerned about negative impacts."

"Since when did you use words like negative impacts?" When she blushes, I can't help smiling. "He wants you in the film, right?"

"Would that be okay?"

"You're a natural, Frances. And in case you don't believe it, you can demonstrate your talents this evening."

"We're not playing charades, are we?"

"Gemma's coming over this evening for a pizza with you and me, but I'll be out with Ashley on a call."

"Why don't you ring Gemma and arrange another night?"

"You didn't see the look on her face when she told me about her mother and new lover going at it in the next bedroom."

Frances chuckles. "Okay, leave it with me."

I spot Adrian's car the moment we pull into Sunshine View Caravan Park. "I knew he'd arranged to meet her here, not Brighton."

Ashley parks a few spaces away. "I thought Miranda had moved on."

"Or is that what she wants us to think? I can't wait to surprise her."

"Not on an empty stomach." Ashley reaches across and opens the box on my lap to extract a wedge of pizza. The cheese stretches across the gap between us for a moment. "What's with the building works?"

"It's an entertainment complex with a restaurant, bar, gymnasium and swimming pool."

The building site, surrounded by wire mesh fencing panels, is still at the groundworks stage, with piles of rusty reinforcing bars between the mounds of clay subsoil. A couple of diggers stand beside a mountain of concrete beams and blocks that will become the ground floor.

She points to the portaloo at the edge of the site. "I'm surprised they brought their own toilet when there are plenty over there."

"The site manager won't want builders trampling into the toilet block."

Ashley helps herself to another slice of pizza. "The site's close to the trees. Did they have to chop any down?"

"There's a bridleway running between the site and the edge of the woods. We could wander down there later. The views are lovely, especially at sunset."

"Is it another of your seduction paths?"

"What?"

"Niamh told me you have certain paths and walks you like to use. When you were younger, she showed you some of the paths leading from Downland Manor estate to Butts Brow, Jevington, and the Long Man of Wilmington. She said you used them all the time when you were dating."

I did, but only Gemma appreciated the beauty and magic of those gentle green hills.

"I never ventured this far," I say.

"Shame." Ashley grins and helps herself to more pizza.

Cars and people carriers come and go while we eat. A few people enter the reception building to buy milk and other necessities, like sweets and ice creams for their children. No one seems to notice us, even though we haven't moved for half an hour. Ashley shifts in her seat and checks her phone for emails. Her attention drifts to the children playing football on the grassy area adjacent to the building site.

"Someone's going to kick the ball over the fence," she says, opening the door. "I fancy an ice cream. Can I get you anything?"

I shake my head and ring Blossom. She picks up within a couple of rings. "Mr Fisher, what a pleasant surprise?"

A football sails over the wire mesh fence and disappears between the diggers.

"Blossom, could look out of your window at the home Miranda rented? Is anyone there?"

"No, it's locked while we clean the place."

"Of course. Thanks, Blossom."

The children run over and tug at one of the mesh panels to make an opening. One of the fathers forces two panels apart and squeezes through the gap, stumbling as he enters the building site.

"Change of plan," Ashley says, returning without an ice cream. "The guy in the shop said Adrian arrived about six o'clock. He headed around the back of the building and down the bridleway. There's a bird hide in a small clearing about a quarter of mile away."

I grab my notebook and join her. "Did he see Miranda with Adrian?"

"No, there's no window at the back of the shop." She grabs her bag and phone and locks the car. She stops,

167

distracted by the man who weaves across the site and disappears from view between the diggers. "I said someone would kick the ball in there, didn't I?"

The man rushes out, shouting and waving his arms. "Call the police! Call the police! There's a body in here."

Thirty-Four

Adrian lies face down between the two diggers, the back of his head a bloody mess. The football lies in the congealing blood that's spreading across the clay. We're standing where someone has detached one side of a mesh fencing panel and folded it back to allow access from the path. Ashley remains in the gap, her face pale and drawn as she studies the scene, phone pressed to her ear. She requests support, scenes of crime and the pathologist.

"Bob, the guy in the shop, is taking care of the father who found the body," I say. "He's going to stay on if you want a word."

She nods, but she's not listening. She's concentrating, looking over the scene, checking for clues, making a mental list of questions she needs to ask. She's already taken plenty of photographs with her phone.

"Do you want me to go down the path and see if Miranda's around? Her body might be lying nearby."

"I don't think Miranda arranged to meet Adrian, do you?" Her voice is sharp, defying me to challenge her opinion. "If his killer escaped down the path, it's part of the crime scene."

"If Miranda's the killer, she's already gone. Or, she could also be fighting for her life."

"You're right, Kent. Sorry, I'm trying to fathom out why anyone would want to bludgeon Adrian to death." She points down the path. "Stick to the far side and return on the same side. If you find anything, stop and ring me straight away."

I jog down the path that skirts the woods. There's nothing to suggest Miranda or Adrian came down here. A minute later I slow to a walk and head through the trees into a clearing. A shed that doubles as a hide has brittle and cracked larch lap panels, a rotting wooden base and an ill-fitting door. Close to the trees, a metal pole supports a couple of empty bird feeders.

Taking care to avoid the flattened grass, I lean through the opening in the hide and peer inside. Apart from a faded condom, there's no evidence that Miranda or anyone else was here recently. Even the graffiti looks old. I reach down and raise the lid of a plastic bin, finding bird seed inside. Though tempted to rummage among the grain for a murder weapon, I resist. After a cursory sweep of the clearing, I return.

Ashley's studying the mesh panels and the metal brackets that couple them together. The tension in her eyes and shoulders ebbs a little when I shake my head. I tell her about the bird seed and she nods, dictating a note to her phone.

"I had a word with Bob about the cars out front," she says. "Apart from my Audi, Adrian's car is the only one not belonging to someone associated with the site. Either the killer's left or he got a lift here."

"He could have come by taxi, walking up from the site entrance."

"It could be one of the builders." She turns her head, hearing sirens in the distance. "Someone lured Adrian here, waited for him to walk along the path, and then enticed him through the opening and between the diggers. He could have operated alone or with help. There are so many builders' boot prints in the clay, it's hard to tell."

"The killer took a chance, attacking Adrian in daylight next to a public path."

"You'd be out of sight behind the reception building. As Adrian walks along, you call out and he comes over. You beckon him through the opening, saying there's something he should see between the diggers. He takes a look and wallop."

"A woman could have done this, right? A woman rang Adrian. Was she pretending to be Miranda, or was it her?"

Ashley shrugs. "Yes, a woman could have done this."

I stare at the opening in the fence. "She'd have to undo the connectors on one side to move the panel aside. That would have taken a few minutes. Someone could have seen her, wondered what she was doing."

"Good point, Kent. So, did she take a risk because she had no choice? Did Adrian uncover something, forcing her to act fast?" She looks back across the site. "Miranda rented a mobile home here."

"But she wasn't staying here."

"She has to be our main suspect. Adrian would recognise her voice."

"If Miranda's the killer, why did she send me a fourth clue?"

"Intriguing, isn't it?" Ashley walks towards the sound of the approaching sirens. "In a few minutes, it's going to look like chaos, Kent. Go back to the car. Stay away from the mobile home Miranda rented. I'm going to be in enough trouble, coming here with you."

"What will you tell your guvnor?"

"The truth. You had reason to believe Miranda Tate was meeting Adrian Peach here and you asked for my support. He won't like it, but at least we were here to secure the scene. Shit, it can't be Miranda."

"Why not?"

"If you were walking past and a builder was fiddling with a fence panel, you wouldn't suspect anything was wrong. If the builder asked you to help move the panel, you'd walk over and ..." Like the excitement in her eyes, her voice fades. "You've got that look which says I'm talking out of my arse."

I look back at Adrian, lying on the ground between two diggers on a construction site.

"If Miranda's not the killer, why kill Adrian here?"

Thirty-Five

On her way back to base, Ashley drops me off at Meadow Farm. Her guvnor, DCI Simon O'Leary, aka Silky Simon, took charge at the scene, sending her to set up an incident room.

"Your guvnor seemed to appreciate your initiative."

She gives me a dubious look. "We call him Silky Simon because he's smooth, not because of the ties he wears. I'm not off the hook yet. In the morning, when he allocates resources, he'll assign me to checking past editions of the *Argus* for leads when I should be out there on the ground."

"Why would he do that when he knows what a good detective you are?"

"He has a problem with our friendship. Your father was a bit of a villain, to say the least. You solved murders we didn't. Now you're part of another."

"He doesn't think you feed me information, surely."

"Of course he does. He can't prove it though. He can't control you either, but he can make life difficult for me."

"I never realised. I'm sorry."

"It's been a blast, Kent, but I need you to promise me one thing. If you solve the case before we do, contact me before you do anything else. We might already be planning an arrest. I need a collar to prove I'm worth my place on the team." She leans across and kisses me on the cheek. "I'll always be your friend, no matter what. Remember that."

It sounds like goodbye, like I'm being dismissed.

I climb out of the car and watch her speed away, not sure what to think.

She wants to sever ties so I don't wreck her career prospects, but if I identify the killer, she wants me to let her take the credit.

I'm not sure that's my definition of friendship.

Once through the entrance, I spot Columbo tearing across the grass. Gemma's trailing behind, taking a more leisurely walk along the path in sandals, shorts and a sleeveless white top that shows off her bronzed skin. A delicate platinum necklace caresses her slender neck. Her smile fades as she draws close.

"What happened, Kent?"

"Someone killed Adrian Peach this evening."

"Why? Who'd do such a thing?"

"I don't know," I reply, a little sharper than intended. "Nothing makes sense."

"Want to tell me about it?"

I want to think not talk. "Maybe later. I don't know." Seeing the concern in her eyes, I try to lighten the moment. "You know me, never sure what I want."

"No surprises there then."

She turns and strides back to the mobile home, where Frances is watching from the deck. Without looking back, Gemma follows her inside and slams the door.

I look down at Columbo and sigh. "I've shut her out again, haven't I?"

Why do I do that?

Why do I always hurt the people who care about me?

Fifteen minutes later, I'm in my study, staring at the whiteboard. The connections Ashley made, the notes and questions she posed, feel like details floating in the ether. Adrian's death and the issues it raises only convince me I'm missing something – in addition to the three clues I never received from Harry or Miranda.

I look down at Columbo, poised on the sofa bed. "Harry went to the party to get more evidence. He wanted Sarah to break her ties with Rathbone and Stephanie Richmond. He wanted to confront Sarah with the evidence."

Columbo barks and rises onto his back legs.

"But she'd already told Rathbone about his planned visit."

"And now he's dead, Holmes."

Gemma slides onto the sofa bed next to Columbo, letting him sniff the pizza box in her hands. "I shouldn't have walked off like that," she says, looking up at me. "Adrian's murder has obviously upset you."

While I've already shared a pepperoni pizza with Ashley, the aroma of jalapeno peppers reminds me I'm still hungry. I sit beside Gemma and accept her peace offering. While we eat and sneak bits of crust to Columbo, I update her on the day's events. Once finished, Gemma settles back, a contented look on her face.

"If you were the killer, Holmes, you'd want to find out what Adrian knew before you killed him. Wouldn't you choose somewhere private where you could beat the truth out of him?"

"Unless the killer had already found what he wanted."

"When he ransacked Harry's flat and Miranda's house, right?"

"Then again, he may not have found what he was looking for. That's the trouble – we've no idea what anyone is looking for."

"Adrian was here this morning, looking for you. Betty spotted him by the entrance to your flat, looking lost."

"He never said he'd called when he rang me later."

I grab my phone from the desk and ring Betty. "Sorry to bother you at home. Did you speak to Adrian Peach from the *Argus* this morning?"

"Yes, he said he would telephone you. Did he?"

"He did, but he never said he'd called round. Did he say anything to you?"

"When I asked him what he wanted, he gave me a strange, enigmatic smile. He said he didn't have a clue, but you did. Does that make any sense?"

"None whatsoever." I thank her and end the call. "Adrian said he didn't have a clue, but I did. Do you think Miranda told him about the clue she sent me?"

I walk back to the whiteboard.

Your fourth and final clue. Timing matters.

Gemma steps up beside me. "Where are the other three clues?"

"Harry died before he could send them – or did he?" I grab the notebook from my desk and flick back to the start of the investigation. "He sent three texts to your mother the night before he died."

I write them in time order on the whiteboard above the fourth clue.

You never gave me a chance, Sarah.
You only had eyes for Kent.

If you'd chosen me, none of this would have happened.
Your fourth and final clue. Timing matters.

I turn to Gemma. "Anything leap out at you?"

"The fourth clue's different from the first three. It's like an instruction. Is it anything to do with the time he sent the texts?"

"Of course." I can't believe I missed what's staring me in the face. When I first saw the texts on Sarah's phone, I wondered why they weren't sent as one text. Then the timings puzzled me. The first two texts were sent within minutes, followed by a delay of a couple of hours before the third.

Gemma rests her head on my shoulder, a twinkle in her eyes. "You've worked it out, haven't you, Holmes?"

Thirty-Six

Back in the kitchen I slide a mug of tea across the breakfast bar. "I know the key, but it's a long way from solving the puzzle."

Gemma looks at the two crossword puzzle books and then at the printout containing the four texts. Next to each one, I've written the dates and times they were sent, transferring the details from my notebook.

"Harry sent the first two texts close together," she says. "Then there's a gap of three hours to the third. Did he think twice about sending it?"

"No, it's deliberate."

"The fourth text was sent six days later, long after Harry's death." She flicks through the first puzzle book and grins. "The dates and times relate to certain puzzles and clues, don't they?"

I nod, delighted she's picked up what's taken me a week to deduce.

"You knew right away, didn't you, Holmes? That's why you made a note of everything."

I didn't know, but she seems so impressed it would be wrong to disappoint her. And I can hardly tell her I made copious notes because her mother can be a bitch when things don't go her way. I also need to make sure Gemma doesn't tell her mother what we're doing.

Sarah Wheeler's too close to Gregory Rathbone.

Gemma pushes her hair behind her ears and leans forward to study the printout. She picks up the first puzzle book. She thumbs past the first twelve puzzles, which he had already completed.

"Harry sent the first three texts on Saturday, the thirteenth," she says. "As the first blank puzzle is the thirteenth, it must be the grid his clues refer to. Why are you smiling?"

"I enjoy watching you concentrate. The bridge of your nose wrinkles and your eyebrows almost meet. When you're really stuck, your tongue pushes out between your lips."

"You click your tongue against your teeth when you concentrate. And let's not forget the way you stroke your earlobe, which is rather sexy."

She pushes her tongue between her lips and looks down at the thirteenth crossword.

"Forget the dates," I say. "Concentrate on the times of the first two texts – 13.25 and 13.28. The third text is 16.21. Those are the puzzle numbers and the clues we need to solve."

She runs her finger down the clues and nods. "Do you think the fourth text relates to the second puzzle book? It was sent at 8.19 and the eighth puzzle in the first book has already been completed."

"Good call."

"If I write out the clues can you get the cakes? With Niamh's tiffin inside me I could crack a case in half an hour."

179

"Since Niamh left I don't have a ready supply of snacks."

"Frances says there are some leftover cakes in the café."

I grab the keys and wander over, giving Columbo a chance to run around outside. While I can manage cryptic crossword puzzles, Gemma's faster at seeing the connections and codes.

In the café refrigerator I find a couple of cream slices. I pop them in a paper bag and return to the flat, joined by Columbo. Gemma takes a slice, licks out a furrow of cream and sighs with pleasure.

"We have four words, Holmes. The first one is *flash*. 'Gordon cleans up in an instant'. Flash Gordon cleans up in a flash. The second one's more obscure. 'Upset stomach could be after prey.' Seven letters."

I consider the clue while I enjoy my cream slice. "Upset stomach could be an anagram"

"How about the runs?" She scoops out more cream with her tongue. "Anagram of the runs is *hunters*, who go after prey. "That gives us *Flash Hunters*. Does it mean anything to you?"

"Nothing." I study the third clue. 'Pelt goes off to find refuge.' Eight letters. "Pelt could be fur, or skin or fleece."

"Or throwing something."

I savour my cream slice, sensing a long struggle with this clue "Goes off means leave, depart."

"It could mean going stale or decomposing. Let's use the thesaurus on the computer."

"And admit defeat?"

Before she can answer, the doorbell rings. Columbo goes from waiting for crumbs to hurtling down the stairs in the blink of an eye. I trot after him, licking some stray cream from my fingers. When I open the door, I'm surprised to see

Savanna. She looks tired, her eyes a little puffy, her hair lacklustre. She's about to speak when Columbo barks, demanding attention.

She kneels so he can lick her face. "If only everyone felt the same way about me."

"What's happened?"

"Johnny left for the Cayman Islands this morning." She looks up at me, her eyes filled with sadness and pain. "He took my younger sister." She rises and straightens her vest top, smoothing it over the top of her ripped jeans. "They've been seeing each other for some time."

"You didn't suspect?"

"I was too wrapped up in my business. Things between Johnny and me have been flat for months. We work long hours. We're often away for days." She manages a vague smile. "Sorry, you don't want to hear about my woes."

"Then why are you here?"

"Would you be surprised if I said I don't know many people I can trust or turn to for help?" She looks at me with those wonderful eyes. "I couldn't face a night alone. This is a sanctuary, a place to hide away and lick your wounds."

"Hideaway. That's it."

"What are you talking about?"

"It's the answer to a cryptic crossword clue." I stop, realising how rock and roll it sounds. "It's linked to a couple of deaths we're investigating."

"More murders?"

"Come and join us. You met Gemma at the grand opening, didn't you?"

She hesitates, looking up the stairs.

Gemma waves. "Hi, Savanna, what brings you here?"

181

"Savanna's solved a puzzle clue. It's hideaway. Hide as in pelt and –"

"I'm already ahead of you," Gemma says. "I hear you're filming next week, Savanna."

"Yes, I'll be here."

"Let's chat upstairs," I say, leading the way. "I'll put the kettle on, unless you want something stronger."

"You don't have anything stronger." Gemma rolls her eyes and turns to Savanna. "He's teetotal."

"Ditto. I got slaughtered so many times, waking up in strange beds, never sure who I'd slept with, where I was. I used to feel like shit every morning, unable to remember what happened. I was the fun girl, the one everyone invited to parties, until I realised why I was so popular with the guys."

Savanna talks about her troubles without any reservation or fear, not worried what we might think of her. She spots the crossword books on the breakfast bar and takes a look. "Do you mind?"

Gemma shrugs. "I've also solved the fourth clue too. It's *Florence*. With hideaway, we've got *flash hunters hideaway Florence*. Any idea what it means?"

I reach for another mug in the cupboard. "Hunter's hideaways were places Harry and I used for leaving messages, video footage and photographs about local hunts. He's saying he's left something for me."

She scoops up some flakes of pastry from her cake. "In Florence?"

Savanna looks up. "Are you talking about Harry Lawson, the guy who drowned in a swimming pool?"

I nod. "You showed me the email he sent to Johnny."

"I should have told you he also rang last Wednesday or Thursday evening, demanding to speak to Johnny. He was furious, claiming Johnny had been in his flat, looking through his things."

"What did Johnny say when you told him?"

"He said Harry Lawson shouldn't go sticking his nose into things that didn't concern him."

Thirty-Seven

In the silence, Savanna's restless anxiety becomes defiance. She stops pacing and turns to face me. "You think Johnny had something to do with Harry Lawson's death, don't you?"

Like ripples in a pond, Harry's death seems to have spread further than I imagined, touching so many people. Sarah Wheeler, the woman he pined for, a member of the EnvirAvengers group we formed, seems to be at the centre. Adrian Peach, Harry's colleague at the *Argus*, may have helped with the investigation into Rathbone. Miranda, the lover Harry intended to marry, once dealt drugs for Rathbone. Now Johnny Spender, property developer and landlord, not averse to searching his tenants' homes, has joined the circle.

"Do you know where Johnny was last Saturday evening?" I ask.

Savanna nods, her expression grim. "He went to an engagement party with my sister. Gregory Rathbone invited him and a plus one. I found the invite in his dinner jacket."

His name wasn't on the list Ashley gave me. Then again, everyone connected to Harry seems to have been at the party.

"Years ago, Johnny had a few brushes with the law," Savanna says, "but it doesn't mean he had anything to do with Harry Lawson's death."

"Did he mention Harry's death?"

"Of course he didn't." Her hollow laugh suggests this was the first of several unpleasant discoveries she made about Spender. "He normally goes to your father's casino on Saturday night. I only found out when two police officers called to interview him on Monday afternoon, but he wasn't home. They asked me for my sister's contact details. That's when I discovered she went to the casino with him."

The casino's CCTV will have recorded their movements, the times they arrived and left.

"When I confronted Johnny, he said Susie wanted to meet Katya. They went to college in Brighton. That's why he took her instead of me." Savanna pauses, blinking back the tears. "And like a fool I believed him. Then she rang me from the airport this morning to say they were running away together."

"How does Johnny know Gregory Rathbone?" Gemma asks.

"Johnny has some properties he wants to demolish and replace with flats. The neighbours are up in arms about it, so he spoke to Gregory and some woman from Planning."

"Steph Richmond." Gemma almost spits the words out. "Why's he talking to her and not the planning officers?"

"Johnny wants to provide accommodation for homeless people. It's been a dream of his since I've known him. When one of his businesses went bust, he was out on the streets for months. He thought the council would back him if they understood what he wanted to do. He met Gregory a couple of times for an informal chat."

A couple of informal chats don't get you an invitation to an engagement party.

What else has Spender kept to himself?

Was it something Harry was interested in? He had words with Katya at the party. She's the one driving the refurbishment of the Travellers.

What if money was changing hands? Is that what Harry discovered?

Savanna drags me from my thoughts, brushing past me to sit on one of the stools at the breakfast bar. She strokes her hair back into shape and looks ready for a photo shoot. "Is the hideaway in Italy, only I know Florence well?"

"We had several hideaways in our hunt saboteur days. It was the 1990s – before WhatsApp, broadband or 4G. Mobile phones were like bricks and none of us had email. We could go weeks without seeing each other, so we left information and photos in hideaways."

"In Italy?" Gemma looks sceptical. "Why didn't you ring each other?"

"We had a lot of documentary evidence. We didn't want it to fall into the wrong hands."

"So where's this hideaway? The word *flash* suggests somewhere posh, and several of the suites in Downland Manor Hotel are named after Italian cities."

"It wasn't a hotel in the days of our hideaway," I say.

"No, it was your family home, filled with secret rooms and passageways."

"How exciting," Savanna says.

"Most of the hideaways were removed when the house was converted into a hotel," I say. "We had a hidey hole in the stable block, but that went up in flames a few months ago, as you know, Gemma. If Harry left anything there, it's gone."

Savanna looks thoughtful. "Why would Harry leave something in a hideaway? Why not email it to you or use Dropbox? Why not put everything on a memory stick?"

"Harry was old school. You can't beat a notebook and pen, he always said. They don't leave trails on computer networks. Emails can be traced. You can recover files deleted from hard drives with the right software. Computers keep logs of what you do."

"Maybe Harry left his laptop in the hideaway," Gemma says. "Or *flash* could mean flash memory or a flash card."

If it's the hideaway I think it is, a laptop wouldn't fit. But a memory card would.

Savanna checks her watch and rises. "If Harry was investigating Johnny, I want to know. I've invested a lot of time and money in his business. If he's been breaking the law, I need to protect myself. I've told you what I know, Kent, so be straight with me. That's all I ask."

Though I suspect she knows more than she's admitting, I nod and escort her down the stairs. At the door she turns. "I understand Wayne didn't quite get what you do here."

"No, not quite. Are you sure you want you go ahead with the filming after what's happened?"

"Johnny's gone to the Cayman Islands with my sister. Good riddance to both of them. I'd much rather be here with you next week." She moves closer, her voice deep and sultry. "Isn't that what you want?"

She seems to have skipped past the tears and recrimination stages of loss and started planning a future –

one without Spender, if her appearance here is any indicator.

She wasn't expecting to find me with Gemma though.

Savanna strokes my cheek with her fingers. "The first time I saw you by the farmhouse, I could feel how much you wanted me."

"Was I that obvious?"

She's close now, her voice like the whisper of her perfume, playing on my senses. "You made me look at Johnny and realise what was missing from my life. But when you didn't get in touch, I wondered if you were teasing, playing games with me."

"You could have contacted me."

"You and Gemma look cosy together," she says, as if she didn't hear me. "Do you really want to spend your time with a child when you need a woman to satisfy you?" She presses a finger to my lips and turns to leave. "You know where I am."

"You want me to collect you from kindergarten?"

She leaves the door ajar and saunters down the path. Gemma joins me in the doorway, resting her head on my shoulder. "I thought you'd turn to jelly the way she was coming on at you. I mean, she's beautiful, intelligent, rich and available."

"You think I'm that gullible?"

"You've grown up, Kent. It suits you."

"There won't be any film now, I guess. I hope Frances will understand." I turn to go back inside. "How long were you listening?"

"Long enough." She hands me my phone. "Ashley sent you a text. I thought you'd want to see it."

Traces of ketamine found in Harry's fluids. Avoid all contact with Sarah Wheeler. Not a word to Gemma.

"Bit late for that," I say, heading up the stairs.

"My mother carries an emergency bag in the boot of her car. She uses drugs like ketamine all the time, but she'd never drug Harry."

"Perish the thought," I say, recalling the night many years ago when Sarah slipped a sedative into Harry's drink.

Thirty-Eight

On Saturday morning, Gemma rises early and emerges from the flat in shorts and a running vest, her hair tied behind her ears. The sun has encouraged the freckles on her nose, giving her an impish look. As she stretches her limbs, her dark eyes accentuate the innuendo in her voice.

"Fancy some strenuous exercise, Kent?"

"You want me to carry your rucksack?"

She slips the small black rucksack over her shoulders. "You never know what you might pick up on a run."

"Like a stitch?"

She moves closer, treating me to the pleasant aroma of her body wash as we walk towards the main entrance. "Depends what Harry's left in the treehouse."

"You know about the treehouse?"

"My mother told me how you and Harry met there when you were planning something she wouldn't like."

"Did she tell you how the rotten floor collapsed when she took a sneaky look round? She ended up on the ground with a bruised bottom and a fractured wrist."

"No chance of us making passionate love there, I suppose. How about here?"

"You refused to come and live here with me."

190

"Niamh's not around to look down her nose at me now, is she?"

"True, but your mother won't approve."

"She doesn't like men." Gemma lets me open the gate for her. As I turn she puts a hand on my arm. "You were right to distance yourself from Savanna. All that guff about Spender and sleeping with her sister is nothing compared to what she's done."

"I didn't realise you were an expert."

"Come for a run and I'll tell you what I've discovered on Twitter. Or am I too childish for you?"

I watch her run until she turns onto the main road and out of sight. Something tells me I should have defended her when Savanna referred to her as a child.

One day, I'll work out how to please women.

When I reach the kennels, Frances is cleaning and disinfecting. We used to share the task before we became 'an enterprise', as my father calls it.

I must ring him about Spender's Saturday evening visit to the casino.

I grab a broom. "I'll make a start next door."

Frances shakes her head. "I've already turned down an offer from Ollie."

"I don't like leaving everything to you."

"That's why you pay me, Kent. Gemma says the filming's off."

I nod. "I don't think we'll be seeing Savanna again."

"Does it mean Gemma's moving in with you?"

"If you're talking about last night, she fell asleep on the sofa."

"In her running kit?" She puts down the antibacterial spray and wipes her hands on the towel, hanging from her belt. "Unless you're planning to marry her, Kent, you can't let her move here. You can't build up her hopes and dash them again."

"What's she been saying to you?"

"Nothing." Frances shifts and focuses on her Doc Martens. "You're my favourite two people in the world. You're made for each other. You always have been. If you'd stop chasing this dream of finding the perfect woman, you'd see she's right in front of you."

"I asked Gemma to move in with me. She refused. She could have handled Niamh, won her over."

Frances looks up. "How could she when Niamh's your idea of the perfect woman?"

"Is that what Gemma said?"

"No, William Fisher said it. He said Niamh should have married you not him."

I don't want to go there.

I miss Niamh more than I thought I would. It's not simply her wonderful cakes, it's the way she makes me feel better with no effort at all. She never judges me, no matter how badly I behave. She's great at everything she does. Everyone loves her, but she's always there when I need her.

"Why didn't Gemma tell me?"

"Would you have asked Niamh to leave? No, of course you wouldn't."

"She's not here now," I say.

"Then you've run out of excuses."

I return to the flat, unable to push Niamh from my thoughts. When I returned to East Sussex, a hormonal seventeen years old, I fell in love with her the minute she introduced herself. She was only eight years older than me, but more sophisticated and elegant than any woman I'd ever met. We shared similar tastes in music, literature and wildlife. She was in awe of the Fisher ancestry and the huge manor house in which we lived. With William Fisher spending so much of his time in Westminster, I saw more of her than he did. I had her to myself.

Until Tara McNamara, who ran the stables, took away the burden of my virginity.

I settle at my desk and focus on the present. It's time to ring my father to break the news that Savanna won't be filming here next week.

He's in his office at the Ace of Hearts in Brighton, an early starter like me. He tells me about the exotic cruises he's planning to take with Georgina, listing all the names of the ships and ports of call.

"Savanna's filmed several of her promotions on cruise ships," he says, effortlessly moving onto his second favourite woman. "I can't wait to check out the filming next week."

"There won't be any filming."

"Yeah, the weather's looking unsettled, isn't it? Has Savanna rearranged?"

"No, Spender took off to the Cayman Islands with her sister yesterday."

"Well, well, well. So that's who he brought to the casino last Saturday night. I thought there was something familiar about her. Savanna's sister." I can imagine him shaking his head in disbelief that anyone could cheat on his favourite *Love Island* contestant. "Savanna must be heartbroken."

Yeah, so heartbroken she made a pass at me. "Can you tell me when they arrived and left?"

"Why, does he need an alibi?"

"He might when the police find out he attended the party where Harry Lawson drowned."

"I'll ring you back in fifteen," he says.

While I wait, I sit on the floor of my study and make a fuss of Columbo, who's returned from his morning tour of the sanctuary. "Do you think I compare women to Niamh?"

His ears prick at the mention of her name. He whines and places a paw on my leg.

"I miss her too, little mate, but I don't think she's coming back."

The phone rings. My father's brief and to the point.

"Johnny Spender arrived and signed in Miss Susie Westcott as a guest at 1.17am. They left at 4.32am, after consuming two bottles of champagne."

"You may get a similar enquiry from the police."

"You're working with Ashley, I suppose." His tone is good-natured, even though he feels uneasy about my friendship with her. "I'll get the CCTV transferred to DVD for her."

I walk over to the whiteboard and move Spender higher up the suspect column. Harry was killed before midnight. That leaves plenty of time to drive to Brighton.

What about the murder of Adrian Peach, Harry's colleague?

Spender ransacked Harry's flat. What if Spender found evidence that Harry and Adrian were working together?

What if Susie Westcott pretended to be Miranda and lured Adrian to Sunshine View Caravan Park?

What if Susie Westcott is Miranda?

Thirty-Nine

Gemma strolls into the study, fresh from a shower after her run. "You look like you stepped in a cow pat, Holmes. Still pining for Savanna or is the pit in your stomach simply hunger? I hope it's the latter because I picked up some sandwiches from Betty."

I follow her to the kitchen, where Columbo's drooling by the breakfast bar.

"I thought Betty cleaned for your mother on Saturdays."

"Steph Richmond's staying for the weekend." Gemma inserts a finger into her mouth. "If it goes well, it might become permanent. You'll have to let me move in then, for the sake of my mental health."

Aware of what Frances said about raising Gemma's hopes, I shrug. "Are you sure it's a good idea, moving here?"

"I don't mind mucking in, or mucking out the animals." She takes a bite out of her chicken salad sandwich, barely chewing it before she swallows. "We also have murders to solve. Admit it, Holmes, without me solving the puzzle you wouldn't be looking in Harry's hidey hole. Are we going there next?"

She's irresistible in this mood. She glows with enthusiasm and self-confidence, her humour infectious, her energy almost boundless.

"We're meeting Wendy Birch at Sunshine View Caravan Park first. She's reporting on Adrian's murder. If anyone knows what he was working on, she will."

"She's the one with the blue hair and nose ring, right? She came to your old sanctuary with Adrian when a kid went down with E. coli. She was rather partial to bacon sarnies, wasn't she?"

On our way out, Gemma collects a pack of BLT sandwiches from the café. I pick some roses, cornflowers and honeysuckle from the borders and slip an elastic band around the stems. She looks delighted when I hand her the flowers, then disappointed when I tell her they're for Harry's aunt.

"You never mentioned his aunt before."

"That's because she guards the hideaway."

We pull into the car park at Sunshine View a few minutes after midday. Wendy's waiting on the public footpath behind reception. Now with long, bottle blonde hair, she's ditched the nose ring and combat clothes for an engagement ring, jeans and a blouse. She stands at the fence, staring at the spot between the two diggers where Adrian's body was found. Her voice is as sombre as her expression.

"His parents were here yesterday. They looked like they'd died inside and I couldn't bring myself to interview them." She nods to Gemma. "DI Goodman looked shaken too, but it didn't stop her questioning them, or me."

I pass her the sandwiches. "She has a murder to investigate. Are you okay to talk?"

"Niamh made the best bacon sarnies I've ever tasted. How is she?"

"Happy in Northern Ireland, safe with her family."

Wendy turns the sandwich pack in her hands and finally looks up. "A couple of weeks ago Harry said you might contact me."

"Did he?" Not for the first time, I wonder if there's anything Harry didn't anticipate.

"He was working on something big that would shake Downland District Council to its foundations." Wendy laughs. "You know how Harry liked to big himself up with dramatic headlines. Have you any idea what he was investigating?"

I shake my head. "Was Adrian involved?"

"I doubt it. They didn't get on. Harry was a chancer, always working alone, refusing to let anyone know what he was doing until he'd filed the final copy." She sighs and shakes her head. "Why did Adrian come here, Kent? Was it linked to Harry's death?"

"I think Adrian was lured here by the person who killed Harry."

She looks up. "So Harry was murdered? Why haven't the police confirmed it?"

"It's only a theory," I reply, realising my mistake. "I could be wrong, which is why I need your help, Wendy. Adrian was meeting Miranda here."

"Harry's ex?" Wendy looks confused. "Why would she want to meet Adrian?"

"I was hoping you might know."

"Were Adrian and Miranda seeing each other?" Gemma asks.

"She wasn't his type, believe me."

"You've met her?"

Wendy nods, turning the sandwich pack in her hands. "Back in June I was sitting on a bench on Brighton seafront, eating my lunch when this woman strolled up. I thought it was Katie Price at first – big black hair, heavy makeup, tight top. She had this slow deliberate walk, like she knew everyone was watching her. She talked like that too, like she wanted to emphasise every syllable."

"You didn't like her," I say, sensing Wendy's disapproval.

"I didn't know who she was. She was wearing dark glasses and the sun was behind her, so her face was in shadow. She asked me if Harry was having an affair with your mother, Gemma. Came straight out with it."

"My mother wasn't interested in Harry – quite the opposite."

Wendy doesn't seem surprised. "When I asked her why she wanted to know, she told me she was Harry's fiancée. I told her I knew nothing about Harry's love life, which I didn't. He never talked about Miranda, which was odd."

"Any idea why Miranda approached you?" I ask.

"I'd written a feature about horses abandoned on roadside verges by people who couldn't afford the upkeep. Sarah examined some of the horses. She had to put one down too. Anyway, she gave me lots of information, so I wrote a feature about her."

"She's got it framed on her surgery wall," Gemma says.

"Miranda asked me if Sarah and I had talked about Harry. I said I didn't know they knew each other. Miranda didn't believe me, accusing me of covering for Harry. A few days later, Adrian told me the wedding was off, but you'd never have known. Harry carried on as if nothing had happened. When I asked him, it was like Miranda never existed."

I'm beginning to wonder if she ever existed. I pull out an image I printed off Facebook. "Is this her?"

Wendy and Gemma study the photo of Susie Westcott, who has big black hair, a pouting smile and a slim, attractive face, disguised by heavy makeup and full lips. Her eyes, the colour of sapphire, seem almost demonic in the image.

Wendy shrugs. "I found numerous Miranda Tates on Facebook, but none of them linked to Harry. Is it Miranda?"

Gemma gives me a puzzled look. "Is it Susie Westcott?"

"Who's she?" Wendy asks.

"Someone of interest," I reply, pocketing the image. "We need to get moving, Gemma."

During the walk back to the car park, Wendy asks me to let her know if I find out anything about Adrian's murder. I tell her I'm not investigating it.

"You're friends with Ashley Goodman," she says.

"Did you tell her about your chat with Miranda?"

She smiles. "DI Goodman asked me about Adrian, not Harry."

Wendy thanks us for the sandwiches and heads for her car. I'm about to climb into mine when a woman's loud voice scares the birds out of the trees.

"You can't park here. This is private property."

A brusque woman with a military haircut and a pinstripe trouser suit that's as loud as her voice strides towards us.

She stops in front of me, her steely grey eyes regarding me with contempt. "Who are you?"

I point to the sign. "We're visitors. Who are you?"

Her back stiffens. "I'm Pippa Castle. I own this caravan park. You were talking to a reporter by the building site. In light of recent events, I'd like to know who you are."

I pull out my ID card. "Environmental Health, Ms Castle. Concern has been expressed about the hide in the woods. The bird food's attracting vermin. I'm sure your residents don't want rats roaming around the place."

"Depends on whether they have fur or not. So, you're not here about the man who died?"

"I suppose it must be the main topic of conversation at the moment. It can't be good for business, I guess."

"No," she says, her hostility fading. "It's a terrible thing, I know, but why would anyone commit murder here? It's a caravan site in the middle of the countryside. It's hardly some unlit back alley in the fag end of a city, is it?"

She's right.

I'm no nearer an answer when we drive into Langney Cemetery in Eastbourne. The cemetery's not far from the shopping Centre and next door to the crematorium. The road runs along the rear of a 70s housing estate. To our left, the graves and headstones fill the slopes. A red brick church with matching tiles stands among the graves about fifty metres back from the road. But for the steeple, it could be a village school. Once past the lane that leads to the church, I stop beside a walled area of the graveyard. Flowers in hand I walk across the grass with Gemma, taking advantage of the shade offered by the mature trees. It takes me a moment to orientate myself.

"Over there," I say, leading the way.

When we reach the grave of Harry's aunt, Florence Mackay, Gemma gives me a filthy look. "So this is the Florence in the clue. You could have told me, Holmes."

I look around, wondering if anyone's watching us. The grave is little more than a faded headstone and an aluminium flower pot, sunk into gravel chippings. A perforated cover keeps the flower stalks erect. I kneel and remove the faded flowers, wondering if Harry put them there.

I remove the perforated cover and slide my hand into the pot, hoping the killer hasn't got here first. My fingers trace around the rough aluminium surface until they encounter a small package, taped to the side. It takes me a few moments to free a sealed polythene pouch, about two inches square.

Gemma kneels beside me. "That's the smallest notebook I've ever seen."

The pouch contains a sheet of paper, folded around something thin and flat. It's the wrong shape and size for an SD Card or a memory stick.

I pass the pouch to Gemma. "Why don't you do the honours while I arrange the flowers?"

She extracts the paper and unfolds it to reveal two keys. "They look like the ones we have for our metal cabinets at work."

"This one looks more like a padlock key. Is there anything on the paper to give us a clue?"

She holds up the paper, revealing a line of small print. Her brow furrows as she reads it aloud.

No hammer required for the wise hooter here.

Forty

Gemma looks out to sea. Flat, blue and sparkling in the sunlight, it draws families onto the shingle beach and into the water. While nowhere near as busy as Eastbourne along the coast, Pevensey Bay has a charm of its own, thanks to the lack of hotels and guest houses. People walk their dogs here or simply stroll along the shingle, breathing in the salty air, taking in the views towards Bexhill and Eastbourne.

She turns her back to the sun. "I don't think this is a good idea."

I walk across to the rubble – all that's left of Mike Turner's garage. After the police investigation into his murder concluded, I knocked down what was left of his garage and placed a bunch of flowers on top. Every so often, I return to replace them. Then I go and sit in the chair on his veranda, remembering all the times we sat there, putting the world right or discussing his doomed love life. He would sit with a Budweiser in one hand, cigarette in the other, masking his loneliness with an enthusiasm and humour I miss so much.

I place the flowers I should have left at Florence Mackay's grave on the rubble and wish my old friend well.

"I turned down another offer on the place," I say. "The older couple from London upped their offer. It's more than the place is worth in its current state, but I can't bear to sell it."

She smiles. "How many offers have you rejected so far – five?"

"Seven. The estate agent's tearing her hair out. I know it sounds sentimental and ridiculous, but I feel like Mike's still here. Maybe I should pull the place off the market until I'm ready to let go. What do you think?"

"Would Ashley be interested?"

I shake my head. "She thinks of it as the place where Mike died. To me it's the place where Mike lived and laughed, where we joked about his non-existent love life and put the world to rights. We had so many good times here."

Gemma slides an arm around my waist and rests her head on my shoulder. Unlike me, she's not afraid to shed tears, to show the sorrow she feels, to talk about her feelings. "I know how much you miss him."

"Sometimes I can feel him with me," I say. "I know it's my imagination, but he's here, rooted in the buildings and garden like an everlasting memory. Does that sound crazy?"

"No, I feel him too. I think of how he made me laugh, how he took a sneaky look down my blouse when he had the chance. Mike always made me feel better when I came to talk to him."

"He never said you came to see him."

"That's because I always talked about you." She pauses, a distant look in her eyes. "He told me not to marry Richard. Mike sat over there, puffed on his cigarette and said you

wouldn't come to rescue me, even if you wanted to. He said
–"

"I'd bury my feelings and carry on as if nothing had happened. I'm sorry," I say, sliding an arm around her waist. "I could never get it right. He said it was because I suppressed so many feelings. He said I'd explode one day. Sorry, bad choice of words."

I pull away and walk over to the veranda, pausing at the steps. I catch a whiff of his cigarettes on the breeze, as I have many times since his death. I can hear his booming voice, his infectious laughter. I could almost kill for his bullshit detector, which cut through my flimsy ideas and speculation when we discussed the murders I was investigating.

"Mike always told me to follow the evidence," I say, sensing Gemma's approach. "Well, we have another cryptic message and two keys that could be for anything."

"We'll work it out, Holmes. We always do."

"Harry's gone to more trouble than usual to hide his secrets. That's why I felt drawn here, hoping some of Mike's logic and wisdom would permeate through the ether and open my eyes."

"How about testing some of my logic and wisdom?"

I look into her eyes, realising she's always here when I need her.

Why has it taken me so long to work it out?

"Okay," I say, turning my thoughts back to the grave. "When I pulled the pouch out of the planter, I thought we'd find an SD Card, containing Harry's investigation notes. When I saw the keys and cryptic message, I couldn't believe he'd thrown another challenge at us. Then I reminded myself that he and Adrian were dead. What had they uncovered that meant they had to die?"

"Drug dealing's pretty cut throat, isn't it?"

"Let's forget about drugs and organised crime, Watson. Let's focus on Rathbone's sphere of influence in Downland – local politics, small businesses, housing developments."

"Johnny Spender." Gemma grins at me. "Didn't Savanna say Harry was giving Spender a hard time? When Harry found out Spender was going to the party, Harry decided to confront him."

"I like your logic, but what about Adrian's murder? Can we link Spender to that?"

"Harry and Adrian both worked at the *Argus*."

"But Harry was a loner. Why did he book a mobile home for Miranda at Sunshine View Caravan Park when they'd gone their separate ways?" I drum my fist on the handrail, thinking back to my conversation with Jeremy West. "Miranda went there on the first day and returned on the final day, last Friday, when she left the key for him. He never saw her. No one saw her there."

I want to bang my head against the wall. Then something in the dust and dirt glints in the sunshine. I climb the steps and push the old sofa to one side. Dropping to my knees, I feel in the dirt until my fingers close around something metallic, familiar and highly symbolic.

"What is it, Holmes?"

I hold up the old and trusted bottle opener. "Mike's lending us a hand."

"You didn't see a puzzle solver down there, did you?"

I'm about to get up again when I notice the way the sunlight catches her hair, creating a fiery chestnut halo. During our first visit to Birling Gap, while she gazed out to sea, the setting sun created a similar effect. Even though I was looking at her silhouette, she was stunning – a lethal combination of mystery and temptation.

When she took a step towards me, the moment was gone, the illusion broken.

"Do you think Harry and Miranda planned a break, a chance to get back together again?"

"Don't move," I call out.

She stops and looks down. "Have I trodden in some dog poo?"

The moment's gone.

I pocket the bottle opener and get to my feet. "I don't know what to think. In spite of his impulsive nature, Harry seems to have anticipated his death and left us a trail to follow. He dumped Miranda and then booked her a holiday home she may never have visited. Yet she seems to have lured Adrian there for a second murder we can't find a motive for. And all we have to show for our efforts are two keys and another clue."

I walk down the steps to join Gemma. "If I didn't know better, I'd say someone's playing games with us, Watson."

Forty-One

I explain my logic during the drive back to Jevington. We take the more scenic route through Pevensey village and past the ruins of the first castle built by William the Conqueror after the Battle of Hastings. If my memory's correct, he was a master tactician – like Harry's killer.

"As I've already said, I knew it was odd when we found the puzzle book in Harry's flat. I thought it might belong to Miranda, but I was too preoccupied with the investigation to give it much thought."

Gemma looks up from her phone. "Why didn't you say so when we started to work out the clues?"

"We'll come to that in a minute. Harry didn't have any patience. If he couldn't get the answer in a few seconds, he moved on." I slow down as we take the double bend around the castle's outer wall. "So, why would he spend hours, solving the clues so he could select the right ones for us to find?"

"He didn't, Holmes. He went through the answers to find the words he needed and that gave him the puzzles and clue numbers." She buffs her fingernails against her blouse. "That's how I got the answers while you were chatting to Savanna."

I laugh, glad we're working together.

"The clever part was using a 24-hour clock to identify the puzzles and clues. Had the texts been delayed for any reason, Harry's plan would have gone astray. I can imagine him in his flat, waiting for the precise minute to send his texts. He knew the texts would prompt your mother to come to me if he died."

"That doesn't explain the latest clue."

"Doesn't it?"

She tilts her phone so I can see the photograph of the clue from Florence Mackay's grave. "This one doesn't come from a puzzle book."

"Go on."

"Harry didn't write it, did he?"

"Okay, let's assume the killer did. If it was me, I'd want to send people in the wrong direction. I'd take the SD card, leaving the keys and clue for us to find."

I glance at the timber framed houses as we weave between the parked cars on Westham High Street. The walls and roofs bulge and twist, as if settling into the earth. Not a straight line or right angle in sight – like our investigation.

"Why not take the card and run, Holmes? Or would you prefer Moriarty?"

"If we found nothing, either the original clues were wrong or we'd assume someone had beaten us to the SD card. By giving us another clue, we think Harry's being extra cautious, that what he's protecting is even more valuable that we first thought. Then we waste a shedload of time on a clue that takes us nowhere instead of hunting for the killer."

"Holmes, you're assuming the killer solved the original crossword clues."

"He ransacked Harry's flat before we got there. He could have looked up the answers like you did."

"He'd have to know the location of your secret hideaway, Kent."

It takes another quarter of a mile before I come up with an answer. "Harry put the card there before going to the party. The flowers hadn't been at the grave for long. The killer could have followed him there."

"And taken the card then."

"Exactly. He pops back later to plant the keys. Then again," I say, certain my head's about to burst, "Harry could have bragged about the hideaways to Adrian, which might explain his murder."

Gemma shakes her head. "Hang on. The killer would have to know about the texts Harry sent to identify which puzzles to check. Only you, me, Harry and my mother know about the texts."

"Harry's phone is missing. The killer took it."

"You think the killer understood the significance of the times the texts were sent? We only worked it out after you got the fourth text from Miranda."

"Miranda's house was ransacked too. The killer could have ... no, there's a simple explanation. What if your mother showed the texts to someone else?"

"Like Steph Richmond? She was at Rathbone's party."

"So were Spender and Susie Westcott," I say. "According to Facebook, she keeps horses in Arlington. Your mother may be her vet."

"You want me to ask my mother if she showed the texts to anyone, right?"

"No, don't say anything to anyone. If I'm wrong, who knows what damage we could cause?"

Gemma returns to checking her phone. "We need to follow the evidence, Kent, as Mike always said."

"So let's go with the keys we found. If they're genuine, they'll lead us to Harry's notes. If they're not, we'll know the killer's had a good laugh at our expense."

She nods. "Mum's the word."

Modern estates flank either side of the road as it rises towards Stone Cross. Houses sprawl across the land and down the slopes like weeds, smothering the natural environment, replacing wildlife with patios and decking. Proud residents then rejoice on Facebook when they add a birdfeeder.

In the silence I wonder if Ashley's connected Harry and Adrian's murders. She should have interviewed the staff at the *Argus* by now. She may have turned up a connection we haven't considered.

I shouldn't dismiss Rathbone's drug dealing from all those years ago. Was it a minor indiscretion or does it warrant further investigation?

While we wait at the traffic lights, my phone rings. Betty sounds breathless.

"I saw a woman coming out of your flat, Mr Fisher. Ollie chased after her, but she got away. Do you want me to call the police?"

Forty-Two

"I hope you don't think I'm speaking out of turn, Mr Fisher, but you should lock your front door."

It's a hangover from my previous sanctuary, which was remote. Most visitors came by appointment and would have to climb a flight of stairs to reach my first floor flat. I never locked the door during the day, allowing Frances to come and go as she pleased, using the facilities or my computer.

I take a sip of tea while we wait for Ollie to join us in the café. Gemma's already on her second flapjack, happy to mop up the cakes we haven't sold today. "Are you sure you don't mind hanging on?" I ask Betty.

"Ollie's driving me home," she says. "I only have my TV and a meal for one waiting for me. As Saturday night TV is nothing to shout about, I'll probably curl up with an Agatha Christie or the latest *Take a Break* magazine."

It's a quarter past four and the last customer left the sanctuary over twenty minutes ago. While someone might stop by before we close at five, it's unlikely. Ollie's clearing away and washing down his gardening tools round the back of the barn. Though we have all the necessary tools and equipment, he prefers to use his own.

"You and Ollie seem to be getting on well," I say.

"He's a kind, thoughtful man, even if he chases after women with little thought for his arthritis."

"Neither of you saw her go into my flat?"

"No, I only saw her coming out." She drinks the last of her milky tea and sits up straight. "She stopped to look both ways, like she was searching for someone. When she saw me watching her she hurried away. When I called after her, she started to run. Ollie came round from the back of the visitor centre and chased after her. By the time he made it to the main gate, she was long gone."

"You didn't see a car or anyone waiting for her?"

"She ran down the lane." Ollie closes the door behind him. "I would have chased after her in my car, but the keys were in my jacket in the changing room." He sits next to Betty and places a small package on the table, wrapped inside a Sainsbury's carrier bag. "A few years ago she wouldn't have got away."

Betty pats him on the shoulder and goes to the counter. She pulls out a plate containing a huge slice of Victoria sponge cake and places it in front of him. "There's tea in the pot if you want some."

I reach for my notebook. "Can you describe the woman, Betty?"

She closes her eyes. "She was slim, dressed in a casual shirt and those tight leggings everyone seems to wear these days. I couldn't see much of her face as she was wearing sunglasses, but she had thick black hair, long enough to go over her shoulders. She was wearing gloves too." She opens her eyes, as if she's realised the significance of this. "No one wears gloves in this heat. That's why I knew she was up to no good."

"What sort of gloves?" Gemma asks.

"Like those running gloves you wear, Mr Fisher – the ones with the white tick. She didn't take your gloves, did she?"

"I doubt it." I wonder if the slim woman in leggings, Nike running gloves, and nifty on her feet, is a runner. "What kind of shoes was she wearing?"

When Betty hesitates, Ollie chips in. "Yellow Nike trainers, like the ones you have," he says to Gemma. "She was pretty fleet of foot – not bad for her age."

"How old would you say she was?"

He shrugs. "Forty something?"

"Would you recognise her if you saw her again?"

"I'd recognise her bottom." He bites off a slice of cake while he thinks. "Actually, there is something. While she ran down the lane, she put her hand on her head – the way you would if your hat was about to blow off."

"You mean she was wearing a wig?" Betty nods to herself considering the possibility. "Her hair was unusually glossy."

I ask if there's anything else they remember. "Did she have a handbag?"

Betty shakes her head. "I was more concerned about stopping her."

"Me too," Ollie says.

"I checked the flat to make sure she hadn't taken anything," Betty says. "I hope you don't mind, Mr Fisher."

"Of course not. I appreciate your concern."

Ollie pushes the package across the table. "I found this in the bushes, close to the main gate."

I open the Sainsbury's carrier bag and slide out the two cryptic crossword books missing from my desk ten minutes ago. Gemma realises the significance straight away. When she looks at me, I give her the slightest shake of the head and turn to Ollie.

"Did our intruder drop them?"

"They weren't dropped. Someone threw them into the bushes. It could have been the intruder, I suppose, but I didn't see her do it."

"Was she carrying the bag, Betty?"

"I only saw the back of her as she escaped."

I slide the books back into the bag and rise. "Thanks for everything you did, Betty, Ollie. Why don't you go home and enjoy your evenings?"

"Are you going to contact the police?" Betty's hands tremble as she takes the cups back to the counter. "Only they'll want to take a statement, won't they?"

"They'll tell me off for not locking the door," I say. "If nothing's missing, there's no point creating paperwork for them."

Gemma follows me out and along the path to collect Columbo from Frances. "What do you make of that, Holmes? Do we think Miranda paid you a visit?"

"If you went to all that trouble to steal two puzzle books, would you toss them into the bushes when you left?"

Forty-Three

Columbo barks long before we reach the mobile home, howling with delight when he hears my footsteps on the decking. As soon as I open the door, he's leaping up at me, encouraging me to pick him up so he can wash my face. Once finished, he wriggles to escape and repeat the process with Gemma, but I keep hold of him. Frances, who's seated at the table, pushes her tablet computer to one side.

"Before you ask, Kent, I was in the woods with the dogs. I didn't see anyone running, but I heard a car speed off and head in the direction of Tollingdon a few minutes after three thirty. Whether it was your mystery woman, I couldn't say. Did she take anything?"

"I don't think so."

"Maybe it was one of your groupies. Did she leave a rose on your pillow?"

Gemma giggles and stares at me. "Groupies? Did someone leave a rose for you?"

Frances nods. "They turn up every so often, wanting to know about the murders he's solved, how he does it, whether he's around for a selfie. One or two look like they're still at school, but most of them come on organised trips from local care homes."

Gemma's laughter sets off Columbo, who barks and wags his tail. "Maybe you could organise some exclusive excursions around Kent Fisher Country," she says. "Savanna could promote it on YouTube."

"Why do I get the feeling you two have nothing better to talk about?"

I set Columbo down and he races out of the door, down the steps and into the grass. Gemma and I follow. She points to the bag in my hand. "Why didn't you tell Betty and Ollie the books were yours?"

"I knew something wasn't right when I saw the bag in Ollie's hand."

"It's a standard carrier bag. You have some in the kitchen."

I shake my head. "Not plastic ones like this. I have the bigger, robust ones. That's why I knew something wasn't right."

"You think the intruder brought this bag along?"

"Yes, but she wasn't planning on taking the books with her and this bag's highly visible."

"She might have dumped them when Ollie chased after her."

"They're hardly going to slow her down."

"She saw Ollie chasing her and panicked."

Once Columbo's through the door, I close it and follow him upstairs. I glance around the kitchen and lounge areas, which look as they should, right down to the squeaky ball Columbo leaves beside the hi-fi speakers. Nothing's disturbed or out of place, but someone walked around here, either looking for something or ...

"Someone wants me to know they've been here," I say. "They want me to know how easy it is to enter my home, to

216

take whatever they want. Maybe they want me to feel vulnerable in my sanctuary."

I'm not sure whether to laugh at the irony.

Gemma walks over. "Are you okay? You look troubled?"

"I'm trying to make sense of what makes no sense. The intruder planned her visit to coincide with Frances taking the dogs for their afternoon walk. Someone's watched for a few days, getting to know her routines."

"Someone must have spotted the woman hanging around. She sounds memorable. You could check the CCTV – see if she's been here a few times."

"If she's disguising herself, there wouldn't be much point. She took a chance today. If Betty or Ollie had spotted her entering the flat, she was in trouble. Maybe she had an accomplice to distract Betty."

"Why didn't you ask her earlier?"

"I didn't think of it then. I'm working this out as I go along, right, Columbo?"

He barks and tilts his head as he listens from his place on the sofa. He often knows what I should do before I do. Maybe it's a sixth sense. Maybe he picks up on my mood or my subconscious. Maybe he senses my emotions or reads my body language.

Or maybe I'm becoming one of those dog owners who insist their pet understands every word they say.

"Why did she throw the books into the bushes?"

Gemma joins Columbo on the sofa, fussing him. "Why did she take them in the first place?"

"Quite. Do you remember Wendy Birch's description of Miranda?"

"Yeah, it's similar to Betty's description of our intruder. Was Miranda checking to see if we'd worked out her final

217

clue? She must have checked the whiteboard in the study while she was here."

If this woman's the killer, she now knows how much we know.

I keep the thought to myself and place two mugs of tea on the small table. I settle the other side of Columbo, wondering how I'm going to solve these murders.

"Harry enjoyed playing games," I say, filling the silence. "I don't know if your mother told you, but he loved playing tricks on me."

"Because he thought my mother was more interested in you than him?"

"Maybe. Harry didn't like the way I came up with better ideas than him. I wasn't undermining him, but that's how he took it. When we were following hunts, he'd give me false information to send me to the wrong venue. Then he'd say his informant rang at the last minute with a change of venue and he couldn't get hold of me."

"Are you suggesting he's laid a false trail to spite you?"

"No," I reply, on my feet and pacing. "Our visitor came here today to intimidate us, to show how easy it was to enter my flat and disappear again. It could have been Miranda. She could be the killer, checking on our progress. She could be dead. She never showed at Sunshine View Caravan Park, did she?"

"You need to chill, Holmes." Gemma's on her feet, a concerned look in her eyes. "All this speculating and analysing is getting us nowhere. Maybe Miranda came here today to find out how we were doing. Whatever happened between her and Harry, she loved him. She wants to know what happened to him."

"Then why not ring? Or arrange to meet?"

"She's scared someone's going to kill her too."

"So scared she comes here in a disguise that makes her stand out? Why take the books and leave them in the bushes in a bright shopping bag? It doesn't make any sense unless ..."

"Unless what, Holmes?"

"I was going to say unless it's meant to mean something. I don't know what before you ask."

Gemma walks over to the window and stares at the Downs, the way I do when I need inspiration. Once again, the sun catches her hair.

"Is she saying the books are useless, Holmes, meaningless? What if she's telling us to forget Harry's clues, the keys we found? Maybe they're a distraction, a false trail." She turns, biting her lower lip. "What if Harry was following the wrong trail?"

Forty-Four

I take Gemma's hand and lead her to the study. "Let's go back to the beginning and see if there's a different trail. Let's start with the engagement party Harry was so keen to attend."

She grins. "For a moment, I thought you were going to take me into the bedroom and make love to me."

"Two people are dead, Gemma. Miranda could be next. And we haven't got a clue what we're doing."

"You think I don't know that?" She wrenches her hand from mine. "You think I'm here to make up the numbers and massage your ego?"

"No," I say, wondering why she flared up like that.

I turn to the whiteboard, tempted to erase all the connecting lines that funnel my thinking. They could be leading me in all the wrong directions while the truth lies hidden on the board, mocking me.

"Harry wanted your mother to help him get into the study," I say, going back to the beginning. "What was he looking for?"

"If Harry followed the wrong trail, whatever he did at the party isn't going to help us, is it?"

"Why are you being so negative? The right trail could still start at the party. Harry was killed there, wasn't he? He went to a lot of trouble to get to the party, pestering your mother, ringing Kelly at the office..."

My throat tightens too late to stop the words tumbling out.

As the look of confusion on Gemma's face turns to anger, I wish life had a rewind button.

How did my tongue get so far ahead of my brain?

"Why did Harry ring Kelly?" Her voice is flat, calm, subzero. She points to the whiteboard. "Where does Kelly fit into all of this?"

When I didn't tell Gemma what I'd learned about Kelly, it was only a matter of time before this moment arrived. I should have prepared for it, worked out my excuses, the higher principles that underpinned my decisions.

I thought I'd get away with it, didn't I? I should have known that lies and deception are ticking bombs.

Where do I start?

I sit on the sofa bed next to Columbo, aware of the anxiety he's feeling. As an abused dog, he endured many temper tantrums from his owners. He doesn't need to be reminded of them now.

"I'm sorry, I should have told you."

Gemma remains standing, arms folded tight across her chest, glaring at me.

"Many years ago, Kelly and Miranda were part of Rathbone's close circle. Please, let me finish," I say, hoping to stop the questions she's going to fire at me like bullets. "I don't know the details, but Miranda broke ranks to give evidence against Rathbone. Kelly stayed loyal to him. She's been feeding him information ever since. I can't prove it yet, but ..."

"Why the hell were you kissing her?"

I wince, remembering the moment Gemma burst into my office. "Kelly tried to kiss me. That's what roused my suspicious."

"You weren't exactly fighting her off."

Thinking about it now, I wonder if my brain had dropped into my trousers. "I wanted to see how far she would go to keep me onside. I think she realised how suspicious I'd become."

"Why didn't you tell me, Kent?"

"I didn't want Kelly to know I was onto her. If you knew what she was doing, you would have behaved differently with her. You might have let something slip."

"And you wouldn't?" The chill in her eyes could reverse global warming. "She's my best friend, Kent. I've told her things I've never told anyone else." Her hands go to her head as if she's regretting everything she told Kelly. "If I'd said anything about our investigation, she would have told him. Didn't that occur to you?"

I ruffle Columbo's fur to keep him calm. "I was trying to protect our investigation."

"No, Kent, you didn't trust me. I'm not sure you ever really have."

She strides away, her heels beating an angry rhythm on the floor and stairs. When the front door slams behind her, I sink back. Columbo stares at me with sad eyes, as if he thinks he's to blame. I stroke his fur, wishing I could tell him how empty I feel.

"I've blown it, little mate."

He rests his head on my legs and lets out a heavy sigh.

Then the front door opens and he's on his feet in an instant, ears pricked, his tail erect.

I scramble to my feet, ready to do anything Gemma wants.

Ashley calls and laughs when Columbo intercepts her. Moments later, still grinning, she steps into the study. "Oh dear," she says, seeming to enjoy my discomfort. "Gemma almost bowled me over. Was it something to do with Savanna?"

"What?"

"Someone only has to mention her name and you start drooling."

The squeal of tyres draws me to the window. Gemma speeds down the lane, ignoring the potholes. She slams on the brakes at the junction with the main road and turns right, heading into Jevington village.

"I haven't seen Savanna since yesterday. Her partner, Johnny Spender, took off for the Cayman Islands with her younger sister."

Ashley shakes her head. "I'm afraid you're a couple of steps off the pace, Kent. Susie Westcott and Savanna flew out to the Bahamas this morning. Single tickets only."

It takes a few moments for my muddled mind to process this. "You mean she was lying to me yesterday?"

"It could be worse than that. Earlier today, officers recovered Spender's body from the basement of a house he was renovating in Lewes."

Forty-Five

I pass Ashley a mug of decaffeinated coffee. "Was Spender murdered?"

She puts her phone down, now up to date with the case. "It looks like he fell from the first floor to the cellar. The ground floor joists and boards had been removed as part of a dry rot treatment. There was nothing between him and the brick floor of the cellar." She takes a sip of coffee. "We won't know if he was pushed until scenes of crime officers and the pathologist have finished. Time of death was late afternoon, early evening yesterday, after the builders finished work for the week. They won't be back till Monday."

"So who found Spender?"

"Go easy with the questions, Kent. I was only informed because Spender's tagged as a person of interest in the Adrian Peach murder enquiry. I've now tagged you too, which means I can talk to you without my guvnor getting suspicious."

"You think he's going to fall for that?"

"Why not? You know Adrian Peach, Savanna and Harry Lawson. I'd say you were central to my enquiries."

"Meaning you can interview me but tell me nothing about your enquiries in case you compromised a future prosecution."

"You reckon? What if I told you one of the subcontractors, a joiner named Kenny, went to do some extra work today and discovered the body? He recognised Spender, and as we have his dabs on computer, his identity was quickly confirmed. Kenny thinks the builders are from Eastern Europe."

"Belarus?" I take a sip of tea, joining the dots. "Rathbone's fiancée, Katya Novik, hails from there. Susie and Spender attended the engagement party for Katya last Saturday. So did Harry."

"The builders are probably from Poland, not Belarus. And to save you any future embarrassment, we're sure Harry's death has nothing to do with Rathbone or drug dealing."

"How sure?"

"Rathbone found cannabis in the staff room of his hotel and reported it to Tollingdon police. He wasn't aware that officers from vice were tracking a couple of couriers, who'd stayed at the hotel. Officers suspected Rathbone of a double bluff and arranged a dawn raid. He was hauled him in for questioning, but the drugs team found no incriminating evidence."

"Did they jump too soon?"

"They misjudged Rathbone. He doesn't have the skills, bottle or contacts to be a player."

"I thought Miranda was due to give evidence against him."

Ashley's dismissive laugh suggests bad news. "Her statement didn't check out. There was no evidence to verify her claims. It looks like she fell out with Rathbone."

"How do you know all this?"

"The detective inspector who led the original investigation is now my guvnor."

"What about Kelly?"

Ashley shrugs.

"She phoned Rathbone and asked him to deal with Harry."

She shrugs again.

"Was Harry murdered?" I ask.

"We believe ketamine was administered at the party or shortly before. It may have contributed to him slipping and falling into the pool."

"You've interviewed everyone who attended the party. Did Harry go there to meet someone else – like Johnny Spender?"

"We'll never know as they're both dead."

"What about Adrian's murder? Any progress?"

No shrug this time. "Why did you meet Wendy Birch at the caravan park, Kent? Wasn't it a little insensitive, meeting her where her colleague was killed?"

"I wanted to find out why the killer chose Sunshine View Caravan Park. Miranda Tate rented a home there, but it's a tenuous connection as she was never there. Have you managed to track her down?"

She shakes her head. "Her family haven't heard from her either."

"Have Adrian's colleagues at the *Argus* told you anything useful?"

"Adrian ruffled a few feathers in his younger days. Like Harry Lawson he fancied himself as an investigative journalist. Unlike Harry, Adrian matured into a respected and reliable reporter."

"Have you recovered Harry's laptop or phone?"

"Still missing. Have you uncovered anything?"

"We've been looking for his notes."

"You and Gemma."

"Harry left us some clues. I'll show you."

Columbo trots beside me, glancing back to make sure Ashley's following. She's checking her phone. When she joins us, she studies the whiteboard for a minute or so. "Do you mind if I take a photograph?"

"Be my guest."

I pause, wondering if our intruder took a photograph. Thankfully, the latest cryptic clue and keys from Florence Mackay's grave are locked inside the top drawer of my desk.

Ashley homes in on the texts Harry sent to Sarah. "How did you know they were clues?"

"The times of Harry's texts correspond with puzzle and clue numbers."

"What does it mean – *Flash hunters hideaway Florence*?"

"It's a secret hideaway in Langney Cemetery. I thought Harry had left his notes there."

"Did he?"

"No, there were no notes there."

It's not a lie. If she asks me, I'll tell her about the clue and the keys. I'd rather not in case they're a false lead. She won't thank me for wasting her time.

"It must be difficult working with Gemma when her mother's part of the investigation. Did you mention the ketamine? Is that why Gemma shot out of here like a bat out of hell?"

"She'll come round," Ashley says when I don't answer. "I can't imagine Sarah Wheeler being involved in Harry's death, can you?"

I glance at the whiteboard, still not sure why Sarah came to me about Harry's death.

Rathbone's not a drug dealer.

Miranda remains a mystery. Was she in cahoots with Harry?

Did Susie Westcott kill Spender? Did Savanna help? Is that why they flew out to the Bahamas?

Who lured Adrian Peach to his death at Sunshine View Caravan Park?

Why was Harry pestering Kelly?

Why didn't I tell Gemma about Kelly?

I have a feeling that question will haunt me for some time to come.

Ashley gives me a concerned look. "Is there something you want to tell me, Kent?"

I shake my head, wondering if I've withheld information that might become evidence in a murder enquiry.

It's too late to backtrack now. I've crossed a line and there's no going back.

I'll be fine, as long as Gemma doesn't tell anyone about the clue and keys.

Forty-Six

On Sunday, it's time to put everything right. I'm not happy about setting aside world peace, nuclear disarmament and global warming, but they'll have to wait until I've put things right with Gemma. After an hour of failing to write a half-decent text, I push my phone to one side, realising what I knew all along – I have to talk to her in person.

Columbo's lying on the sofa. He was sitting on the floor with me while I went through my problems. After listening to a minute of my soul searching, he jumped up onto the sofa and went to sleep.

Says it all really.

I pick up my phone and ring Gemma. When her phone goes to voicemail, I'm not sure what to say. I ask her to ring me.

I'm not the only one who's behaved badly.

"She was going to marry Richard, even though she didn't love him." I glance at Columbo to see if he's listening. "She dragged Kelly with her to the Cotswolds ... Damn! What if Gemma confronts Kelly?"

I scramble to my feet. Columbo leaps off the sofa, thinking we're off for a stroll. I grab my phone and car keys and head outside, making it as far as the visitor centre. I stop and return to lock the front door, waving to Betty in the café. Then I realise she doesn't normally work Sundays. Maybe she's bored at home.

After a quick word with Frances, I drive off to visit Sarah Wheeler. Columbo takes up his usual position on the parcel shelf, watching the world go by. When we pass Olivia Haynes' riding school, he barks at the horses. He continues to bark at anything that moves as we head through Filching, shaded by the canopy of trees, and on towards Tollingdon.

When I pull into the car park at the veterinary surgery, there's only Sarah's Volvo. Stephanie Richmond isn't here. Neither is Gemma. Her mother might know where she's gone.

"I thought she'd moved in with you." Sarah stands in the doorway. The smear of marmalade on the corner of her mouth suggests I've interrupted breakfast. "Have you fallen out already?"

"Do you know where she is?"

"I'm not her keeper, Kent. I've been telling her you're a waste of space since she was fifteen, but she never listened."

"Fifteen?"

Gemma was eighteen when I first met her. I had no idea she was Sarah's daughter because Gemma took her father's surname. Years later, I found out she lived with her father in London until she was seventeen. While Sarah, Harry and I were saving the environment and putting the world right, she never once mentioned she had a daughter.

"She saw photographs of you in the *Tollingdon Tribune,*" Sarah says. "We'd won the battle to prevent the housing development at Plover's Farm. After her father died, I found her diary and a collection of photographs of you in a box file. She'd kept all the press cuttings of you, printed out photos from the internet. She'd even written you a letter, which she never sent."

The revelations knock the wind out of me. When I walked in to inspect *La Floret* and saw Gemma for the first time, she already knew who I was. No wonder she flirted with me. She'd been waiting for the moment, maybe even planning it for at least three years.

"Why didn't you tell me, Sarah?"

"I didn't know you'd spent any time together until years later. When she went back to her father in London, I didn't know you'd dumped her. She told him, of course, but he was no better than you." She licks marmalade off her finger. "So, what's happened? Did Gemma find you in bed with the woman from *Love Island*?"

I bite my lip, weary of her sniping. "You came to me about Harry's death, so why didn't you tell me who was at the party."

"I was Steph's guest. I hardly knew anyone there. They were Katya's friends and family."

"What about Johnny Spender? Wore a dinner jacket, bit of a ladies man? He was there with Susie Westcott – long blonde hair, blue eyes, butterfly tattoo on her shoulder."

"I saw them leaving. They didn't stay long. He was talking to Gregory and she looked bored. They left before Harry drowned."

She closes the door.

I stand there, not sure what to do. If Gemma's not here, where is she?

My new stepmother, Lady Georgina Rhys-Jones, has the answer when she stops by the sanctuary at two in the afternoon. Though in her sixties, expensive surgery, a healthy appetite for all things sinful, and meticulous breeding by her ancestors mean she looks twenty years younger. Well-versed in attracting attention, she turns quite a few heads as she slides out of her white Mercedes convertible. She strolls towards my flat in a short skirt and vest top, her stilettos punching holes into the crushed gravel path.

Ollie steps up, receiving a smile he won't forget, and escorts her to my front door. Columbo greets her with excitement, but doesn't jump up. His tail swishes the floor as he sits and waits, drooling as he anticipates the treat in her elegant fingers. Once the treat is in his mouth, he heads upstairs to devour it. She looks me up and down, mild disapproval across her face. "You're such an idiot, Kent."

"What are you talking about?"

"Savanna's a beautiful woman. She's intelligent, charming and completely ruthless. I don't know what signals she's giving you, but she's after your money. Take this film she wants to make. Once it's shot, she'll want your help with the costs of marketing, converting your vanity into funding."

"How do you know?"

"I stopped your father agreeing to a film about his casino. Savanna's business is going down the pan thanks to Johnny Spender."

Aware of several people nearby pretending not to listen, I usher her inside. "Spender's dead and Savanna's gone, so there's no film."

"Excellent news." Georgina smiles, a twinkle in her eyes. "Gemma's already eating me out of chocolate and cakes. I don't suppose you've got anything unhealthy in your cupboards."

"Gemma's with you?" I follow her upstairs, wondering why I'm so slow sometimes. The two of them have been on several shopping sprees of late.

"She's staying with us while you come to your senses. With Savanna Westcott out of the picture, that leaves Ashley Goodman. Do you really want a woman who'll run your life?"

"My father doesn't seem to mind."

Georgina's deep, husky laugh betrays a lifetime of cigarettes. "He trusts my judgement. I hope you will too. Ashley's drawn to you because she craves excitement and adventure. What happens when there are no more murders to solve?"

"Ashley and I are friends."

"As our friends across the pond would say, wake up and smell the coffee. Stay away from Ashley, if only to lower your father's blood pressure. You know how twitchy he gets with the police around."

"He can stop twitching because Ashley will be moving away soon."

Georgina sinks into the leather corner unit, looking pleased. "So should you. Separate home and work. I love what you've done to this old barn, but if you and Gemma are going to grow old together, you need your own space away from the sanctuary."

Columbo jumps up to join her, giving her his 'haven't eaten for days' look. He's canny enough to know there's always another treat.

"Did she tell you she's kept photographs of me since she was fifteen?"

"That's sweet."

"It's obsessive and unhealthy, Georgina. She's created a fantasy I can never match up to."

"Then stop faffing around. The most wonderful young woman you've ever known worships you and you're like a rabbit caught in headlights. Admit it, Kent, no other woman comes close." She gets to her feet and walks over to me, resting her hands on my shoulders. "Gemma's the only woman you've ever loved. Everyone else can see it, so why can't you?"

"You didn't see the way she looked at me last night."

"No, but you deserved it. Honestly, Kent, you're hopeless with women. That's why I have a plan. Listen carefully."

Her plan involves treating Gemma to some intense retail therapy tomorrow, followed by a meal in the evening. All I have to do is pay a surprise visit in the evening to see my father and tell Gemma how much I love her.

"She won't believe me."

Georgina kisses my cheek. "Why not? Not once have you protested or told me you don't love her. You've agreed to everything I said. See you tomorrow."

She strolls to the stairs, Columbo at her heels. When her hand grips the handrail, she stops. She frowns as she examines her fingers. "If Gemma's going to live here, you need to clean the place and run the hoover round."

Outside, Ollie's waiting. He escorts her to her car, opening the door for her like the gentleman he is. In the café, Betty watches with a face like thunder.

I chuckle and head for the cupboard where I keep my Dyson.

That's when I realise how careless and stupid I've been.

Forty-Seven

My plan takes shape when I remember Scooby Cam from my last investigation. In order to discover who was placing threatening notes on my car windscreen, Ashley had a small camera fitted inside the Scooby Doo soft toy that sits on my dashboard. I go straight out to my car, open the boot and retrieve the holdall that contains my spare running kit. I slip Scooby inside and return to the flat, pausing only to wave to Betty.

It takes me a few minutes to remove the camera, put it on charge and switch it on. With the app on my phone activated, I test the camera, delighted when it transmits a clear image of my desk and the whiteboard. While the battery charges, I plan the trap. If nothing else, it takes my mind off Gemma.

At a quarter to four, I'm ready to go. After trying several locations, I hide the camera on the top shelf of my bookcase, appropriately nestled on top of a Miss Marple DVD collection. After checking everything is in order, I change into my running clothes and take Columbo to Frances. On my way back, I stop to talk to Ollie.

"Thanks for looking after my stepmother earlier."

"My pleasure. She's a remarkable lady, isn't she?"

"Indeed. Will you also be escorting Betty home?"

He nods and checks his watch. "She shouldn't be long now."

Back in the flat I slip on my back pack and grab my empty running bottle. In the café, Betty's wiping down the tables. I wave my bottle and nip around the counter. "I need some chilled orange squash."

"Was that Lady Georgina Rhys-Jones I saw earlier?" she asks.

"Yes," I reply, filling my bottle from the jug. "She brought me some news about Harry Lawson, the journalist who drowned last weekend. Seems like I got it all wrong. That's why I'm going for a run over the Downs to clear my head and focus my mind."

"Don't forget to lock your door," she calls as I leave. "You need to get into the habit after what happened yesterday."

I retrieve my keys and lock the door before I set off. I wave to Betty and Ollie as I jog past, taking it easy until I'm on the track that runs alongside my sanctuary. Within minutes, I'm under the trees, enjoying the shade and the gentle breeze that rolls off the Downs. As the track splits, I take the right turn for a change, following the path that runs along the back of the sanctuary. When I reach the boundary between my land and the field belonging to the riding school, I stop and remove the back pack. With my binoculars in my hand, I jog down the side of the hedgerow, hoping I don't bump into any riders.

A few minutes later, I stop at a gap that gives me a clear view to the main barn and the café. It looks like Betty's still cleaning, though I can't be sure. I take a few glugs of orange while I keep watch. About ten minutes later, Ollie emerges through the door and walks towards the main entrance, disappearing from view when he rounds the visitor centre. Betty leaves the café, locking the door behind her. She checks her bag, glances up at the sky and follows the same path as Ollie.

I lower the binoculars, wishing she hadn't insisted I lock the door. I'm sure she was nosing around my flat before she offered to clean for me. That's how she knew I had a Dyson in the cupboard.

I'm not sure why she's interested in my investigation or what she hopes to find. She only started as a volunteer a few months ago, moving from general work to running the café in the blink of an eye. Ollie started at the same time, which makes we wonder if they're working together.

I glug back more orange, wondering why she insisted I lock the door. I thought she'd jump at the chance to take a look around while I was out running.

Then she returns. She stops at my front door and checks around her. For a moment, I could swear she's spotted me watching her. Then she inserts a key into the lock and enters my flat.

I should have known she'd have a copy of my key.

Though tempted to run back and challenge her, I need to video her in my study before I confront her. It shouldn't take her long to find the cryptic clue and keys I recovered from Florence Mackay's grave. I placed them on top of the desk, leaving my notebook locked in the drawer for safe keeping.

My notebook contains far more information than the whiteboard, including my thoughts, ideas, and suspicions about Harry and Adrian's deaths. I've speculated about

Miranda's role, Spender's links to Rathbone and possible dodgy property deals.

Then there's Kelly.

Tomorrow at the office, I'll have to confront her. I've no idea what I'll say or do, but I can't afford any mistakes.

Then I realise I've already made a mistake.

If Betty made a copy of my front door key, she may have one for my desk.

She could be reading my notebook right now.

Ramming my binoculars into the back pack, I start running.

Forty-Eight

Betty's sitting on a stool at the breakfast bar, a large glass of orange squash and a handbag before her. Sweet Betty Cooper with her Margaret Thatcher hair and precisely pressed trousers and jackets. If she sat behind a desk, stroking a cat with demonic eyes, she'd be the perfect Bond villain. She withdraws two keys from her handbag and places them on the breakfast bar.

I meet her unblinking gaze. "How long have you been spying on me?"

"Long enough to know you've fallen into the same trap as Harry Lawson."

She's cool, I'll give her that. "How long have you had a key to my flat and my desk?"

"The second key's for the rear door. It's easier to sneak in and out that way."

"While Ollie cleans his tools and stands watch?"

She smiles. "Yes, he has a very shiny spade."

"So why didn't you escape through the rear? You must have seen me running over."

"I thought it was time we had a chat." She sounds like a manager about to start an appraisal. "I knew you'd rumbled me when you came into the café for orange squash. You have plenty in your fridge and your back pack's far too big for a small bottle."

It's another dent to my chances of graduating from detective school.

She pulls the camera out of her handbag. "I haven't tampered with it. I liked the way you set it on top of your Miss Marple DVDs. Very apt." She jumps down from the stool and walks over to the fridge. "I've brought a couple of cream slices with me. I don't know about you, but all this sneaking around makes me peckish. Do you find that while you're investigating?"

"Who's the third slice for?" I ask, spotting a spare one on the shelf.

"I was hoping Miss Goodman might be with you, but relations between you seem strained." She places the plates on the breakfast bar and retrieves two napkins from her handbag. "You don't mind if I stand, do you? The stools are a sod to mount for someone my age and size. But you should sit, Mr Fisher. I'm not going to attack you. I'm not even going to reprimand you for making the same mistakes as Harry. You were following his investigation, which was flawed. I was hoping you'd correct your error after my last hint."

From the way she talks, she sounds like a controller, directing her spies. "Are you talking about the discarded puzzle books?"

She smiles and nods. "You picked up on that. That's encouraging."

Now it's sounding like an appraisal.

"Did you and Ollie set it up to make me think Miranda came here?"

"Of course, and in case you're wondering, we haven't seen or spoken to her. If we had, we wouldn't need to trouble you."

While she nibbles at the cream slice like a mouse, I ponder her words. "Are you saying Miranda's the key to solving Harry's death?"

She continues to nibble, in no hurry it seems. "This is not about Harry Lawson's demise. Had he not drawn you into his investigation, we would have approached you the way we sought Harry's assistance. But in answer to your question, yes, Miranda Tate could well be the key that unlocks the mystery. Had Harry not overreacted and split up with her, we wouldn't have needed his services."

"You want me to find Miranda Tate. Is that why you're here?"

"You're already trying to find her, Mr Fisher, but you're relying too much on Harry's work. You need to know the bigger picture, as they call it. But first, you're probably wondering why Harry was working for Ollie and me."

While she attacks the filling of her cream slice, I think about what she's told me. Why didn't she approach me direct? Why sneak around in my study, following my progress? Did it give her a thrill, a sense of power and control?

Hopefully, her approach will make more sense after she's explained herself.

She sets the cake aside and wipes her fingers on the napkin.

"Harry was a freelance reporter who took an interest in a drowning at Ashdown Activity Centre near East Grinstead in 2009. He was based in London and investigated PlayAway Adventures, a local Croydon charity. They took children from poor families and care homes on activity breaks in the countryside. During one visit, a seven year old girl in their care drowned in the swimming pool."

"Yes, I remember hearing about the incident. Environmental Health Officers from Mid Sussex District Council investigated."

She looks up sharply. "If you know about it, why haven't you updated your whiteboard?"

"I didn't know it had anything to do with Harry's death."

"Then how do you know about it?"

"We have a county liaison group where we share information. If my memory's correct, the activity centre was prosecuted for health and safety offences." I pause, wondering why she's so agitated. "Are you related to the girl who drowned? Is that what this is all about?"

Betty shakes her head. "We we're interested in an employee at the activity centre who'd agreed to talk to Harry. She claimed she knew what happened on the day, but then vanished. That's what he told me when we spoke."

"You don't believe him?"

She shrugs. "The official investigation was a shambles. Officers from Croydon investigated the charity, saying it didn't make appropriate checks into Ashdown Activity Centre. But the charity had taken children there for years without any problems. The charity blamed the activity centre for not providing lifeguards on the day. The activity centre blamed the charity for failing to keep control of their children."

"Did Croydon take legal action against the charity?"

She shakes her head. "No, Croydon were looking after the girl in one of their care homes. The council funded the charity that took her to the activity centre."

"They didn't want their own environmental health officers prosecuting and making this public, right?"

"Something like that. The media, including Harry, tore into them, but no one was ever held accountable. The council survived, naturally, but the media destroyed PlayAway Adventures."

"Betty, this was ten years ago. Why have you waited so long?"

"You're aware of the new swimming pool and gym at the Travellers, I'm sure. When Mr Rathbone applied for planning permission there were objections from virtually everyone who lived nearby. The media took an interest when objectors claimed Mr Rathbone was using his position as leader of the council to influence the planning decision."

"Did that include Harry Lawson?"

She nods. "I didn't realise he'd left London to work for the *Argus* in Brighton. When I read his features in the paper, I rang and asked to meet him. While he didn't remember me, he recalled the drowning at Ashdown Activity Centre. I asked him if he'd ever tracked down the missing employee, but he hadn't. He said he knew someone who used to work there and could make a few enquiries for me on a freelance basis."

"He wanted money."

"I didn't mind. If I was paying, I could make certain demands."

"Did he find this missing employee?"

"No, he became obsessed with Gregory Rathbone, certain he was the key to the whole mystery."

"But you don't think that's the case."

"Harry said he could link Mr Rathbone to the girl's death, but he died before he could give us the details. Then we realised he'd left you information so you could finish what he started. But you haven't made a great deal of progress, have you? All those suspects and connections on your whiteboard and you're no closer to the truth than Harry was. It's so disappointing."

"What do you expect when I don't have Harry's notes? I didn't know about the activity centre drowning till you told me. I'll follow it up."

"I'll follow it up? That's what social workers say before adding your complaint to the pile on their desks. Don't worry, Mrs Cooper, we'll look into it and get back to you."

"I understand your frustration, Betty, but I'm not a mind reader."

"On the day Chrissy Jones drowned, a lifeguard deserted her post. We want to find her so we can take action."

"What kind of action?"

"Legal action, of course. We want everyone to know what she did. We want her to pay ... Ollie, no!" she cries, a look of horror in her eyes.

I look over my shoulder and catch a glimpse of a spade swinging towards me, a split second before it makes contact.

Forty-Nine

I find myself on the floor, next to a prostrate bar stool. I hear footsteps, a door slamming shut. Dazed and disorientated, I raise my head, setting off a throbbing pain at the base of my skull and between my shoulders. A damp sticky mess is soaking into my running vest and shorts. It's too thin for blood. I sniff my damp fingers. They smell of orange. Turning, I feel the rucksack pressing into my back.

Did my rucksack absorb some of the impact of the spade?

More jabs of pain hinder my progress as I kick away the bar stool and clamber to my feet. Peering through the window I see Ollie and Betty driving away from the car park. The keys to my flat are still on the breakfast bar, lying between the two cream slices.

"I don't think we'll be seeing them again, Fisher."

While I still don't understand their role in Harry's investigation, they're connected to someone involved in the drowning at Ashdown Activity Centre. Harry's death in Rathbone's swimming pool is an echo of the earlier drowning. It means someone at the engagement party has a connection to the activity centre death.

Harry went to see that someone.

Without his investigation notes, I'll have to work it out myself.

Hearing Columbo's claws clicking on the stairs, I turn to greet him as he bounds across the floor. Frances follows a few steps behind and stops, staring from me to the stool and pool of orange on the floor.

"What happened, Kent? I've never seen you look so pale. What's dribbling down your leg?"

"Ollie whacked me with a spade," I say, struggling to ease off my rucksack without generating more pain in my neck and back.

She helps me remove it, setting it on the breakfast bar. She extracts my binoculars and phone, which are wet with orange squash, but otherwise undamaged. Then she pulls out the cracked and empty plastic bottle. "You should have filled it with water," she says.

Columbo's already sniffing the orange squash on the floor. While he'll consume almost anything, he turns away and jumps up onto the corner unit to watch from there.

"Shall I call Ashley?" Frances asks.

I shake my head, setting off more dull pains. "I'll live."

She steps up, looking into my eyes while she runs her hands over my head, checking for damage. "You were lucky the spade didn't hit your head," she says, checking my arms and shoulders. Finally, she examines my neck and back. "Why did Ollie attack you?"

"It's a long story. While I shower and freshen up, can you call up Betty and Ollie's addresses from our staff records? I need to pay them a visit."

She shakes her head. "What if you have concussion? What if you pass out?"

"Then you drive."

246

"And who's going to look after this place. It's late Sunday afternoon and everyone's gone home. I've got dogs to feed and walk, horses to tend to. I can't see Betty and Ollie fleeing across the channel overnight, can you?"

I head for the shower, realising she's probably right.

The rush of water helps to clear my head. I'm going to have a few bruises, but the ache's worse than the damage. I doubt if Ollie intended to kill me, but why strike me if he and Betty wanted my help? It makes no sense.

Back in the lounge, armed with a mug of tea, I explain Ollie and Betty's interest in Harry Lawson's death and my investigation. Frances listens, watching me as if she expects me to pass out at any moment. When I finish, she thinks for a moment.

"Betty must be related to the girl who drowned."

"She says not, but she could have worked for PlayAway or the activity centre. Or she's the mother of someone who does."

"So why does she think you're making the same mistakes as Harry? She can't possibly know all the details you've uncovered from looking at the whiteboard."

"She thinks Harry was fixated on Rathbone, even though he'd reported on the drowning at Ashdown Activity Centre. Thanks to my job, I can speak to the officers who investigated and find out what really happened."

Eager to return to my investigation, I get to my feet – too sharply.

Frances places her hands on my shoulders, steadying me. "If you can speak to your colleagues, you don't need to visit Betty and Ollie, do you?"

It's a fair point. "Okay, let's go the study and see what else we can work out."

Columbo follows us, leaping onto the sofa bed. I slump into my chair and make myself comfortable. The top drawer is locked, thankfully. I open it, relieved to find my notebook inside. If Betty had a key to the drawer, she wouldn't have had much time to check my notebook.

Frances walks over to the whiteboard. "Where does Miranda fit it?"

"I'm not sure. She was Harry's fiancée once. She probably met Adrian. She worked for Rathbone and she's been hiding since Harry's death. And we all want to find her."

"Could she be connected to PlayAway or the activity centre?"

"If she is, I won't know until I ring Environmental Health at Mid Sussex tomorrow. They investigated the drowning and interviewed the staff."

"Would you need lifeguards round the pool?"

"It depends on so many risk factors, Frances. If the charity workers were in the pool with the children, maybe you wouldn't need a lifeguard."

"If I was a parent, I'd want a lifeguard. Charity workers are fine – if they're trained in life saving."

"I'll check when I ring Mid Sussex. We should also check if Ashdown Activity Centre is still trading. If it had to close down after the drowning, there could be some disgruntled owners or staff who lost their jobs. Hang on," I say, thinking back, "Betty said Harry knew someone who once worked there."

We're back to his missing notes. I pass the cryptic message from the grave to Frances. "While I search Google, see if you can make sense of that."

While she puzzles over the clue, it takes me seconds to find Ashdown Activity Centre, which is still operating. It provides a range of outdoor activities, including ball games, archery, swimming in the outdoor pool, orienteering and rock climbing. The centre also has a gym, sports hall, pool tables and sauna indoors. With excellent Trip Advisor ratings and commendations from Scouting and Guide groups, it looks like the perfect place to send children and teenagers, as long as it's not Christmas or Boxing Day.

No mention of lifeguards though.

I refine my search to include drowning. A news feature from the *Argus,* dated 21st May 2010, reported on the Crown Court case between Mid Sussex District Council and Ashdown Leisure Activities Ltd, following the death of Chrissy Jones, aged 7, on 10th August 2009.

"The activity centre pleaded guilty to not carrying out a comprehensive risk assessment for the use of the swimming pool. They also failed to take reasonable precautions to prevent unauthorised entry," I say, looking up. "Are they saying the girl broke into the pool?"

"That's what it sounds like. Does it say anything else?"

"Not really," I say, skimming through the words. "That's the trouble when companies plead guilty – most of the detail never gets heard in court or reported. There's the briefest mention of a missing lifeguard. I'll get more details tomorrow."

I click on the link at the bottom of the article, which takes me to another feature from the following week. The moment I see Adrian Peach's name in the byline, the back of my neck tingles.

"Come and read this," I say, leaning back so Frances can take a look. "Adrian's rubbishing Ashdown Activity Centre.

He claims it's poorly managed and maintained, accident reports are not made or are missing, staff are only paid the minimum wage, but expected to cover all duties without the proper training. Morale is rock bottom, standards have slipped and so on."

Adrian then goes on to say that parents and those sending children there have the right to expect high standards. They don't expect their children to come home in body bags. He also asks why environmental health officers didn't close the place after the drowning.

I read on in silence.

Chrissy Jones lost her parents in a tragic road accident a few months before her visit to Ashdown Activity Centre. She was in the care of a local authority home at the time of the visit. She wasn't a strong swimmer or a sociable child, and missed the swimming session. No one remembers seeing her until she was found later at the bottom of the pool.

How did she find her way into the pool from wherever she was hiding? Had a lifeguard been on duty, Chrissy would be alive today with new parents and her life ahead of her.

The owners declined an interview. In a written statement, the company informed me that the management failures at the time of the tragedy had been swiftly corrected and a new regime put in place to ensure such a tragedy could never happen again.

Chrissy drowned. Harry drowned.

If someone's trying to make a point, why bludgeon Adrian to death?

"We have a possible motive for Adrian's murder," I say. "When I talk to Mid Sussex tomorrow and find out who was running the place on the day, we may have our killer."

Fifty

On Monday morning, my neck and shoulders ache, but otherwise I feel fine. Frances stops by to tell me she's arranged for a couple of volunteers to do some extra days to cover the café.

Armed with Betty and Ollie's home addresses, I set off at seven, calling at Tollingdon Town Hall first. I'm not the first to arrive, but with few people around, I make it to my office without passing anyone. It takes me a few minutes to find the best place to hide my tiny camera. I tuck it within the folds of the hi-vis tabard I keep on the window sill behind my desk. A quick check with my phone shows it has a good field of view across the office, including the door.

A few minutes later I'm on my way to the outskirts of Tollingdon, close to the boundary with Eastbourne. Betty lives on a small estate of 1950s semi-detached bungalows – or she would if 13 Downland Way existed. Unfortunately, the builders didn't leave enough room to squeeze it between 11 and 15.

While not surprised, I'm annoyed we didn't check the address when we took her on as a volunteer.

From here, it's a short drive into Eastbourne and Meads on the western edge of town. Not far from the seafront,

Ollie has a top floor flat in a large house with three floors and steps down to a basement. It looks like one of those houses owned by a Victorian family who travelled to the coast with their servants to sample the sea air. There's no bell for Flat 9 because there are only eight flats.

On the way back to the car, I make a note to talk to Frances about improving our vetting procedures.

It's too early to inspect any kitchens, so I drive down the seafront and find a space near the Devonshire Park Theatre. I walk to the seafront and get a takeaway tea from one of the small cafés on the promenade. The tide is out, revealing stretches of sand beyond the shingle beach. A few dog walkers enjoy the morning sun, which sparkles and winks on the gentle waves. The pier, with its white buildings and gold domed roofs reaches out across the sea on sturdy iron legs. Pigeons roost on the iron girders beneath the boardwalk, waiting for the tourists.

You only have to drop a chip on the promenade and gulls and pigeons materialise, screeching and squawking as they battle for the morsel. A seagull once swooped down from behind, passing my head and shoulder as it liberated the ice cream scoop from my cone.

I sit on a low wall and think about Ashdown Activity Centre, knowing it holds the key to Harry's murder. But if he was following the wrong trail, as Betty suggested, then why was he killed?

What if Betty's wrong? What if Harry found a link between Rathbone and Ashdown Activity Centre?

Would that be enough to warrant killing Harry?

Then there's Adrian's scathing attack on Ashdown Activity Centre. Did it warrant his murder? Why lure him to Sunshine View Caravan Park to kill him?

At nine, I phone Environmental Health at Mid Sussex District Council and ask to speak to Penny Reid, an EHO who specialises in health and safety at work. She's now working part time for Hastings Borough Council, but she's at her desk and delighted to speak to me. After a few minutes to catch up on her new family and job, I ask her about Ashdown Activity Centre. It prompts a deep, mournful sigh.

"It was one of the worst investigations I've ever had to make," she says. "Chrissy Jones was seven years old. No one should die that young. Why are you interested, Kent?"

"The incident cropped up during some inquiries I'm making."

"Are we talking dead bodies? How do you keep finding them, Kent?"

"They find me."

"Well, I hate to disappoint you, but no one was murdered at Ashdown Activity Centre. The girl drowned because she couldn't swim. I don't know why she didn't join the other children in the pool. No one seems to know what happened to her while everyone else was in the pool. We believe she entered the pool area after everyone had gone inside to dry off and change. We think she found her way through a gap in the fence near the deep end. She went into the water, not realising it was deep, and drowned, poor soul. The people who brought her down from London didn't even know she'd gone missing."

"Did the centre have lifeguards?"

"Yes, a couple of the staff had received training, but they carried out other duties as well."

I'm starting to get an impression of what happened on the day. "Were either of the lifeguards on duty during the swimming lesson?"

"No, the people from the charity were in the pool with the children. After everyone had gone inside there was no need for a lifeguard. The health and safety systems and practices were a bit vague and rather hit and miss, which is why we prosecuted."

"Would you say PlayAway Adventures failed to keep an eye on Chrissy Jones?"

"Our colleagues at Croydon wanted to prosecute the charity, but politics got in the way. The council ran the home where Chrissy was staying. They were aware she couldn't swim, but never told anyone. It never appeared in any official reports either."

"A reporter from the *Argus* wrote a scathing piece about the centre."

"Are you talking about a pushy young guy called Adrian Peach? He pestered me for days, claiming we'd gone soft on Ashdown Activity Centre because one of our councillors was a director and employed as a leisure consultant."

"Do you recall his or her name?" I ask, pen poised.

"I'll find out and let you know. Why are you so interested, Kent?"

"Adrian Peach was murdered last week."

She gasps. "You don't think it's because of the article he wrote?"

"I don't know, Penny, that's why I rang. Can you remember who was in charge at the activity centre on the day Chrissy drowned?"

"Oh yes," she says, as if it wasn't a pleasant experience. "It was the managing director herself. She was a nasty piece of work, constantly attacking our investigation, complaining that we should be going after the charity instead of hounding her. I don't know if Pippa Castle's still there, but why don't you pay her a visit and give her a hard time?"

If it's the Pippa Castle who got stroppy when Ashley and I parked at Sunshine View Caravan Park, it might explain why Adrian went there.

I thank Penny for her help and walk back to my car. As I settle in the driver's seat, my phone pings with a text from her.

It was Councillor Gregory Rathbone. He's one of yours now, isn't he?

Harry wasn't on the wrong trail, after all.

Fifty-One

A few more texts establish that Gregory Rathbone quit as a councillor before the Ashdown Activity Centre prosecution was heard in the Crown Court. I'll need to check, but I'm guessing he became a Downland councillor not long after.

I ring Sunshine View Caravan Park and ask to speak to Pippa Castle. Erin Perkins tells me Ms Castle hasn't arrived at the office yet. "She has a meeting with the builders at ten. Can I take a message?"

"Tell her I'm coming straight over."

As I turn the key in the ignition my phone rings.

"Hello lover," Kelly says, "where are you this bright and sunny morning?"

"On the district," I reply, sensing an opportunity. "If anyone asks, say I'm on food hygiene inspections till lunch."

"But today's audit preparation day. That's why I'm here in your office for you."

"An unexpected lead came up about Harry Lawson. He's the one who drowned at Councillor Rathbone's party. I'm following it up, so not a word to anyone, okay?"

"You know me better than that, lover."

Better than you think, I want to say.

If she tells Rathbone I'm moonlighting, I'll find out soon enough. It should be interesting watching the video of what she gets up to this morning. It's a pity I can't record sound or get the camera to follow her to Rathbone's office.

But I can find out if she rings him straight after talking to me. I make a note of the time and set off for Alfriston via East Dean and Jevington. It takes about twenty minutes to reach Sunshine View Caravan Park, where all traces of the police and crimes scenes investigation have gone. The builders are back on site, continuing with their works. When I enter reception, Erin looks up from behind her desk and gives me a warm smile.

"I told Ms Castle you were on your way, but she doesn't want to be disturbed. She suggested I make an appointment for later in the week."

"I need to speak to her now, Erin."

"I thought you'd say that. Leave it to me."

She knocks on the door at the rear of her area and enters. While I wait, I examine and photograph the public liability insurance certificate on the wall, as well as a couple of notices which contain details of Downland Activities (Sussex) plc.

When Erin returns to usher me inside, I've already checked online to discover Ashdown Activity Centre was run by Downland Activities (Sussex) plc before it was sold this year.

Ms Castle's office is small, beige and organised, with only a desk, filing cabinet and a small table, piled high with folders and brochures. A venetian blind keeps out the sun and rattles against the glass in the breeze. She rises from behind her computer monitor to reveal a black trouser suit

257

with creases that could cut paper. Her aggressive stance and scowl could halt a charging elephant.

"I really am very busy, Mr Fisher. The police investigation has severely disrupted my schedules."

"Why didn't you tell me you knew Adrian Peach?"

"I didn't know Mr Peach."

"He came to Ashdown Activity Centre when he followed up on a drowning ten years ago. You must remember Chrissy Jones."

Her scowl deepens. "The girl drowned because the people looking after her failed to do their job. The Coroner exonerated us of any wrong doing."

"Adrian Peach wrote a scathing article about your activity centre and how it was run. Then he's murdered at your new business, Ms Castle."

"Are you suggesting I had something to do with his murder, Mr Fisher?"

I can see she's not going to tell me anything in this frame of mind. Maybe I should have taken a softer approach, tried to get her on my side.

"What if someone believes you are responsible for Chrissy drowning, Ms Castle? I'm not saying you are, but people are always looking for someone to blame. With a child as young as Chrissy dying, you could be in danger."

Her defiance melts away. "I'll ask Erin to make tea."

While she's in reception, I look at the plans for the building works. It takes a few moments to relate the excavations outside to the architect's drawing, but it reveals a connection that confirms my suspicions about Harry's death.

Adrian Peach was killed on the site of the new swimming pool.

Fifty-Two

Three deaths – all linked to swimming pools.

The murders relate to Chrissy Jones' drowning, not drugs or employing illegal immigrants. Rathbone's connection appears to be linked to his role as a councillor at Mid Sussex.

Ms Castle returns before I can give it any further thought. She walks up beside me and admires the plans. "It's going to be a magnificent leisure complex with a bespoke gymnasium and fitness studio, swimming pool, bar and restaurant, dancefloor for cabaret. No doubt you'll want to inspect the kitchens before it opens next year."

"You realise Adrian Peach was killed where the swimming pool will go."

"Was he?"

"You don't see the significance?"

"I fail to see what it has to do with me, other than bringing Sunshine View more unwelcome publicity."

"I didn't know you were unpopular."

"The green wellie brigade kicked off about the environmental impact, claiming the complex would destroy valuable habitat and ecosystems. It's nothing but empty fields, filled with wild flowers. Downland Council's

Planning Committee gave them the chance to voice their objections before unanimously dismissing them. The council are more than happy with the number of trees I'm going to plant."

I have a vague memory of a feature in the *Argus* in March, detailing a heated and lengthy debate before permission was granted on the casting vote of the chair, Stephanie Richmond.

Hardly unanimous.

I sense another connection. "Was Adrian Peach at the planning meeting?"

Erin enters with a tray of tea and biscuits, which she places on the desk. Once she's left, Pippa Castle looks at me and sighs.

"He tried to accuse me of colluding with councillors to get permission."

It seems to be a common thread where Rathbone's concerned.

"Why would Adrian Peach do that?"

"He came to Ashdown Activity Centre to make me the scapegoat for that girl's death."

I take the cup of tea she offers me. "Are you suggesting he had a grudge, Ms Castle?"

"Of course he had a grudge. His father, Edgar Peach, fought a bitter battle with Gregory Rathbone to be elected onto Mid Sussex council. There were accusations, smears, even a story about smuggling tobacco. Then rumours started about Edgar abusing his wife, causing her mental breakdown and dementia. Edgar was finished before the ink dried on the paper."

"I guess people thought Rathbone started the rumour."

"People always think the worst, don't they? Gregory took it on the chin, but was forced to stand down after the article about the activity centre appeared in the *Argus*. It suggested he was using his influence as a councillor to help us, which couldn't be further from the truth. Gregory has a lot of experience in the leisure industry, Mr Fisher. He's also my cousin, which is why he wanted to help me. He never took any money or shared any secrets."

"Was Adrian Peach aware of the family connection?"

She nods.

I take a sip of tea, not sure where this takes my investigation. If she's right about Adrian's grudge, she's more likely to be a suspect in his murder, not the next victim.

"Would you tell me about Chrissy Jones, Ms Castle? I'd like to hear your version of events."

She doesn't look happy. After a mouthful of tea, she straightens in her chair and speaks in a deliberate, steady voice. "We did nothing wrong, Mr Fisher, no matter what Mr Peach or Mid Sussex Council claim. The Coroner exonerated us. The charity workers supervised the children. Our lifeguards weren't needed, so they carried out other duties. PlayAway lost sight of the poor girl for an hour, but no one took them to court. We had an exemplary safety record. No accidents in eleven years, thousands, maybe millions of happy customers and members. Then one disgruntled casual worker makes some offhand remark and suddenly I'm in league with the devil."

"Who was this casual worker?"

"We employed hundreds of casual workers over the years. You can't expect me to remember their names. It had nothing to do with the drowning, before you ask."

She's definitely protesting too much. "What did the casual worker say?"

"She made a false allegation about my behaviour and told Mr Peach."

I think back to the story I read yesterday. "I don't recall any allegations."

"He never printed anything because she vanished that afternoon."

"Vanished?"

Didn't Betty tell me about someone who vanished before Harry could interview them?

Could this be the same employee?

Were Harry and Adrian pursuing the same story?

"Vanished as in ran off and never came back. I think it tells you all you need to know, Mr Fisher."

"What did she accuse you of, Ms Castle?"

"That's none of your business, Mr Fisher. It had nothing to do with the drowning."

"Adrian Peach didn't think so, did he? And now he's dead. I imagine Detective Inspector Goodman would be interested, especially if she thinks you're withholding information in connection with a murder enquiry. It would cast doubt on everything you've said so far."

Ms Castle sits for a while, her fingers as restless as her eyes. "She made spurious accusations about my conduct and then vanished."

"Who, Ms Castle? Who vanished?"

She almost spits out the words. "Miranda Tate."

Fifty-Three

I should have realised it would be Miranda Tate. Everything comes back to her. No matter where I look or which way I approach the murders, everything comes back to her. She's associated with Rathbone. She was engaged to Harry. She knew Adrian. She worked for Pippa Castle. And she sent me a text with a clue.

What prompted Harry to dump the woman he loved? Was it her association with Rathbone's dodgy deals?

Or did she play a part in Chrissy Jones' drowning? Maybe she was the lifeguard who should have been on duty?

Maybe Miranda killed Harry, Adrian too.

Whatever happened, Betty wants me to finish what Harry started. So why didn't she simply ask for my help? She must have known I've solved a few murders.

And if she wanted my help, why did Ollie whack me with a spade. It's hardly an incentive.

Detouring back to Meadow Farm, I nip into the café to thank Andrea for taking over on her day off. A quick word with Frances reveals she's hasn't managed to contact Betty or Ollie. Back in my study, with Columbo looking on, I stare at the whiteboard, hoping something will suddenly make sense and leap out at me.

When inspiration fails to materialise, I recall Mike's mantra to follow the evidence. The drowning at Ashdown Activity Centre may well be the event that led to Harry's death, but where do I start? There could be any number of employees at the centre with a connection or a motive. The same goes for the PlayAway charity. What are the chances of me finding the one person out of them who was at Rathbone's engagement party?

Maybe Harry found the person.

Could it be Rathbone after all? He has a connection with Ashdown Activity Centre and he was at his own engagement party.

If Harry was on the right trail, he left the clue at Florence Mackay's grave.

I pick up the keys on my desk and look at them. If I can solve the clue and find the locks these keys will open, I might find the evidence Harry collected and hid for safe keeping.

I ruffle Columbo's fur. "It could be evidence that puts Rathbone behind bars."

He barks, enjoying the attention.

"I may have some video evidence from this morning," I say, remembering my hidden camera.

I slip the two keys into a karabiner, which I attach to my key ring. With Columbo blazing the way, I exit the flat, lock the door and take him to Frances. I decline a cup of tea, having drunk gallons in the last few days. When I spot the sheets of paper scattered across the table, I realise she's also trying to solve the clue.

No hammer required for the wise hooter here.

"Any progress?" I ask.

"I've come up with two words that mean hammer – mace and mallet. I've tried no mace and no mallet, malletless and maceless, and nothing. Gemma would solve it in minutes," she says. "Why don't you ring her? She must be missing you."

I doubt if Gemma's even thought of me during her retail therapy with Georgina. "I should be seeing her this evening."

"That's good. Isn't it? You don't seem too sure."

"I can't see Gemma wanting to see me, not after the way I treated her." Sensing Frances wants to find out more, I tell her I need to get back to the office. "If you solve the clue, let me know."

On the short drive to the office, I wonder what I'll find on the video. Without sound, or the services of a lip reader, I could spend a monotonous two hours watching Kelly answer the phone and send emails – on the basis she hasn't discovered the camera.

Once parked, I head up the stairs and stop outside my office. A quick check of the app on my phone gives me an image of Kelly at her desk, chatting on the phone. She's relaxed, animated and flirting, I'd say. She flirts with most of the men at the council, especially the older ones.

It's how she knows more gossip than anyone else.

I switch on the voice recorder app, slip my phone into my jacket pocket and enter the office. She ends the call abruptly and returns to her keyboard, as if she's been working hard all morning. She gives me a big smile.

"I wasn't expecting you till lunchtime, lover. There's been a couple of calls, details on your desk. Councillor

Rathbone wants a word. I hope you haven't been doing anything naughty."

The minute I left Sunshine View Caravan Park, Pippa Castle will have rung her cousin to complain about me.

"What about you, Kelly? Have you been doing anything naughty while I've been out on district?"

She averts her eyes for a moment before regaining her composure. She looks straight into my eyes and runs her tongue over her lips. "Do you have anything in mind, lover?"

"We'd need to be careful," I say, turning to the windowsill. "You never know who's watching these days."

I lift the tabard to remove the camera before holding it up to the light where she can see it.

"What's that?" she asks. The nervous tremor in her voice suggests she has a good idea what it is.

"The truth." I slip the camera into my pocket and walk towards the door. "Have you heard the saying, the camera never lies? Well, this hi resolution camera will show me whether you have been naughty this morning."

The colour seems to drain from her face. For once she has no cheeky response. I reach the stairwell before she calls after me. "Wait. Let me explain."

I push through the door and walk down the stairs.

She chases after me. "I had no choice."

I stop on the half landing and turn to face her. "We always have a choice."

"You've never had to turn tricks in a lap dancing club to feed a heroin habit." She slumps back against the wall, her breathing heavy. "Greg rescued me. He helped me kick the habit. He gave me back my self-respect, my life."

"And what did you give him in return?"

"Oh, it's much more than sex, Kent, but you wouldn't understand, the way you treat women."

I ignore the slur, the venom in her voice. "Harry found out about you and Rathbone, didn't he? That's why he came to the party. What did he want?"

"What you all want." She peels herself off the wall, treating me to her sultry eyes and seductive smile. "I've seen the way you look at me. I know you've wondered what it would be like, undressing me, exploring me. Well, you don't have to fantasise anymore. I know what you like, lover. Gemma told me."

She smiles, knowing she's hit the target. "You'd be surprised what us girls talk about when we've had a few glasses of wine. I'm sure you don't want everyone knowing what you and Gemma got up to."

I've no idea whether she's bluffing or serious, but if she's threatening me, there must be something she doesn't want me to see on the video.

"Go to hell, Kelly."

I trot down the stairs to the ground floor, half expecting her to make more threats. I'm about to push open the door, when she calls out once more.

"I know where to find Miranda Tate."

I should walk out of the door, but I don't. I want to know how she knows I'm looking for Miranda Tate. When she stops on the stairs, a couple of steps above me, I stare straight into her eyes.

"Why would I be interested in Miranda Tate?"

"She killed your friend, Harry Lawson."

That wasn't the answer I expected. "I'm listening."

She holds out her hand. "Camera first."

I shake my head. "Convince me."

"Miranda worked with me in the lap dancing club. We shared a flat and got to know each other quite well, shared all our secrets. When Greg offered us a way out, she didn't want to know. She enjoyed the attention and the sex. I don't know what happened to her until she contacted me to say she was marrying this guy called Harry, a hot shot reporter in London."

Kelly pauses, an angry scowl on her face. "He found out about her past while he was investigating Greg. The bastard dumped her and cancelled the wedding without telling her. He sent an email to all the people invited, telling them what she'd done. I'm not surprised she killed him."

"I am," I say, certain Sarah would have told me about any malicious emails sent by Harry. "I'll be in touch once I've watched the video, Kelly. Or should I call you Kira?"

I push open the door and stride across the car park, hoping I'm right about Sarah.

Fifty-Four

Sarah's confirmed she didn't receive any malicious emails from Harry about Miranda. It doesn't mean he didn't send any, just not to her. If Kelly's right and Miranda killed Harry, I can always trade the video for her location.

Armed with a cheese and onion baguette from the café and a glass of cold milk, I settle down in my study to watch the video footage. When I started to investigate, I was hoping Kelly was the victim, manipulated by Rathbone. Her performance on the stairs revealed her to be not only a willing accomplice, but maybe the instigator.

When she said, 'Oh, it's much more than sex, Kent,' she was talking in the present tense.

She and Rathbone are lovers, even though he's engaged to her sister.

The video footage confirms it. I've had to watch and fast forward through three hours of Kelly on the phone, Kelly applying lipstick, Kelly walking over to the window to watch the world and Kelly checking her phone every few minutes. It's not till twenty past ten that the footage becomes interesting. Rathbone saunters into the office, a huge grin on his face. He locks the door and strolls over to

Kelly, who's sitting at her computer. Standing behind her, he nuzzles her neck while his hands cup her breasts.

When he unbuttons her blouse, I stop the video.

No wonder Kelly wanted to recover the footage.

I slip Columbo some cheese. "Will Rathbone offer me my department back or slip ketamine into my Becks Blue?"

A few minutes later, Rathbone drives into the car park, tyres squealing. He's out of the car and striding towards my flat like a man on a mission. A few moments later, he hammers on the front door. Columbo barks and races down the stairs. When I open the door, he jumps forward, baring his teeth. Rathbone retreats a few steps, giving me time to haul Columbo back inside and close the door.

Rathbone looks harassed, angry and tired. His greasy black hair falls across his forehead as he stares at me. His voice is strained as he struggles to keep control. "What are you going to do?"

Having only just watched the footage, I haven't considered what I plan to do. "What are you going to do?" I ask.

"Whatever it takes."

"Whatever it takes to keep your job as Leader of the Council?"

"I'll reinstate Environmental Health as a separate department. You'll be in charge and I'll make sure you get the staff and support you need."

"And I give you the video footage?"

He nods.

I shake my head. "You don't get it, do you? For years, you've been spying on me and my colleagues, undermining the work we do. Now I've been spying on you. How do you think Katya will react when she finds out you're screwing her sister?"

"Katya doesn't mind. She has her own lovers."

For a moment, I'm lost. "How do you think Frank and your fellow councillors will react when they discover you've been screwing Kelly in my office? Or the newspapers, come to that."

His face pales. His shoulders sink. The fight seems to leak out of him like air from a balloon. "There's no need to twist the knife."

"Resign today and I won't. Reinstate Environmental Health by all means, but without me. And in case you ever think of doing anything stupid, I'm keeping the video footage. Now go and resign with your dignity and reputation intact. If Frank rings me to confirm it by the end of the afternoon, I'll keep your secrets."

I turn and go back into my flat, scooping up Columbo before he races out to bite Rathbone. Upstairs, I watch him drive away, wondering if it's the last I'll see or hear of him. An hour later, Chief Executive Frank Dean rings. His tone is sombre.

"Gregory Rathbone's resigned as Leader of the Council."

"Wow," I say, feigning surprise. "Did he say why?"

"Personal reasons. I don't understand it, Kent. At ten o'clock this morning, I got a call to say we'd secured some significant government funding for a project to open up more of the countryside for leisure pursuits. Gregory was delighted, dancing around, talking about the things we could do, how we could celebrate."

I smile, well aware of how he celebrated with Kelly.

"Then, a few minutes ago, he walks into my office, hands me an envelope, and tells me he's resigned. His hands were

271

shaking and I could tell he was struggling to hold it together. He said the decision was final and non-negotiable." Frank sighs. "I tried to get hold of Kelly to see if she knew anything, but no one can find her. Have you spoken to her?"

"I think she had a migraine. Anyway, thanks for letting me know."

"Actually, I rang to tell you Gregory deeply regrets incorporating Environmental Health into the Planning Department. He said he'd misjudged you and your team. He wants us to reinstate Environmental Health at the earliest opportunity. Would you be willing to return as the head of service?"

"That's for the future, Frank. Right now, I imagine you'll need to prepare a media release."

After the call I copy the video and sound files onto my computer, saving additional copies on the cloud. For added security, I might hide a memory stick at Florence Mackay's grave.

The idea brings me back to Harry's murder. I wish Gemma was here to confirm my suspicions and help me like she used to do. When I close my eyes she's lounging on the sofa like she's always lived here. Her laughter fills the room. Her smile lights up the place. It feels so natural and comfortable having her around, sitting with Columbo between us.

Only it's not going to happen, thanks to my stupidity.

Rather than berate myself, I drag thoughts back to the investigation. I have murders to solve. Kelly said I'd never find Miranda without her help. Kelly wanted me to believe Miranda was hiding, afraid of being arrested for murder.

I think she's dead.

Kelly had a smug, untouchable air about her when she spoke about Miranda.

Was Miranda killed before Harry?

If she was, it answers my doubts about Miranda helping Harry after he dumped her.

It means the killer sent the fourth text that led us to Florence Mackay's grave. Either the killer wanted me to solve the puzzle for him, or her, or send my investigation down the wrong track. Betty and Ollie said as much.

Did Harry go to Rathbone's party to find out what happened to Miranda?

Without a confession from Kelly or Rathbone, I'll never know, but Harry's murder supports the idea.

Why kill Miranda?

She worked at Ashdown Activity Centre at the time Chrissy Jones drowned.

What did Miranda see or know that meant she had to die?

The answer to this question is the key to solving the murders.

This is what prompted Betty and Ollie to ask for Harry's help. This is what led him to Ashdown Activity Centre and a link to Rathbone. But Harry also homed in on the drugs and discovered Miranda had been a lap dancer.

I look up at the whiteboard. "If Miranda worked at Ashdown Activity Centre, how did she end up lap dancing? Or was it the other way around?"

Columbo tilts his head from side to side, earnestly considering the question.

Pippa Castle claimed Miranda made spurious accusations. Enough to get her killed?

If Pippa Castle was at Rathbone's engagement party, it might.

Like Johnny Spender or Susie Westcott, Pippa Castle's name is not on the list of attendees.

Coroner's Officer Beth Rimmer picks up on the third ring, her greeting amiable but suspicious. "Are you ringing about Harry Lawson or Adrian Peach?"

"I wondered who compiled the list of people at Gregory Rathbone's engagement party."

"His fiancée, Katya Novik. She arranged everything, including the invitation cards they sent out, the catering. She printed off the list I sent to you and Ashley."

"How come Johnny Spender and Susie Westcott weren't on the list?"

"She told me Rathbone had a habit of inviting people verbally and not telling her. It played havoc with the catering, though from what I saw, they had enough to feed an army. Anything else or do you have enough to solve the case?"

"I wish. Thanks for your help, Beth."

I end the call, aware there's still one avenue to check.

No hammer required for the wise hooter here.

No sledgehammer, no mallet, no mace, no lump hammer. I leave out the spaces between the words, wondering if Gemma's trying to solve the clue.

Thoughts of her distract me for some time as I think about seeing her tonight at my father's house. What if she doesn't want to see me? What if she's unhappy about Georgina's deception? Gemma's already upset because I didn't trust her.

Can I win back her trust?

Columbo makes no comment.

I scoop him up and walk over to the window. Frances is with Lucy, one of our older volunteers, lifting potatoes in the kitchen garden. Lucy suggested we could start or sponsor a community allotment for people on low incomes or without gardens. While Frances supports the idea, she doesn't want it at Meadow Farm.

I open the window and call down. "You should get an allotment, Frances."

She looks up at me and shrieks. "That's it," she says, becoming animated. "We're looking for an allotment."

She runs around the barn and up the stairs. "I've solved the clue," she says between breaths. "It's an allotment. *No hammer required.* Not mallet. It's an anagram of allotment."

I hesitate, wondering why Harry would hide his notes on an allotment.

Then I picture Miranda's body at the bottom of a compost heap.

Fifty-Five

If Harry thought Miranda's body was lying in an allotment, he would have called the police.

Frances is undeterred. "The rest of the clue must tell us which allotment. A wise hooter must be an owl. Is it an anagram of owl and here? Or is that too obvious?"

While I don't want to quash her enthusiasm, there's a simple answer. "Tollingdon Town Council will have a list of allotments. So will Downland District Council. Ditto Eastbourne."

When I return with two mugs of tea, she's scrolling through the Eastbourne Garden and Allotments Society home page. A separate Google search reveals the allotments page on Tollingdon Town Council's website. There are three allotments – one at Western Road, a second at Marsh View and a third at Nether Way.

"Go for the third," I say. "I can see the word *here* in Nether Way. That leaves the letters N, T, W, A, Y."

She whoops. "Tawny, as in owl."

"Click on the link and get some contact details."

The web page tells us there are no allotments available, but we can join the waiting list. Frances gives up the seat so I can send an email to Edward Rogers of the Tollingdon

Allotments Society, asking him to ring me as soon as possible.

"Why don't you drive over there, Kent? There's bound to be someone who's had an allotment for over fifty years and knows everyone. It beats sitting around here."

I grab the two keys that came with the clue and head out of the door. With Google Maps to guide me, I drive off, opening all the windows to get some air circulating. While a few clouds take turns to obscure the sun, the temperature holds in the mid-twenties, twice that inside the car. Though excited to see what I'll find at Nether Way, I can't believe Harry owned an allotment.

He was always on the go, desperate to prove himself, but his determination brought out a vindictive side to his nature. Unforgiving of his own mistakes and lapses, he took an equally uncompromising view of other people's errors and misfortunes. He expected them to work to the high standards he set himself.

Unattainable standards, as Miranda must have found when he discovered her past. He wouldn't have cared about why she chose to be a lap dancer. She became damaged goods, not a suitable wife. It's difficult to believe he could be so black and white, considering his own weakness with alcohol.

Then again, none of us are perfect. I lost the plot over Savanna. My emotions were all over the place after my brush with death during the last investigation. It's no excuse for the fantasies I spun, but maybe they were a sign that I needed someone. Savanna strolled into my sanctuary and my hormones did the rest.

Only it wasn't Savanna I wanted, was it?

Nor did I want to be a head of service at Downland.

That's why I've had enough of fighting bad management, government spending cuts and corrupt councillors. Maybe it's time to focus on the animals that need my help. I can't eradicate cruelty, but I can give more animals a better life.

I can educate children to understand that all life matters.

The sound of a car horn reminds me I have a murder to solve first. I release the handbrake and drive through the traffic lights into Tollingdon. When I pass the town hall, I wonder how Frank Dean's coping with the fallout from Rathbone's resignation.

The footage of him undressing Kelly is damning.

What would Katya do if she saw her fiancé undressing her sister?

Within five minutes, I've reached the other side of town. The houses from the 1930s and 50s give way to modern estates, nibbling into the countryside. The exception is the small estate near to a former landfill site. Once social housing, tenants bought the houses at low prices during the 1980s and 90s, selling them later for a healthy profit. Nether Lane continues beyond the houses and becomes a rough track that leads to the allotments. The views across the marshes towards Herstmonceux and Wartling are breath taking.

The allotments are surrounded by mesh fencing, topped with barbed wire. The entrance gate is controlled by a digital lock. With rural thefts on the increase, the allotment owners want to protect their equipment. I park outside the site and walk up to the gate, admiring the busy mixture of allotments, separated by earth and gravel paths. Some plots have poly tunnels or greenhouses, nearly all have sheds of some description, and the volume of plants and vegetables could stock a supermarket. Someone has a caged area with chickens. Another allotment is a giant cage, protecting a variety of fruit bushes, but each one has its own character.

With plenty of people tending their plots, the gate isn't locked. I push through and stroll across to a water trough. An elderly man with rolled up shirt sleeves and a roll up cigarette pinched between his lips, is filling his watering can. His shirt looks likes it doubles as a cleaning rag and his trousers must be held up by willpower. He adjusts his cap as he turns to face me, his blue eyes sunk beneath heavy eyelids.

"I'm looking for an allotment that belonged to Harry Lawson," I say. "Do you know him?"

The man puts down his watering can. He sucks on his flattened cigarette before speaking. "Don't know anyone with that name. What's he like?"

"He died recently."

"If you want to take over his plot, you need to speak to Ted Rogers. That's him with the pink shirt and sunhat. He's our chairman."

I nod my thanks and take the path that leads past the chicken run to an immaculate plot, split between raised beds and a large greenhouse, draped in netting to keep out the sun. Though I'm no gardener, I recognise the main vegetable crops, bursting with vitality. Ted has the deepest tan I've ever seen, which suggests he spends most of his time here.

"Mr Rogers," I say, holding out my hand. "Kent Fisher. I emailed you earlier."

"Aye, I saw it on my phone." His accent is broad Yorkshire, which means I should get some straight answers. "Couldn't you wait for me to contact you, lad?"

"Harry Lawson, a friend of mine recently deceased, may have had a plot here. He was a reporter for the *Argus*. You may have read about him in the paper. He drowned the weekend before last."

Ted removes his hat and fans his face. "That's as may be, but he didn't have an allotment here."

I pull out the keys from Florence Mackay's grave. "He left me these. One's for a padlock, I think."

"Plenty of padlocks round here, Mr Fisher. Can't say what your second key might open. What makes you think your friend had an allotment here?"

"You wouldn't believe me if I told you," I say, sensing another dead end.

"I might, seeing as you're not the only one looking for Harry Lawson." He chuckles, enjoying his moment. "A woman rang me yesterday, asking questions like you. I was at home so I could check my spreadsheet. That's how I know Harry Lawson never had an allotment here."

"Did she give you a name?"

"Aye." He runs his hand over his fine silver hair and replaces his hat, in no hurry to tell me. "She said her name was Miranda Tate."

"Are you sure?"

"I'm not deaf and I'm not stupid, Mr Fisher. When I asked her why she was interested in Harry Lawson, she said he was dead. She'd always wanted an allotment, she said, and wondered if she could come and view his and take it over. That was her big mistake."

"You have a waiting list, right?"

"Aye, but that's not what I'm getting at. Harry Lawson may not have an allotment, but Miranda Tate does." He points towards a corner, shaded by ash and sycamore trees.

"You think she'd know about her own allotment, wouldn't you?"

Fifty-Six

Ted looks so pleased with himself, he has to confirm what he said. "The woman who rang me yesterday wasn't Miranda Tate."

While I'm happy to agree with him, the conclusion only poses more questions.

Who rang Ted yesterday, posing as Miranda Tate?

How did she know about the allotment, referred to in Harry's cryptic clue? Frances and I took a while to work it out, but this woman knew yesterday.

Betty Cooper would have read the clue on my desk, but could she have solved it so soon?

Harry could have mentioned the allotment to Betty.

Someone could have followed me to Florence Mackay's grave. Someone like Ollie.

For the first time during the investigation, I feel vulnerable. Betty and Ollie have been monitoring my progress, watching me, going into my flat to check my whiteboard. I even let Betty clean the place.

I think back to Langney Cemetery. I checked there was no one nearby, but did I really pay attention? I was so busy searching the flower bowl, anyone could have snuck up. And when I found the keys...

Someone behind the wall or a tree could have heard Gemma read out the clue.

Am I letting my imagination get the better of me?

It's Mike's voice in my head, urging me to be rational.

Is there a more rational explanation?

If someone knew about the allotment, how did they find out? Did they overhear Harry talking about it? Did he tell someone about the allotment, someone he thought he could trust?

Was it someone at Rathbone's engagement party?

"Ted, can you tell me anything about the woman who rang you? Did she have an accent? Did she sound young or old?"

"Hard to say," he says, rubbing his chin. "She sounded ordinary, no real accent. Pleasant to talk to, polite."

"You must have 50 or 60 allotments here, right?"

"We have 86," he says with pride, "and a waiting list of over 50 people."

"How did you know about Miranda Tate's allotment?"

"I keep an eye on the ones that are uncared for. Sometimes there's a bereavement or illness. Sometimes people don't realise how much time and effort it takes to maintain an allotment. We see them for a couple of months then they don't return."

"Like Miranda Tate?"

"I wrote to Miss Tate a few weeks ago and got no reply. I wrote again last week. When she rang, I thought it was in response to my letter. When she asked about Harry Lawson, I became suspicious."

"Would you give me her address?"

"I don't know if I'm allowed to, but I can show you her allotment."

He leads the way, pausing to chat to everyone we pass. He has an upright bearing, which suggests a former military career, a no-nonsense manner and a sense of humour that's as dry as chipboard. As we reach the shady, less desirable part of the site, it's clear no one's tended Miranda's allotment for a while. The greenhouse glass supports healthy colonies of algae and moss, while the weeds are impressive, especially the thistles. At the back, tucked into the corner, there's an old shed with peeling linoleum on the roof.

Ted pushes through the weeds and goes up to the door. When he rattles the padlock, I sigh in relief. No one's beaten me here.

"Do you want to try your key, Mr Fisher?"

Though stiff, the key opens the padlock. I pull open the door to reveal a damp and untidy interior, inhabited by flies and spiders. The smell of rotten wood and plants fills the air. The shelves on either side hold a variety of used plastic pots, seed trays, various pesticides and fertilisers and a small camping stove and gas. Underneath the shelves, rusted tools and bags of compost fill the spaces, leaving a narrow passageway down the middle. At the other end, I notice an old wooden bedside cabinet, stained by water marks.

Looking at the undisturbed dirt and dust on the floor and shelves, I know I'm ahead of the killer and Betty and Ollie. If Harry's hidden anything here, I'll be the first to see it.

While I look through the pots and bottles of insecticide on the shelf, Ted squeezes past. "What's a bedside cabinet doing on an allotment?"

He opens the door to reveal a space divided into two by a shelf. The small drawer above is locked and refuses to open.

He hauls the cabinet up onto the shelf, sending a couple of spiders running for cover. When he grabs a nearby lump hammer, I step forward.

"Let's try this key, Ted."

I insert the smaller key into the brass lock. At first the key refuses to turn. Then, as I'm ready to admit defeat, the lock gives. Inside the drawer, cloaked with cobwebs and dead insects, there's a rusty metal cash box.

Ted places the cash box on the shelf and steps back so I can open it. He shuffles closer when I raise the lid, his chin almost on my shoulder. "It's empty," he says, sounding disappointed. "Anything taped underneath?"

There's nothing. Maybe there never was anything.

"What were you expecting to find, Mr Fisher?"

"Answers."

He chuckles. "Nothing important then."

He activates the torch on his mobile phone and shines the beam into the cabinet, checking every corner. He bends and does the same in the space below the shelf. Then he chuckles and gives the shelf a couple of sharp raps. A final strike with the heel of his hand frees it. He slides the shelf out and turns it over to reveal a photograph of Pamela Anderson from her Baywatch days, printed on a sheet of paper.

He peels it away and passes it over. "If that's Miranda Tate, I can see why you want to find her."

On the reverse of the photograph, there's an image of a sick bay with the curtain pulled back. There's a bed, first aid cabinet on the wall, a trolley containing boxes of disposable gloves and bandages and a waste bin on the floor.

"Ted, did you ever meet Miranda?"

"No, but we always take new people round, show them the facilities, explain the rules. I can ask around, find out who dealt with her originally."

"No, you've done more than enough. I can take it from here."

Harry's telling me to focus on lifeguards, maybe a particular female lifeguard. It must be the lifeguard who should have been on duty the day Chrissy Jones drowned at Ashdown Activity Centre.

Betty and Ollie misjudged Harry.

But did he know who she was?

Is that why he was killed, to stop him revealing her identity?

Fifty-Seven

It's my job to finish what Harry started.

Betty and Ollie said I was following the wrong trail like Harry. The trail didn't lead to Gregory Rathbone. Ashley told me the same thing. Yet Rathbone's connected to Ashdown Activity Centre through his cousin, Pippa Castle, and Miranda Tate.

Harry's brought me to Miranda's allotment. It means he left the clue and keys at Florence Mackay's grave.

Why didn't he tell Betty and Ollie what he'd uncovered? Was he concerned they might take action against the lifeguard? Or did Harry want to confirm all the details before he published his story?

Was the lifeguard at Rathbone's party? Did Harry go there to confront the lifeguard?

I flip the paper over and look at the image of a sick bay.

Was the lifeguard sick on the day Chrissy Jones drowned?

I place the paper on the passenger seat and phone Penny Reid, the EHO who investigated the drowning at Ashdown Activity Centre.

"Last time we spoke, Penny, I got the impression you interviewed one of the lifeguards at Ashdown Activity Centre. Can you remember who it was?"

"No, but the name will be on file. You need to talk to Mid Sussex."

"Can you remember how many lifeguards there were at the centre?"

"Two, I think, but neither was on duty the day of the drowning."

"One more question. Did the centre have a sick room?"

"They had a first aid area, curtained off in the corner of an equipment store, would you believe? That's where they kept the accident book. I wanted to check their past history of accidents, as we always do, but there were no entries in the book – not even the drowning. Can you believe it?"

"Sadly I can. Did you speak to anyone from PlayAway Adventures?"

"The London Borough of Croydon handled that side of the investigation. Cameron McLean, the senior EHO at the time, kept hitting brick walls. The woman who ran the charity was related to one of the local councillors, or something like that, so it got rather messy."

I make a note of the name. "Is he still at Croydon?"

"I doubt it. He became so disillusioned he was talking about becoming a consultant. I don't know if he did, but I still have his mobile number. I'll ring him and pass on your details."

"Cheers. Tell him it's urgent."

"Everything is." There's no resentment in her voice. It's simply a comment on staff cutbacks, leaving fewer people to do more work in less time.

I drive back to Meadow Farm, my head buzzing with connections and ideas that wouldn't be out of place on *Jonathan Creek*. But this is no TV drama. I need evidence not fanciful ideas.

Cameron McLean provides a possible answer when he rings at five. "Penny says you're interested in the death of Chrissy Jones at Ashdown Activity Centre."

"I'm interested in PlayAway Adventures. I understand Chrissy was in their care on the day she died."

"Yes, they lost track of her for at least an hour." From the tone of his voice, it sounds like this still irks him. "Her parents died a couple of months earlier and this was her first trip since going into care. She was quiet, timid, nervous. You'd think someone would take special care of her, wouldn't you? But none of the adults from the charity realised she wasn't in the pool with the other children. They got dried and dressed in the changing rooms and went for lunch. That's when they realised Chrissy was missing. But they were too late. Chrissy was already dead in the deep end."

"Who found her?"

"Can I ask why you want to know?"

"A friend of mine was killed recently. He was a reporter, investigating the drowning."

"Would that be Harry Lawson?"

"You know him?"

"I read about his death in the papers, but yes, our paths crossed. Anyway," he says, after a brief pause, "you wanted to know who found Chrissy Jones. It was one of the staff at the centre – Miranda Tate. She worked on the reception desk. They couldn't get hold of the owner so she went to find her. After checking her office and the usual places,

Miranda went down to the pool. That's when she spotted a pile of clothes by a gap in the fence that enclosed the pool. When she went to take a closer look, she saw Chrissy in the pool and raised the alarm."

"You've got a good recall," I say, scribbling notes on my pad.

"Injustice improves your recall. And a copy of my report always helps. I had this idea of seeing if I could do anything after I left Croydon, but life got in the way." He clears his throat before continuing. "Penny told you about the trouble we had with PlayAway Adventures. Geraldine Nash, the chief executive of the charity, gave me grief for months. She was determined to shift responsibility for the accident onto the activity centre. No lifeguard on duty, that kind of thing. I felt the charity had failed in their duty of care and put a case forward to prosecute.

"The day after the report went to committee, the *Evening Standard* published an interview with Geraldine Nash. She blamed Ashdown Activity Centre for the death and claimed EHOs, meaning me, were harassing her and her wonderful charity, threatening to prosecute them. Someone tipped her off. My report wasn't included in the public side of the meeting, so how did she know about it? I did some detective work and found out the deputy chairman of the committee was her uncle."

"You mean he didn't declare a conflict of interest?"

"No, he declared an interest and took no part in the discussion, but he'd still read my report and passed the details to his niece. When I confronted him, he got nasty. The following day, the boss took me off the case."

"They can't do that."

"We both know it's illegal to interfere with an inspector's investigation, but you have to work with these people afterwards, don't you? And Geraldine Nash hadn't finished with me."

I swap the phone to my other ear and turn the page of my notepad.

"My wife had left me a few months earlier. We'd grown apart, the usual thing. It had nothing to do with the case until Harry Lawson asked to speak to me about it. Naturally, I refused. Two days later, I'm in the *Evening Standard*, the disgraced EHO who was taken off the investigation. He suggested, as only reporters can, that I'd had an affair with the owner of Ashdown Activity Centre, Philippa Castle. This had caused the breakdown of my marriage and explained my determination to blame PlayAway Adventures for the accident. Honestly, Kent, you couldn't make it up."

"No smoke without fire, you mean."

"Apparently, a member of staff at the centre spotted us having sex in the first aid room. I'd never been to the activity centre, for God's sake. But no one believed me, not even my colleagues. That's why I left and set up my own consultancy."

And no action was taken against PlayAway Adventures.

"Did you talk to Pippa Castle?" I ask. "I imagine she wasn't pleased to have her name in the paper."

"She didn't want to know. She accused me of not prosecuting PlayAway, leaving her activity centre to take the blame. Penny was prosecuting them, as you know, and Ms Castle didn't want any more adverse publicity. Turns out she was a lesbian, so why would Lawson suggest she had sex with me in a first aid room of all places? Where did that come from?"

"Maybe other staff used it for sex. Maybe someone spotted a couple in there and mentioned it to Harry."

"It hardly matters now," he says, a resigned tone to his voice. "At least Geraldine Nash got what was coming to her. A few months later the *Evening Standard* investigated her uncle and discovered he'd awarded several large grants to her charity over a ten year period. They coincided with her luxury holidays. She posted photos on Facebook and Instagram. Can you believe that?"

I've heard worse from Ashley. Some people believe they'll never be caught.

"So Harry redeemed himself."

"No, another reporter wrote the story. Adam Peach?"

Is another piece of the puzzle falling into place?

"Do you mean Adrian Peach?"

"That's the chap," Cameron says. "He rang me after the police prosecuted the councillor. He got a suspended sentence, but Geraldine Nash was sentenced to three years. Apparently, she couldn't help dipping into the charity's funds. She took her own life shortly after."

"What happened to the charity?"

"Her mother and her partner kept it running. Mrs Cooper contacted me a few days later. She looked like a zombie, but she wanted to go through my investigation and what happened at the activity centre."

"Would she be Betty Cooper?"

"Yes, Elizabeth Cooper. Has she been in touch with you?"

"She's down here, still searching for the truth with her partner, Ollie."

"Oliver Nash, Geraldine's father. I never met him, but he pestered me for information. That's about all I can tell you."

"You've been a great help, Cameron."

I give Pamela Anderson pride of place on the whiteboard, redirecting all arrows to her.

Identify the lifeguard, solve the murders.

Was the lifeguard fooling around with Pippa Castle in the first aid room when Chrissy Jones drowned?

It would explain why Ms Castle never retaliated to Harry's story in the *Evening Standard*.

It also gives her a motive to kill Harry, Adrian and Miranda.

Fifty-Eight

The drive to Sunshine View Caravan Park is hampered by rush hour traffic. The slow journey, however, gives me more time to consider Pippa Castle as the killer.

Harry's story about her and Cameron having sex, on top of all the other bad press she was enduring, meant he had to go. She had motive. She had means. She was at Cousin Rathbone's party. She may even have arranged to meet Harry there – or earlier to slip him the ketamine.

Adrian Peach wrote a scathing story about standards at her activity centre. She invited him to the caravan site, met him by the diggers and bludgeoned him to death, calmly returning to her office afterwards.

Miranda stumbled on Pippa Castle having sex with the lifeguard. Maybe Miranda heard them through the curtain. Maybe she saw them. Whatever she witnessed, she was killed so she couldn't reveal what really happened on the day Chrissy Jones died.

It all fits, but how can I get Pippa Castle to confess?

She's tough, used to running successful businesses with large budgets. She owned and ran Ashdown Activity Centre, surviving the prosecution and bad publicity. She's bought Sunshine View Caravan Park, happy to spend millions to build a leisure complex to compete with the national companies. She calculates risks, negotiates deals, holding her nerve in a ruthless drive to get what she wants.

She's not going to capitulate now.

Drusillas roundabout looms up, creating a long tail of traffic. Most of the traffic continues across the roundabout towards Lewes and Brighton. I take a left, passing the zoo park a few seconds later, swinging through the bends, enjoying the shadows on the South Downs. When the road narrows on the northern approach to Alfriston, I ease off the accelerator. Visitors and tourists are still wandering along the narrow High Street, taking photographs of the old buildings with their Tudor beams, leaning walls and wavy roofs. Over the years, I've inspected every food business in the village, some several times. I've shared the boom years and helped businesses through the lean ones. I've run through the centre during the Seaford Half Marathon and walked alongside the Cuckmere River. I've seen it flood and spill over the main road.

Once through the village, the road meanders and climbs. The land drops away, revealing the thin ribbon of the river that once took boats of contraband from the coast to Alfriston. When this investigation is over, I'm going to walk beside the river with Gemma until we reach Cuckmere Haven on the coast. We'll pause for lunch in the Plough and Harrow at Litlington, as we did during the first week we spent together.

Damn! I'm supposed to be going to my father's for supper.

I pull onto the verge and ring Georgina. "I could be late. Will it cause a catering problem?"

"No, I'm using the crock pot. Gemma's not back yet, so don't worry. She went out a couple of hours ago. She's been working on that clue about hammers and wise hooters. How long do you think you'll be?"

"No idea, but I'm outside Alfriston, only ten minutes away. I'll text when I'm on my way."

A few minutes later, I reach Sunshine View Caravan Park, surprised by how many people are milling around. Most of the activity centres on the play area adjoining the construction site. A couple of families are playing cricket, with competitive dads taking control of the bowling and batting. Another group are playing boules beside a sand pit. Some kids are bombing around on motorised scooters.

In the reception area, Erin's behind the till. "Good evening, Mr Fisher. If you're looking for Pippa, she's out at the moment. She likes to watch the goldfinches on the bird feeders."

I follow the path and reach the clearing a few minutes later. The birdfeeders are empty. The same goes for the hide. Not even a burnt out portable barbecue or empty takeaway coffee cup. Pippa Castle didn't stop here. Either she continued along the path or she went into the woods. I head over to the flattened grass between two birch trees.

A few metres ahead, something in the brambles catches my eye. I inch my hand between the thorny stems and extract a smartphone. Behind the app icons, the wallpaper on the screen is a photograph of a young Stephanie Richmond in an Ashdown Activity Centre polo shirt.

Has Pippa Castle invited her over to kill her?

There's no evidence of a struggle – but the phone could have been dropped here.

Though tempted to take a closer look at the phone's contents, my gut tells me I need to hurry.

I drop the phone back into the brambles, in case it becomes evidence in another murder. If not, I can collect the phone on my way back. I hurry along the vague path, shielding my eyes from the sun, which occasionally punctures the canopy above. It's not long before the trees thin and I reach the edge of the wood. Ahead, a hedgerow blocks my way. I look both ways and spot a gap about twenty metres to my right.

Once on top of the wooden stile, I have a much better view of the field ahead of me. It slopes down into the valley and then up again to more woodland on the other side. Lambs graze in the field, not far from a cluster of trees and a water trough.

They seem oblivious to the body on the ground, only scattering when I run over. Pippa Castle lies face down in the grass, her hair sodden and plastered to her scalp. The collar and top of her blouse are soaked. While I check her neck for a pulse, I'm aware of two thumbprint-sized marks, close together on the back of her neck. Further finger marks on either side, suggest her head was held down under the water.

Someone's determined to make a point.

Fifty-Nine

Ashley insists I stay with the body. She doesn't ask me what I'm doing in the middle of a field at a murder scene. I'll have plenty of time to explain when she interviews me. In the meantime, I need to make sense of what happened.

If Pippa Castle isn't the killer, who is?

How did the killer lure her out here?

She must have known, even trusted, the killer.

Was the phone left to point the finger at Stephanie Richmond or was it a signpost to the body?

Aware that I could be assisting the police for the rest of the evening, I ring Georgina.

"I can't get hold of Gemma and Sarah's not answering. Her surgery phone goes straight to a message about who to contact in the event of an emergency. I rang Frances, but Gemma's not at the sanctuary. I'm guessing she's not with you, is she?"

If Gemma solved the cryptic clue, she could have gone to the allotment on Nether Way. If she spoke to Ted Rogers, he would have told her about the images we found earlier.

Would Gemma work out the significance and identify the lifeguard?

"Are you still there, Kent?"

"Sorry. Do you know Stephanie Richmond?"

"We've never met, but I know she's one of Gregory Rathbone's golden girls."

"I need to talk to her urgently. Can you get her phone number and text it to me?"

"Gemma said she'd moved in with Sarah."

"All the same, Georgina, her phone might help to track her location. Can you get me Rathbone's home number in case she's there?"

"What's going on, Kent? Is Gemma in trouble?"

"I'll find her, Georgina, don't worry."

Before I set off, I use the *what3words* app on my phone. I find the three words that will identify the location of Pippa Castle's body and text them to Ashley. In the time it takes me to reach my car and buckle up, she's phoned four times and left three voicemail messages. I should warn Erin about what's going to happen, but I need to find Gemma.

To stop my mind from conjuring up all kinds of scenarios, I go through the implications of Pippa Castle's murder. I need to reconsider what I've learned and what I know. Until now, only Miranda Tate and Pippa Castle knew the identity of the lifeguard.

I'm sure both are now dead.

If Pippa Castle revealed the lifeguard's identity to her killer, there's not much time to prevent another murder.

Am I sure Stephanie Richmond was the lifeguard?

There's the image on the phone, of course. Then there's the detail from Harry's drowning at Rathbone's party. Stephanie plunged into the pool when Harry was spotted. She pulled him out and tried to resuscitate him, which suggests her old lifeguard training kicked in.

She's also gay, which would explain the attraction to Pippa Castle.

"Did Harry work this out or did he go to the party to find out?" I ask, thinking aloud. "The killer gave him ketamine, which suggests planning and preparation. In his determination to identify the lifeguard, he may have revealed his hand too soon."

As I reach Sarah's surgery a little after eight thirty, Georgina texts the numbers I requested. Though there are no cars parked at the surgery, I knock on the door. When I get no response, I ring once more.

It looks like Stephanie Richmond's phone is switched off.

I ring Rathbone, but he doesn't answer either.

Trusting my instincts, I drive to Nether Way. Ted Rogers is still there, removing weeds from between his sturdy dwarf beans. When I ask if he's seen Gemma, he smiles. "I spoke to your young lady no more than an hour ago. Have you got time for coffee?"

"I need to find her, Ted. Did she say where she was going?"

"No, but she asked if you'd been here. When I told her about Pamela Anderson, she asked me if you'd started drooling." He chuckles, clearly enamoured with Gemma. "She also asked me when Miranda Tate took on the allotment."

He pulls out a small notepad from his shirt pocket. "Luckily, I popped home for tea after your visit and did some checking. The allotment was originally let to Robert Tate, her father, twelve years ago. About two and half years ago he became ill and indisposed. He asked if the allotment could be transferred to his daughter. Bill, one of our more seasoned members remembers them being regular visitors at the weekend. He also thinks she brought her fiancé on one occasion."

"That was Harry Lawson."

"Of course," he says, as if it answers several questions he had. "He wrote a feature about our allotments and the characters here."

"When was this?"

"May, early June? My wife was in hospital at the time, so I didn't get down here much. Bill remembers a woman visiting Miranda here. They had an argument. It was the last time we saw Miranda. Gemma showed me a photograph on her phone, hoping to identify this other woman, but I didn't recognise her. We showed it around, but no one did."

"Did Gemma tell you who it was?"

"Yes, Stephanie Richmond. She's a local councillor, isn't she? Then Gemma's mother rang and she roared off in her car like Lewis Hamilton."

"Did she say where she was going?"

He shakes his head. "She looked frightened though."

She's not the only one.

For a moment I can't think. I don't know where Gemma could be. With Pippa Castle dead, I've no idea who the killer could be.

Back in the car, I settle in the seat and take a deep breath. I need to calm my thoughts, work out the killer's identity. The killer was at the engagement party. I'm sure about that. The killer must be linked to Chrissy Jones. She was in the care of the local authority after her parents died.

If the killer's linked to the charity that took her to Ashdown Activity Centre, Betty and Ollie are the main suspects. Their daughter, Geraldine Nash, took her own life.

301

They've monitored my investigation from the start, it seems. They even tried to set me on the right course.

If they're the killers, why point me in the right direction?

They wanted me to identify the lifeguard and I led them to Pippa Castle. Now she's dead and a watery death awaits Stephanie Richmond.

Then all the people considered responsible for Chrissy Jones' tragic death will have been dealt with.

Will they try to silence me the way they did with Harry?

Only Betty and Ollie weren't at Rathbone's party.

Or were they? Spender and Susie Westcott weren't on the list. Nor Pippa Castle.

I reach for my notebook, wishing Gemma was here to help me.

Flicking back, I try to remember the little details that don't fit or seem right. Sarah withheld information from the start, though I never figured out why. Rathbone's account of what happened at the party revealed nothing of interest. He didn't even care how Harry accessed his back garden to get to the swimming pool.

Is that because Rathbone already knew Harry would be returning that way?

His fiancée, Katya, said Harry was drunk and reeked of whisky.

The post mortem revealed he hadn't touched a drop of alcohol.

I cast my mind back to my conversation with her, wondering if I've missed any details. Harry accused her of being an illegal immigrant, which understandably rankled. Terry, the chef, said she'd escaped to this country to work in a Brighton Hotel. He said the people who organised it raped her and put her to work in the sex trade.

There's nothing in my notes. I was chatting to him after my hygiene inspection and forgot to make a record.

I close my eyes, taking myself back to Terry's cramped office. He spoke fondly of Katya, who'd triumphed over her troubles to become the manager of the pub and hotel. On arriving in England, she'd lost touch with her sister, lost her child.

I assumed he'd meant a miscarriage.

What if she'd given up the child for adoption?

Before I jump to too many conclusions, I ring Ashley. Immediately, she launches into a tirade about me abandoning a crime scene and not returning her calls.

"Shut up, Ashley, and listen!"

To my surprise, she falls silent.

"Have you looked into Chrissy Jones, the girl who drowned at Ashdown –"

"I know who she is, Kent. We also know how to investigate murders. What do you want to know about Chrissy?"

"Was she adopted?"

"Hang on. I'll check." I hear the clicking of her keyboard as she looks for the answer. "Yes, she was adopted. The couple who adopted her died in a traffic accident and Chrissy was taken into care. A few months later she drowned at the activity centre, as I'm sure you know."

"Have you identified her natural mother?"

Ashley lets out an exasperated sigh. "It's hardly a major line of enquiry."

"It is if her mother's killing everyone who let her daughter down."

"You know who it is?"

"If I'm right, she has a new swimming pool. It was empty last week. I have a terrible feeling it's full now."

Sixty

Despite Ashley's instruction to leave everything to her, I drive straight to the Travellers, parking out of sight. By the time she's briefed her guvnor, organised a team and driven from Eastbourne, we could be too late.

I run along the grass verge until it opens out into the pub's main car park. The lawn area between the car park and pub is filled with tables and bench seating, already occupied by happy groups of people, enjoying the last of the sun before it dips away. It seems surreal to find the pub running as usual while Katya kills Stephanie Richmond.

Then again, the pool's in the basement of the hotel annex, shut off to the public and well away from the pub. No one's going to know what's happening inside.

I want to follow the boundary hedge to the back of the pub, where I can approach the hotel without being spotted. Unfortunately, the customers on the outside tables are bound to notice me. There's a service road on the opposite side of the site, but I have a feeling there's a gate to prevent unauthorised access.

Aware of time ticking by, I walk through the car park, looking for Gemma or Sarah's Volvos. I can't see either car as I meander towards the main entrance. The laughter and frivolity at the tables grows louder and more raucous as I approach the building.

When I reach the lawn, I swing right, grab an empty glass from a table and weave my way to the building. Once by the wall, I dump the glass and walk along the path towards the hedgerow, glancing through the windows as I pass. The restaurant's busy for a Monday evening. Waiting staff move among the tables like ants with trays.

I spot Katya in her work suit, chatting to a couple at a table close to the kitchen.

What the hell's she doing in the restaurant?

Have I made a complete fool of myself?

A hostage negotiating team and an armed unit could be rushing over here, based on what I told Ashley. They'll have to empty the pub, hotel and grounds before surrounding the hotel, breaking down doors and who knows what while customers and staff film events on their mobiles.

As Katya turns, I duck out of sight and move around the corner.

When my heart rate returns to normal, I hurry along, hoping the people inside won't notice me as I pass the windows. The kitchen doors are open, folded back against the wall, allowing staff to access the outdoor fridge and freezer stores. The smell of steak, onion and fries reminds me I haven't eaten since lunchtime. The ventilation system reeks of burnt cooking oil, reminding me why I don't eat fried food.

Hearing voices, I run across the grass and out of sight behind the cold store. Terry Phelan's familiar scouse tones precede his arrival outside. The smell of cigarettes fills the air.

"In a couple of hours, we'll be on our way to the airport," he says, sounding like he's about to embark on the holiday of a lifetime. "Then it's you, me and a South American beach."

I edge closer to the corner so I can hear more clearly above the noise of the extractors.

"Are you sure the other two will drown?"

"Don't worry, Katya. They'll be dead long before the pool fills to the top.

I sprint down the service road to the back of the pub. Around the corner, I find Gemma and Sarah's Volvos, parked next to a hotel service van. I pay no attention to the view across the gardens and marshes that reach almost to the coast.

If I'm too late Gemma will never see the view.

In that moment, I realise how foolish I've been. I've wasted the last eight years, drifting, denying what I feel inside, looking for someone better.

There is no one better.

I hope I'm not too late.

I race across the car park and across the lawn as if my life depended on it, leaping over the orange plastic barrier that surrounds the pool building. I take the steps down to the patio two at a time. When my foot hits the bottom step, the stone flags tips forward, sending me across the patio. A plastic table and chairs halt my progress, sending me sprawling to the ground. Winded, I look up at the sky, aware of a pain in my rear. With a flurry of arms, I disentangle myself and get to my feet. The French doors are locked, the view inside blocked by condensation.

I free the loose flagstone from the bottom step. With the flagstone in both hands, I smash it into the glass. The whole door shakes. The glass splinters, but remains intact. A second strike penetrates the outer pane. The third turns the glass in the inside pane into tiny pieces. I dump the flagstone and kick away loose glass. As the inner pane falls away, the humidity and reek of chlorine surge out like an acrid tsunami.

In the distance, I hear sirens.

Inside, I spot Gemma and Sarah sitting back to back in the shallow end of the pool, water up to their chins, gags stifling their voices.

There's no sign of Stephanie.

I run along the side of the pool to the shallow end, narrowly avoiding the patio table and chairs next to a bar. I leap into the water and wade over to Gemma and Sarah. Their hands and legs are bound by tape. A rope runs around their waists, binding them together.

"Hold on," I say, untying the napkin that's gagging Gemma. "I'll see if I can find something to cut you free."

She cries out. "He's got a knife."

Terry clambers through the door, brushing glass out of the way. He's brandishing a carving knife and breathing hard, as if he's run from the kitchen. I haul myself out of the water, jump to my feet and grab a plastic patio chair. With its legs pointing at him, I walk towards him as he swishes the knife from side to side.

"I've always wanted to get my own back on environmental health officers."

He's still breathing heavily. Despite his bravado, there's fear in his eyes. When he raises his knife arm, ready to lunge at me, I thrust the chair into his chest. Pushing for all I'm worth, I propel him back until he falls into the pool.

As he tumbles the knife falls from his fingers, dropping into the water. I leap in to retrieve it, pushing him out of the way. As my eyes adjust, I see Stephanie Richmond, lying bound and gagged on the floor of the pool.

I grab the knife and swim towards Gemma and Sarah, leaving Terry to thrash around.

It takes me a few moments to saw through the rope to separate Sarah and Gemma. I cut the tape to free her hands and help her to her feet. She grabs hold of me for support, struggling to stand with her legs strapped together.

In the background I'm aware of people shouting and piling into the pool area.

Shouts of "Police, stay where you are!" echo around the building, but they're no more than a blur in the background.

"What took you so long?" Gemma asks.

"I thought I'd lost you." With one arm around her waist, I bend and lift her legs until I'm cradling her in my arms and gazing into her eyes. "I don't ever want to feel like that again. Will you marry me?"

With the chlorine stinging my eyes, it's difficult to tell if she's surprised or stunned.

"Are you sure, Kent? There's so much you don't know about me. Things I wished I'd never done. Things I shouldn't have done."

"I don't care, Gemma. It's taken me eight years to realise how much I love you – how much I've always loved you. I don't want to waste another minute."

"There are things I need to explain," she says, a pained look in her eyes.

"All I care about is our future. Nothing else matters. So, what do you say?"

When she urges me to help her mother, I have a sinking feeling Gemma's going to turn me down.

Sixty-One

When Ashley rings, I'm buttering toast and looking out of the kitchen window of a self-catering cottage in Stratford-upon-Avon. The bird feeders on the small tree in the yard have drawn a few blue tits and sparrows. The clear blue sky suggests another unusually mild October day to end what's been a glorious honeymoon.

It's hard to believe over three months have elapsed since I proposed to Gemma.

Ashley interrupts my thoughts, coming straight to the point as usual. "We've found Miranda Tate – or what's left of her. Katya's finally dropped her plea of manslaughter on the grounds of diminished responsibility and admitted murder. We should be able to proceed much quicker with the prosecution now. Naturally, she's still claiming all the victims contributed to the death of her daughter."

"What about me? I led Katya to Stephanie Richmond."

"Pippa Castle identified Stephanie, not you. They were having sex in the sick bay while the kids were swimming. Miranda saw them and did nothing. I'm pretty sure that's why Katya killed her."

"If Miranda had told Katya, she could have killed Stephanie Richmond first. Maybe Harry and Adrian would still be alive."

"Maybe Miranda wanted to protect Stephanie. Maybe Stephanie helped Miranda later. I'm not sure we'll ever find out as they're both dead." Ashley pauses, clearly affected by the case. "Do you want to know how Katya kept track of your progress?"

"Betty Cooper and Ollie Nash, right?"

"Betty approached Katya after she'd persuaded Harry to do some digging. When it was clear he hadn't identified the lifeguard, Katya killed him."

"Once she crossed that line, there was no going back until everyone who let her daughter down had paid the price." I pause, saddened by the events that had driven Katya to kill. If the charity workers had kept an eye on her daughter at the activity centre, none of this would have happened. "Then again, she had to kill Harry or he would identify her as the killer."

"But he guessed what she would do and left you some clues."

"Hang on. Betty and Ollie were working at my sanctuary months before Harry was killed."

"Katya said they were thinking about employing you to identify and find the lifeguard. Katya persuaded them to select Harry, realising he'd be less trouble than you."

I laugh. "Instead, they got two for the price of one."

"I thought you'd want to know," she says, and rings off.

It feels like Ashley couldn't wait to end the call. I'm not sure why she rang when she could have waited till we were back from the honeymoon.

Gemma comes down the stairs, wrapped in a dressing gown. "Who were you talking to?"

"Ashley. They've found Miranda's body."

I relay the details once we're seated at the small breakfast table. Gemma says little, still troubled by memories of being left to drown in the swimming pool. The nightmares have reduced since that terrible day, but it doesn't take much to trigger the memories.

"One thing still doesn't make sense," she says, looking at the last slice of toast. "If Katya invited Harry to the party, why did he pester my mother for an invite? Why didn't he simply turn up on the night?"

"He wanted to make sure your mother came to me if he died. Insurance in case she didn't realise the significance of the text clues."

I reach across for the toast, only to find Gemma's beaten me to it. With a grin of triumph she snatches it away. Once smeared with raspberry jam, she cuts the slice in two and passes half to me. "I'm not always going to be this generous, Mr Fisher."

"I'm not always going to make you toast, Mrs Fisher."

"Do you think they'll find Betty and Ollie?" she asks, once she's devoured her toast.

I lick the jam off my fingers and shrug. "That's enough talk about murder. This is the last day of our honeymoon and I'm finished with sleuthing."

She laughs. "And when Savanna returns, all bleary eyed and lost, asking you to find out who killed Johnny Spender?"

"I mean it, Gemma. I'm through with sleuthing. The thought of you drowning in that swimming pool was more than I could take. You're my future," I say, taking her hands

313

in mine, wishing she'd believe me. "We're going to develop Meadow Farm to its full potential. We can expand, rescue more animals, offer more experiences to visitors and children, improve our online reach."

"What if I want to become an environmental health officer?"

"Then you'll have the best personal tuition you could wish for."

"All your short cuts and bad habits? No thanks." As the laughter subsides, a shadow seems to fall over her. "Are you sure it's what you want, Kent?"

"When you agreed to marry me, my life finally made sense. Nothing's going to spoil it."

A tear runs down her cheek. Apologising, she leaves the table and runs upstairs.

It's not the first time her emotions have got the better of her. Though we've known each other for eight years, on and off, the last three months have felt like a whirlwind romance. Neither of us expected the pressure the approaching wedding would bring. In the end, I left Georgina to organise everything, including the guests, the meals, the choice of wines, the DJ for the evening.

Two weeks ago, we married in the Mike Turner Visitor Centre at Meadow Farm. Gemma looked so stunning, I had tears in my eyes. My father stood beside me, speechless for once. It seemed perfect as Mike once admitted how much he'd like to be my best man. He also liked the idea of walking Gemma down the aisle.

Hopefully, we fulfilled both his wishes that day. I felt his presence several times during the proceedings.

Even Tommy Logan enjoyed himself, giving the wedding a centre page spread in the *Tollingdon Tribune*. He promised to have a full set of photos ready for our return. Despite their reservations, and lack of input into the proceedings, Niamh and Sarah attended in all their finery.

"Isn't it all a bit sudden?" Niamh asked when I broke the news.

Sarah said, "I hope you're not expecting me to treat your animals for free."

Now it's our last day in Stratford-upon-Avon and Gemma doesn't want to go home.

Columbo jumps down from the sofa when I put water, treats and poo bags into his rucksack for the day ahead. He's not interested in the old timbered buildings that keep history alive and give the town its unique atmosphere. Like me, he knows nothing about Shakespeare, though he enjoys chasing squirrels in the gardens adjacent to the theatre.

We were lucky to find the holiday cottage in a terrace close to Holy Trinity Church, where Shakespeare's buried. The parking's a nightmare as visitors compete with residents for spaces, but we're a short walk from the river, the town centre and the main attractions.

Gemma comes down the stairs, looking gorgeous in a bronze roll neck sweater, jeans and tan boots. As it catches the sunlight from the window, her auburn hair shines like a fresh horse chestnut. She pulls on an anorak and grabs Columbo's lead from the windowsill.

"Are you okay?" I ask.

She nods, but there's a nervous look in her eyes. "I want everything to be perfect, Kent. It's easy for me because you're the only man I've ever wanted. But what if I don't live up to your expectations? What if I'm not the woman you think I am?"

"It's me who doesn't deserve you." I wrap my arms around her and pull her close, wishing I could calm her anxieties. "Now let's get going before Columbo wears a hole in the carpet."

Her kiss is so passionate I'm tempted to take her upstairs, but Columbo has other ideas. Once through the front door, he's off like a rocket, straining at the lead, barking at another dog across the road. Gemma locks the door and hands me the keys.

"We won't go too far," she says, gesturing towards a traffic warden. "We need to move the car before ten."

Hand in hand, we walk down the road and cross to Holy Trinity Church. In the graveyard, Columbo spots a grey squirrel and hurtles across the grass until his extendable lead reaches its limit. He stares up at the tree, barking as the squirrel scurries along the branches.

He repeats this several times as we walk around to the rear. People of all ages, races and denominations fill the cemetery and riverside path, snapping with their cameras. We stop by the low stone wall and look down on the River Avon, rippling with activity. A tour boat chugs past on its way to the weir, where it will turn. Several visitors are struggling with rowing boats, causing mayhem among the local swans and ducks.

Gemma taps my arm. "I left my camera in the house. Can I have the keys?"

She hurries back, weaving through the tourists. Columbo's on a mission to cock his leg against as many gravestones as he can. I pull him back and keep him on a short lead as he drags me around, still hunting for squirrels.

Realising ten minutes have passed since Gemma left us, I steer him back towards the church. Maybe she's talking to someone or taking photographs. When we reach the main gate, she's nowhere to be seen.

"Come on," I say, dragging Columbo away from a cocker spaniel.

We hurry back to the holiday cottage. I open the door and step inside, spotting her camera and phone on the coffee table. Calling out, I run up the stairs, hoping she's not had an accident.

But she's not there.

Back downstairs, I check the rear garden.

Then I notice my keys are missing.

When I step out onto the street, so is my car.

THE END.

If you would like to find out more about the Kent Fisher mysteries and be the first to find out about new releases from Robert Crouch, you can sign up to his email newsletter at his website. You'll also receive a free copy of *Dirty Work*, a short story featuring Kent in his days as an environmental activist.

I hope you enjoyed this book. As an independent author, I don't have the budget that big publishing houses possess to market their books, but I have you. If you could please leave a review on Amazon, it would make my day. Reviews need only take a few minutes of your time, but will inform other readers indefinitely.

Thank you.

Other books by Robert Crouch

No Accident	Kent Fisher mystery #1
No Bodies	Kent Fisher mystery #2
No Remorse	Kent Fisher mystery #3
No More Lies	Kent Fisher mystery #4
No Mercy	Kent Fisher mystery #5
No Love Lost	Kent Fisher mystery #6

Fisher's Fables A collection of humorous blog posts

Author's Note

Thank you for taking this journey with me. I hope you enjoyed reading No Going Back as much as I enjoyed writing it.

Writing the novel is a solitary process, but I'm lucky to have the company of the characters I create. While they are the product of my imagination, they become real when I'm writing, often going in directions of their choosing not mine. I live their lives with them, sharing their hopes, fears and desires as they deal with the complex murder mysteries I throw at them.

Once the writing is completed, I'm helped by a team of people who help turn the manuscript into the finished novel.

My thanks go to my wife Carol and advance reader Kath Middleton, who provide valuable feedback and help me fine tune the novel; to my editor Liz Bailey, who casts an expert and objective eye over my manuscript and helps me strengthen the plot, iron out weaknesses and add a final polish; and to Jane Prior of String Design, who produces another great cover in the series.

I'm indebted to a trusty team of bloggers, who selflessly give up their spare time to read books and write honest, objective reviews, helps me with the launch. Many of them have been with me from the first novel in the series, encouraging and supporting me and my books, helping to bring my work to a wider audience.

And finally my thanks go to you the reader for choosing my book among the many millions of novels out there. I'm always delighted to hear from you, whether by email, social media or directly through my website.

Printed in Great Britain
by Amazon